John Rankin Rogers

Looking Forward

Or, the Story of an American Farm

John Rankin Rogers

Looking Forward
Or, the Story of an American Farm

ISBN/EAN: 9783337009168

Printed in Europe, USA, Canada, Australia, Japan

Cover: Foto ©Andreas Hilbeck / pixelio.de

More available books at **www.hansebooks.com**

LOOKING FORWARD

OR

The Story of an American Farm.

—

BY

JOHN R. ROGERS.

———

SPIKE PUBLISHING COMPANY
1898

DEDICATION.

———

I dedicate this book to the woman who never lost faith in me—my wife.

THE AUTHOR.

PREFACE.

This Story of an American Farm first appeared in 1889 as a serial in the columns of *The Kansas Commoner*, then published at Newton, Kansas, under the management of the writer. Recently it has been revised and partly rewritten without, however, changing the design and arrangement of the book, or the character of the narrative, which, as may be surmised, is largely drawn from actual experiences among the farmers of Kansas.

JOHN R. ROGERS.

OLYMPIA, Washington.
January 15th, 1898.

CONTENTS.

CONTENTS—Continued.

Home Scene at the Farm.

LOOKING FORWARD,

—OR—

The Story of an American Farm.

"For, brother, men
Can counsel, and speak comfort to that grief
Which they themselves not feel; but, tasting it
Their counsel turns to passion, which before
Would give preceptial medicine to rage."

CHAPTER I.

THE FARMER AND HIS FAMILY.

"MOTHER, do you think I ought to go? Oh I hope I can."

"Why Mary, you know as well as I that all depends upon the crops and the weather. Your father wishes you to go and if it is possible to raise the money necessary to send you, you will certainly be sent, but it is so uncertain about the crops."

Mrs. Grafton sighed as she said this, for she well remembered how often her hopes had been raised, only to be destroyed by the failure of the crops upon which the family depended for a living.

The daughter was a sweet faced, brown haired girl, apparently about sixteen years of age; the mother a care-worn woman of forty, with a refined and intelligent face, bearing the marks of a faded youth which evidently had not been without personal attractions.

Mrs. Grafton was a farmer's wife and bore the imprint of her class. Hard work, care and wearying responsibilities of her position had caused her to lose the light hearted gaiety which had been a prominent trait in her character as a girl, while in its place there now appeared a chastened and somewhat constrained cheerfulness which, somehow, gave the beholder the impression that tears might readily flow from her eyes upon slight provocation. "A sweet woman who has seen trouble," came almost involuntarily to the mind of the beholder on first meeting her. The daughter, as became her youth, was yet free from the marks of that care which destroys so much of the life pleasure of and so early gives to most Americans that sorrowful expression, seen when the countenance is in repose, startling even to those closely connected, if unexpectedly encountered.

Mary was a pleasant faced girl of about the usual height. Her figure was trim and shapely and her full brown eyes glistened with a light which betokened intelligence and vivacity. She was the daughter of a farmer in humble circumstances, burdened with debt and struggling wearily along the path of life, who yet cherished for his daughter the highest asperations. Nothing, indeed, seemed to Mr. Grafton too much to hope for Mary, and in pursuance of his design of giving her the best educational facilities possible, she had been encouraged to think of leaving home to attend a superior school which was located in a neighboring town.

Mr. Grafton was himself a well informed man, having in his youth attended the higher schools attainable in the immediate vicinity of his early home and these studies having been followed through life by an earnest endeavor to inform himself at every opportunity. He had been an omnivorous reader and, being possessed of a good memory and endowed by nature with a vivid imagination, his descriptions of what he had read were eagerly listened to, and he had thus easily influenced his daughter in her tastes and in her choice of books. Unconsciously to herself her thoughts and aspirations had been directed toward a higher education than seemed possible at home, although, thanks to her father she had already advanced much farther in general literature than is usual with country girls of her age.

Mr. Grafton well knew that as a pupil in an educational institution she would acquire more from her surroundings and the minds with which she came in contact, than from the books which she might study. At best, the theories and facts accumulated there, form only the tools with which future work may be done.

Fortunate was it for Mary that her parents possessed the qualifications which distinguished them. Mrs. Grafton's gentle manner and retiring disposition was yet tempered by a firm and unwavering advocacy of whatever she regarded as lovely in character or elevating in tendency. Mary was the eldest child and the only daughter; a younger brother, a mere child, completing the family.

Mr. Grafton had emigrated to Kansas from Ohio some ten years previous to the opening of our story. He had been engaged there, in one of the towns of that state in mercantile business. The failure of a friend whom he had heavily endorsed at one of the banks, occurring at a critical time in his affairs caused his own business overthrow. But he was comparatively young, and having been himself a farmer's son, his thoughts seemed irresistably turned toward the life to which he now looked back with regret.

A change must be made; that was sure, and gathering up the remnant of his means he came to Kansas and bought the farm upon which he now resided. He was a grave and thoughtful man possessed of great depth of feeling, which however was not to be noted on the surface. For his family he had the sincerest affection, which it is needless to say was fully returned.

Mrs. Grafton deeply sympathized with her daughter in

her desire for an education and intellectual advancement and yet, mother-like, feared to have her darling leave her, even for so short a time.

While mother and daughter were still engaged in discussing the probabilities regarding the wheat crop upon which in large measure would depend the ability of the family to send her away, Mr. Grafton came hurriedly into the house and said:

" It is going to storm mother."

" Why so it is," said she, hastily looking out of the window. " Come Mary, you must help me get the chickens safely into the coop, and we can talk about going away at another time."

Mr. Grafton went out to make everything fast about the stables and mother and daughter hastily caught up the smaller chickens in their aprons and drove the larger ones, with the bustling hens, before them to their place of refuge.

Before they could finish their errand the rain, accompanied by a fierce looking cloud and a heavy wind was upon them. Running hastily to the house they managed to get inside the door just as the heavily charged cloud burst upon them with all its fury. The lightning with its blinding glare, a furious wind which drove the rain up under the shingles and fairly shook the little cottage with its fury, accompanied by peal upon peal of thunder caused all thoughts of anything but the violence of the storm to leave them.

A moment later Mr. Grafton rushed in, wet to the skin, and amid the noise and roar of the storm, the voice of a child, crying with fear, came from the next room. " Poor Charley !" came simultaneously from all three, just as the little fellow threw open the door and ran sobbing to his mother for protection. He had been asleep in an inner room and wakened by the storm, at once sought that wonderful refuge—a mother's arms.

The storm ceased almost as suddenly as it came. The sun soon shone out and the family went out to see how much destruction had been wrought. Mrs. Grafton, however, returned with a box full of half drowned chickens, which she placed under the kitchen stove, that the warmth of the fire might revive the feeble spark of life which barely fluttered in their naked and chilled bodies. The force of the wind had been so great that although the large hay stack containing Mr. Grafton's entire stock of hay, had been crossed at top by wires attached to heavy stones at the side, its top had been blown off by the wind and the hay wet to the center. Mr. Grafton made the circuit of his wheat field, and found that while the growing wheat was much of it felled flat to the earth by the violence of the wind and rain, yet as it had not advanced far enough to make a falling down final, no great damage had been done. It was yet green and would in a day or two resume its upright position. Feeling thankful that he had escaped a visitation of hail which might have pounded his crops into the ground, he slowly made his way to the house.

As usual, the storm had come up towards the close of the afternoon, and night now began to fall. Mr. Grafton having only himself to depend upon in the work of the farm; and his wife insisting that she "would just as soon milk as not;" Mary and herself had this homely duty in charge. Mr. Grafton busied himself with the horses, fed the squealing pigs, helped in separating the cows and calves, made all snug for the night, and only as it became too dark to see did he retreat in doors, where "mother," as he affectionately called her, was busy in quieting little Charley, who was fretful and sleepy, and at the same time endeavoring to put away the milk in the cellar and sweep out the water, which had been blown, by the violence of the storm, under the door of the kitchen. Mary employed herself in getting supper and talking to her father, as he sat near the stove, at which she was at work, of the damage done to the wheat.

"Will it hurt it much, father, do you think?" said she.

"Why no, I hope not," he replied. "Still all is uncertain and there are yet many chances for loss."

"If we cannot raise the money for you, Molly, this

year, we will try to do so next, and you will only be seventeen then."

"Oh dear!" she sighed; "the very idea of putting off another whole year what I have looked forward to so anxiously, is so disheartening."

"I know it is, and we will hope for the best, but you must not set your heart upon going so strongly as to be unable to bear the disappointment of a failure of our plans."

Supper was now ready, and although it was nearly nine o'clock, the family sat down to the evening meal at the earliest possible moment at which it could have been made ready. Before it was ended, little Charley was fast asleep in his weary mother's arms and although it was very late, the dishes were yet to be washed and put away. When all was done and the family sought repose, it was with aching bones and weary hearts, filled with nameless forebodings of possible misfortune in store.

"I believe, Sir, said she, that I do not need your assistance."

CHAPTER II.

MARY GRAFTON.

ORNING found the Graftons early astir. And as the air, refreshed by the shower of the previous evening, was most delightfully invigorating, laden as it was, with the odor of vegetation springing into life, they cheerfully and hopefully began again their daily round of duties. After feeding the animals, Mr. Grafton could not refrain from taking a hasty look at the wheat field, the boundaries of which were not far distant from the stables. The wheat was still very largely flat upon the surface of the ground, but a close examination convinced him that it was uninjured by the rough treatment it had received. Each blade glistened with moisture in the rays of the rising sun and as the slight breeze of the early morning caused it to flutter gently, for a moment there came over him a sense of the beauty and loveliness of nature, causing his heart to rise in thankfulness to the great and incomprehensible source of the world of beauty spread out before him.

Just then he heard little Charlie calling him, at the stable, where he had been sent to summon his father to the morning meal.

"Here I am Charlie," said he, as the little fellow came into sight, in the search.

"Mamma say dinner weady, Pa."

"Well I am ready too," said he. "What has she got for us."

"Oh mos' eversing, I dess."

Taking him in his arms Mr. Grafton walked slowly towards the house, amusing himself meantime by talking to the child, whose opening mind was eagerly seeking to know the reason for all which met his wondering gaze.

"What made the lark sing? and why had he a yellow breast? Was he glad? Did birds sing when they were glad? Was that what made Mary sing? Did God like little birds? and if a b-a-d man shot the little bird would God be sorry?" And finally, "What made mens be bad?"

Mr. Grafton could not answer, and he realized that the child, who was just learning to talk, had already propounded the question of the origin of evil, which staggers the mind of the philosopher.

One thing distinguished the Graftons; as the family met around the table, whether well or scantily spread, each strove to make it a season of light and innocent gaiety. Whatever of disquiet might be weighing upon them, it was thrown off and each endeavored to bring something to the common fund of enjoyment. This, which had become a habit with them, had unconsciously become not only a source of pleasure, but also served to draw the members of the little family more closely together in thought and feeling.

Seated about the breakfast table, little Charlie began to tell his mother of the "buful" little bird and how nicely it sang. "Oh!" said Mrs. Grafton, "that puts me in mind of one of Charlie's speeches yesterday morning. We were out in the garden and I was planting some seeds and had forgotten him for a moment, when I found that he had stuck a feather in the ground, which he had picked up, and smoothing the dirt carefully around its base he said: 'Now see, Mamma, it will grow up a hen, won't it?'"

All laughed good-naturedly at Charlie and his "hen," while the child appeared in no wise cast down at what now seemed the probable failure of his crop.

"Mary you must go up to town and get some groceries," said Mrs. Grafton.

"I did not know that we were out of coffee until this morning, and there are some other things that we must have."

"I would go," said Mr. Grafton, "but I must finish cultivating the north field."

"O! I will go," said Mary, "I can ride old Jim and that will leave father the good team to work with.

Thus it was arranged that Mary should have the side saddle placed upon a large old horse which had long been the property of the family and was now only occasionally called upon to perform a portion of the work of the farm.

After breakfast Mr. Grafton saddled the old horse and brought him to the door where Mary was ready to mount. Mr. Grafton helped his daughter into the saddle and Mrs. Grafton stood near with a basket containing some choice butter which was to be carried to a lady in town, who had requested it sent upon the first opportunity.

The big old horse made but a sorry mount for so fair a burden, and as Mr. Grafton assisted in handing up the basket and looking to the security of the various straps and buckles he sighed as he realized how rough and uncouth a figure the old horse and rather shabbily dressed girl, would make in the eyes of the fastidious. As he placed the little shoe in the stirrup and noted the rough and well-worn leather, a suspicious dimness came into his eyes as he felt how little he was able to assist in the training of one for whom he thought nothing too good.

Mary saw nothing of this; she was a country girl, unspoiled by the fashionable follies of the day, and while she dearly loved beauty and beautiful things, she was yet able to put away all thoughts of what she knew she could not obtain.

Old Jim was honest and true and gravely jogged along. The morning air was like wine to Mary's naturally joyous spirit, and she hummed softly to herself the strains of the

ballads she loved, until almost before she thought it possible
she was at the hitching rack in town where she had been
told to leave her horse, while she busied herself with the
business of the morning.

Plainville was a little town of some 500 inhabitants.
It had a railway station and boasted of a dozen stores, a
bank, a grist mill, two or three churches and the usual
amount of scandal and jealousy. People of all kinds were
there ; some good, a few bad, and many quite indifferent.
It was an ordinary village, neither town nor country, without the advantages of either, and having some of the evils
of both.

As Mary drew near the rack, which was just at the
edge of the sidewalk and near the store she intended patronizing, she saw among the loungers standing near, the
swaggering form of John Busteed, the worthless son of the
wealthy man of the village. Mary had often, with her
mother, visited at several residences in the town and knew
many of the people. Of Busteed she knew enough to
despise him.

Seeing that she intended stopping, John came forward
and proffered his assistance in helping her to dismount.
This she instantly determined to prevent.

" I believe, sir," said she, " that I do not need your
assistance; Mr. Weldon will you please take my basket a
moment ?"

" Why certainly, certainly I will, Miss Mary," said
Weldon.

John colored with anger and slunk away, to meet the
derisive winks and nods of the bystanders.

As soon as relieved of the heavy basket, Mary sprang
lightly to the ground and tied old Jim in a way that convinced the onlookers that she had often done the like
before.

Mr. Weldon was the village blacksmith, a man of
vigorous frame and speech, who, though now growing old,
did not hesitate, if need be, to back up his rather free

way of speaking, with muscular force. As this was understood to be his way, from traditional reports of a former time, and as his manner gave promise, upon occasion, of an instant "falling from grace," "Uncle Bill," as he was familiarly called, was allowed to do and say pretty much as he pleased.

Mary pinned her riding skirt to the saddle and taking the basket from Uncle Bill, at once sought the home of the lady to whom the butter had been sent.

She had gone but a short distance when one of the loafers spoke up:

"Well, John, you got the mitten that time."

"G—d d—n the little minx, I'll get even with her for that. I wouldn't a cared if it hadn't a been for this crowd a standing around."

"Pooh! John, she is too smart for the likes of you."

"Well now," said John, with a meaning leer, "I've got even with girls just as smart as she is, afore now."

"You'd better make your peace with God, if you harm George Grafton's girl," said Uncle Bill.

"Who's George Grafton? He aint nobody. Just one of them poor farmers that you can buy for ten dollars a head."

"George Grafton is what you never can be—a man—and if men were selling for ten cents a head you couldn't buy the little finger of a man, if it wasn't for your dad's money. Grafton is a quiet man, but that girl is like the apple of yer eye to him and if he needs any help—why he can get it—that's all."

A chuckle of endorsement of Uncle Bill's little speech went round just as the elder Busteed approached, who was gradually made aware of what had occurred.

"George Grafton is bringing up that girl with too high and mighty notions," said he. "There he is, poor and in debt further than he can see a way to pay. He haint got no help. His boy is a girl, and they tell me he is talkin' er sending her to college or some such fool no-

tion, and they say he spends at least fifty dollars a year
for books and papers and sich. It is well enough for a
man to have a decent education. I suppose he's got that,
now why don't he stop fooling with books and try and
make some money?"

"Grafton is a good worker," ventured one of the
loungers.

" Yes, maybe he is, but he don't manage right."

" Well, how ought he to manage?"

"Well, he aint no use for so many books. They say
he's got a house full now, and he don't need more'n one
good newspaper. The *Tribune* is enough for any farmer
to read. Then them reform notions er his is enough to
put any man down. Let the farmers tend to their business an' we'll tend to ourn."

Mr. Busteed was a director and reputed heavy stock-
holder in the local bank; his business consisted, as he
himself expressed it, in looking for "soft snaps." He was
a speculator, a buyer of grain and an occasional loaner of
money at unmentionable rates, standing ready to buy up
property of any kind, when its owner stood in direful need.
Although all his efforts were directed towards taking
advantage of the necessities of his needy fellow creatures,
he veiled his deeds with a thin gloss of very ordinary
religion. He made no pretentions to sanctity, and,
although a member of the Presbyterian Church, he seldom
attended the prayer or official meetings of the society, but
when it came to cash support, he gave more than any
other five members and thus came to be the most influ-
ential member the Church possessed. Indeed, without
him it seemed impossible for the Church to exist. His
son was an idle, worthless rake of twenty, who as a boy
had been guilty of all the meanness possible to mean boys
and who as a man bid fair to eclipse his youthful record.

" Now there's that girl," he continued; "she ought to
help her folks; no use of her readin' po'try, or anything
er that kind. She ought to work out; she could earn at

least two dollars a week; then if she was away from home her board would be saved and that's two more; that's two hundred dollars a year; for ten years that alone is two thousand, but handle it right, put the savings of each year out at interest, or employ it more profitably, and instead of two thousand, in ten years it would be four or five— more than Geogre Grafton is worth. Yes, she ought to work out; there is Miss Busteed wants a girl now."

"You and me," said Uncle Bill, "aint fit to have that girl in our houses; we wouldn't know how to treat her; why blame your old hide there is the real glory-look in them great brown eyes of hers. I aint got no son, but if I had one like John there, I'd know better than to mention such a thing."

It was Uncle Bill, and Mr. Busteed ventured no reply; he noted sharply, however, the actions of those whose looks and nods betokened approval of the free speech, and muttering something like, "you'll see, you'll see," he strode hastily away.

CHAPTER III.

"WHO MAKETH THEM TO DIFFER."

S Mary returned to the store, after leaving the butter at the house to which she had taken it, the loungers, who still remained where she had left them, moved very politely out of her way as she entered the store. Mr. Baker, the keeper, who was also the village postmaster, saluted her quite pleasantly:

"Good morning; awful nice morning aint it? Got lots of mail for your folks."

"Ah, is that so; are there any letters for us?"

"Why I believe so," said he; "but your box is more'n full of papers; you see, the magazines is come."

Mary expressed pleasure at having the magazines to read: the coffee and other articles were soon purchased and all placed in the basket she had brought; she led old Jim up to the sidewalk, which answered the purpose of a horse block; a moment more and she was in the saddle, Mr. Baker brought out the basket and handed it up to her and she was on the road home.

As soon as she got out of the village, the horse moving gently along, she took from the basket in front of her, the various newspapers and magazines, looked each over hurriedly, reading a little here and there. Opening a magazine she read what a wealthy lady had given as a description of her mode of life, and this is what she read:

"We breakfast about ten. Breakfast occupies the best part of an hour, during which we read our letters and pick up the latest news in the papers. After that we have to go and answer our letters, and my mother expects me to write her notes of invitation or reply to such. Then I have to go into the conservatory and feed the canaries and parrots and cut off the dead leaves and faded flowers from the plants. Then it is time to dress for lunch and at two o'clock we lunch. At three my mother likes me to go with her when she makes her calls, and we then come home to a five o'clock

Who Maketh Them to Differ.

tea when some friends drop in. After that we get ready to take our drive in the park, and then we go home to dinner, and after dinner we go to the theatre or the opera, and then when we get home I am so dreadfully tired, that I don't know what to do."

Mary had read very much more than most girls of her age; she knew that the life thus described was lived by but very few in our largest cities, but as she closed the book and strove to imagine the life thus brought before her, the utter vacuity of such an existence was most fully impressed upon her. How could sensible people live such a life? Ah! hers was a preferable life, she thought. The dear faces at home rose up before her, and with a glow of exultation she patted poor old Jim as the only representative at hand of the little band, dearer than all the world beside.

Turning over the newspapers, her eyes fell upon a paragraph, and this is what she saw:

"In a New England town the other day, a newsboy, hardly higher than the platform, was run over by a horse-car and fatally hurt. What did the self-supporting baby of six years do, when writhing in the last agonies of a terrible death? He called piteously for his mother. Why? To shriek piteously upon her breast? That she might clasp him while the surgeon worked? Ah, no! It was to give her his day's earnings. 'I've saved 'em, mother!' he cried. 'I've saved 'em all! Here they are!' When his little clenched, dirty hand fell rigid it was found to contain four cents."

Mary's eyes filled with tears. Were there people like that? Did God care for the poor? How could He if such things were permitted to continue? And yet she knew that this was but one of a thousand daily incidents in the life of the cities, where brilliant sights and horrid scenes are so inextricably commingled. What a world this was! How much of happiness, and ah! how much of misery!

As she rode up the lane and came near the house, her mother, who had been on the watch, came out to meet her; giving her the basket she sprang lightly from the saddle, and throwing her arms about her mother, impulsively kissed her.

The watchful mother noted the tear upon her daughter's cheek, although her eyes were laughing and her face was wreathed with smiles.

"Why Mary," she began; "has anything happened to you?"

"Oh no, mother dear; but I was just reading something which made me feel so sorry, and when I saw you and thought what a pleasant home I had and how much I loved you I couldn't help hugging you just a little."

Mrs. Grafton was too wise a woman to make many enquiries. She knew her daughter's impulsive spirit; she had full confidence in her, and for the moment busied herself in helping Mary as they tugged at the dry old straps and rusty buckles of the saddle. Taking it off, she placed it upon the spacious back porch, while light-hearted Mary led the old horse to the pasture, swung open the gate, and stripping off the bridle, turned the faithful beast loose, to crop the short grass.

Just then she espied her father coming into dinner from the field. By going across the corner of the pasture she could readily intercept him as he came up the farm road, and this she did, actually running part of the way, that she might meet him at a certain bend in the road.

Mr. Grafton was driving the team, which with dangling chains and rattling harness, were swinging heavily along, while he walked behind. Mary came up, and putting her hand in that of her father, they walked along "swinging hands" like a couple of school-girls.

At first neither spoke a word; at last Mary broke the silence, saying:

"Father, what makes such a difference in the conditions of life in which people are found."

"Why, what makes you ask that?"

Mary then related what she had been reading, saying that the great difference between the very rich and the

very poor was to her a mystery, if all were the children of
God, who loved all alike.

"Opportunity makes people, and the lack of it prevents them," said he.

"Don't you know what Gray says:

> 'Full many a gem of purest ray serene
> The dark unfathomed caves of ocean bear;
> Full many a flower is born to blush unseen
> And waste its sweetness on the desert air.' "

"Oh yes," said she; "so many people never have a
chance; opportunity doesn't come to them. Why is it?"

"Up to a comparatively recent period, orthodox people comforted themselves with the theory of Rev. Dr.
Malthus, as an answer to this question," said Mr Grafton.
"This theory held to the belief that the increase of population in the world tends to outrun the means of subsistence. That more people are born into the world than
can properly be cared for. That wars, pestilence, famine
and hardships generally, are the God-appointed means of
thinning out an undesirable increase. That God has
created more people than he can care for and that He then
sets men to killing and destroying one another, in various
ways, as a means of getting rid of His own mistakes.
This theory was very convenient and consoling and laid
all blame—if blame there was—upon God. Great generals
and small persecutors consoled themselves with the idea
that they were co-workers with Deity in the necessary
work of the world. In much the same way the people
who held slaves, in this country, a while ago, found a
passage in the scriptures which they took a great fancy to.
Old Noah cursed one of his grandsons, saying: 'Cursed be
Canaan, a servant of servants shall he be to his brethren;'
and the southern divines held, without the slightest
authority, that Canaan symbolized the black race, and
that as Noah in the Bible had cursed Canaan, they were
carrying out the work of the Lord in America by holding
negroes in slavery. It was a very slim foundation, but
what there was came from the Bible and they made much

of it for the reason that they could lay the blame on Noah or the Bible. The real truth then was, as it is now with the poor creatures you were pitying, a while ago: the whole trouble comes from the insane and murderous greed of man.

"Now-a-days there is another passage that people who are engaged in 'keeping poor people in their places' are very anxious to quote, and that is Christ's saying at a particular time: 'The poor always ye have with you but me ye have not always," as though He meant people to assist in the work of making poverty permanent, but if these will only look it up, they will find that this was really said in opposition to a protest of Judas, and a preceding verse exactly describes the people who are repeating what Jesus said without noting the circumstances. It is found in the twelfth chapter of John:

'This he said not that he cared for the poor; but because he was a thief, and had the bag and bare what was put therein.'

"'Man's inhumanity to man makes countless thousands mourn!" That's the foundation of the whole trouble."

They had now arrived at the stable where Charlie was awaiting them, and as Mr. Grafton stooped to take the little fellow in his arms, Mary drew the reins from his hands, tied them in the proper rings and deftly unharnessed one horse before Charlie had finished telling his father a wonderful story relating to a little bird which the house cat had caught and eaten. The other horse was quickly stripped, Mary led them to the trough, while her father pumped the water for the thirsty beasts. Soon they were placed in their stalls and all then went in to dinner.

Just as they reached the back door they saw a man driving a pair of ponies before a buggy, moving rapidly along the public highway. As he came to the entrance to the Grafton place he turned and came up at a smart trot.

"It is Busteed," said Mr. Grafton. "I wonder what makes him come in."

"Howdy, Grafton," said the man of business. "I was going out to Barnes' place on a little business, and I just drove in to let you know that I'll have to have that money sooner than I thought, fact is I need it bad; you haven't it by you, I s'pose?"

"No," said Mr. Grafton, "I haven't, and I did not try to get it, as you told me that it could run until after harvest, just as well as not."

"So I did, but I didn't know what was coming. Well I'll have to have it."

"Why," said Mr. Grafton, "I don't see how I am to get it for you unless I borrow it."

"No, I s'pose not; but you can do that, can't you?"

"Possibly I can. But I do not know whom to go to for a loan. Can you tell me?"

"Well," said Busteed, "I expect the old Squire is the only chance."

Mr. Grafton made no immediate reply, for he knew, as did every one in the vicinity, that old "Squire" Clinch, as he was called, was but a creature of Busteed's, and of others, who, having no capital of his own, did a precarious business as loan agent, and was expected by his employers to take advantages which they were ashamed openly to extort.

"Well," said Mr. Grafton, "I'll try what I can do for you in a day or two." Busteed whirled his ponies about, and, with a parting injunction to "be sure and fix that matter up," he was gone.

Mrs. Grafton had been a listener to the colloquy just related, and as the family sat down to dinner, the knowledge of the serious financial straits they were in, and the uncertaiuty of the future, was for once too weighty to be thrown aside.

"Why don't you laugh to me," said little Charlie, noting the grave and silent faces.

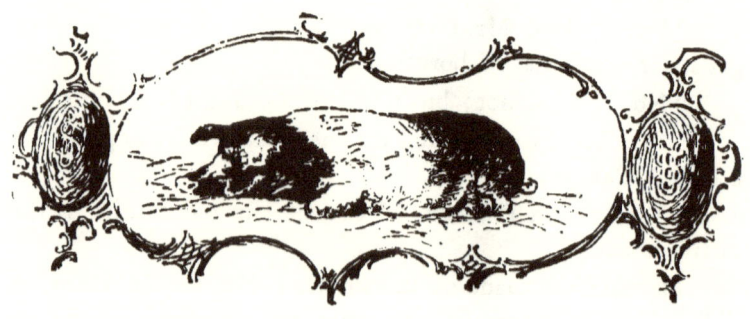

CHAPTER IV.

"MONEY ANSWERETH ALL THINGS."

GEORGE Grafton had for some time been "running behind," as the neighbors said. The loss of a crop, followed by a long-continued time of low prices, had reduced his means of living to the lowest possible point.

When the farm, upon which he lived, was purchased, he had bought it on "payments," and as the crops raised had not enabled him to pay the balance of the purchase money at the appointed time, the farm was mortgaged and the money raised for that purpose. The mortgage drew a heavy rate of interest and formed a serious annual charge. He did not look upon life as a mere opportunity to collect a store of dimes and dollars and so, out of regard to what he considered the higher interests of himself and family, many opportunities for accumulating money were allowed to pass as unworthy the sacrifice which he felt they would be called upon to make in obtaining it. It thus happened that he found himself the subject of many criticisms, on the part of his neighbors, regarding his management of affairs, most of which were in the same line as that of Mr. Busteed, regarding Mary's services. It thus came about that, although he had been reasonably successful in his business of farming, so far at least as raising crops was concerned, yet he found that he was not only not gaining financially, but was actually running astern. And when he compared his condition with that of the farmers about him, he found that his condition was fully as good as the average. Those who had raised more had also taken greater risks, and lost more. Those who had been raising cattle had lost heavily in their operations by the fall of prices as controlled by the manipulators of the great markets.

The next morning Mr. Grafton went to the village,

resolved to make some arrangement, if possible, to obtain the money to pay off Busteed, hoping that the crop might turn out so favorably as to relieve his necessities, at least for the time.

Arrived in the town, he at once sought the bank, and was there told that "they were not loaning now," but that they had in the vault some funds belonging to a private party which might possibly be gotten with a good, well-secured note; " but," said the cashier, " if the note suits, he will discount it; he don't loan at a specified rate; says he'll buy good notes. How much do you want?"

" I have a note out for a hundred dollars that I want to pay," said Mr. Grafton.

" You will have to have an even hundred, then?"

" Yes."

" Well, then, I expect the best plan will be to make a note for one hundred and twenty-five, and get a good signer and we will submit the note and see what can be got; I suppose sixty days time will suit you?"

" Yes, I can pay it then, I hope, but what amount will I realize from the note you describe?"

" Well, the party who has this money is pretty hard, and he is a close shaver."

" Yes, I presume so, but can't you give me an idea of the amount he would allow on such a note?"

" Well, Grafton, this man loans money for what he can make, and he makes all he can, and I don't reckon you would get much over the amount you need. Might some."

" You mean to say, then, that he would not give much over a hundred for such a note?"

" Well, that's about it."

" Let's see," said Grafton; " that is twenty-five per cent. for two months time, or twelve and a half per cent. per month."

" O, you needn't go wild now; that aint the way to look at it, it is simply buying the note for what it will

"LET'S SEE," SAID GRAFTON; "THAT IS TWENTY-FIVE PER CENT. FOR TWO MONTH'S
TIME, OR TWELVE AND A HALF PER CENT. PER MONTH."

bring. You see money is scarce and a thing is worth what
it will bring. You make your note and if anybody will
give more for it, take it to 'em; there's no force to this
thing. This is a free country."

"You know very well that there are so few who have
any money that they are able to take what advantage they
please," said Grafton.

"Oh, well if you want to get huffy about it I don't
believe this party would loan to you anyhow; he don't
want no trouble with anybody."

Grafton turned upon his heel and left the bank; he
knew as well as he cared to know, that the mythical personage who had the money was none other than the
cashier himself, who thus sought to "turn an honest
penny."

But the money must be had and Grafton was determined to secure it, if possible. He had borrowed it of
Busteed at "legal rates," or twelve per cent. per annum,
and he was aware that as harvest was approaching and the
farming community being called upon for unusual expen-
ditures, were at this time nearly all borrowers of money
in large or small quantities, and that he should be obliged
to pay a heavier rate than the note now drew. Resolving
to know the worst, he went at once to Squire Clinch's
office and made known his business.

"What security have you to give?" said Clinch.

"Well," said Mr. Grafton, "I guess I would as soon
give you a chattel mortgage, as to ask anybody to go on
my note."

"What on?"

"Well, on my big team of horses."

"You want a hundred dollars?"

"Yes."

"For sixty days?"

"Yes."

"Well, you make out a note and mortgage for one
hundred and ten, and I'll get the money."

"Why, that's five per cent. a month," said Grafton.

"Pooty near it, that's a fact ; but the fellows I loan
for is sharpers; they have to have their interest, and then
I must get a little for my work of making loans. Best I
can do for ye, Grafton; fact is, money is scarce."

"Well, I'll see," said Grafton, as he turned and went
out.

He went at once to the shop of "Uncle Bill" Weldon,
the blacksmith.

In small villages and country places the blacksmith
shop is a source of neighborhood gossip unequalled. Men
go there to have work performed, and, being away from
home, are obliged to wait upon it. Conversation is certain to ensue regarding neighborhood news, scandals and
quarrels, and topics ranging from the last message of the

President down to the legitimacy of the latest child born in the "settlement" are fully discussed and decided.

Uncle Bill was hammering away at a piece of iron, and barely glanced at Grafton as he entered; having finished his "heat" and returned the iron to the forge, he straightened up and began to pump at the bellows.

"Uncle Bill," said Grafton, "I want to speak to you a moment!"

"All right, say ahead!"

Grafton walked to the further corner of the little shop, Weldon followed, and in a low tone the farmer said:

"I've got to have some money and I've been over to the bank and around to the old Squire's, but they all want rates that no man can long stand to pay; do you know of any one who has a little by him that aint in the regular thieving line?"

"No," said Weldon, "I don't. I did a while ago, but being as it is getting so near harvest and every body having to have more or less, I don't think you can do better than to take up with their offers."

"Well," said Grafton, "if I must, I must."

"Yes, there aint no other show, least ways, not now."

Turning about, Mr. Grafton went at once to Clinch's office, made out the mortgage, secured the money, paid his note, which he found at the bank; thinking as he paid it that possibly the mythical party who was willing to loan at twelve and a half per cent. per month had now secured another hundred dollars to loan at an increased rate. He went immediately home. As he drove up to the stable Mary came out and began to unharness the team upon one side while her father was engaged upon the other; practice had enabled her to do this very quickly, and she had "her horse" unhitched and was leading it to the water trough before her father had finished the one he was engaged upon.

" Pretty smart boy I've got,"
said M^r. Grafton.

" I wish I was a boy, then I
could help you."

" Why, don't you help me
now?"

" O, I try to do what little I
can; but it is so little and there
is so much to be done."

"Ah! Molly you are a great
help to me as it is. I don't
know what I would do without
you and the folks in the house."

During this little colloquy
Mary had been engaged in narrowly watching her father's
actions and manner, hoping thereby to gain some inkling
of the condition of his mind. She knew very well the
purpose of his visit to Plainville, but she chose not to ask
him directly regarding this, as she was well aware that in
case he wished her to know, he could readily tell her, and
then, if from any cause he did not wish her to be informed
she had too much regard for his wishes to seek to pry into
the matter.

Presently she said: " My plan of going to school will
have to be given up, won't it, father?"

"Not if I can help it," said he. " Perhaps the wheat
may do wonders for us."

" But that is so frail a hope. It isn't possible, is it,
for us to receive enough from that to meet all demands
and send me away, too?"

" Oh, yes, it is possible."

" But it isn't probable?"

" Why, I fear not; I wish I could say something more
encouraging, but I can't. You must be a brave girl,
Molly, I know you can be. You are young. The world is
all before you and I feel sure that what we all so much
desire for you can somehow be accomplished."

"Then you don't think I am one of the flowers,

'born to blush unseen
And waste its sweetness on the desert air.' "

" Bless your heart, you are one of the flowers, at any rate," said Mr. Grafton. "There comes mother and Charlie for us now."

It was but a little way from the kitchen door to the front of the horse stables, and Mrs. Grafton, having finished her preparations for the noonday meal, came out to hurry them in to dinner; little Charlie running down the path before her.

"Father," said Mary, "you go in with mother and I will feed the horses. I can just as well as not ; you know I am your boy now;" and she set her straw hat jauntily upon one side of her head and saying, "come, old fellows, you've drank enough," she led the horses toward the stable, whistling a few bars from "Suwanee River."

Mr. Grafton stood looking after the brave-hearted girl, and as his wife came up, said: "That girl is a wonder to me sometimes; isn't she a jewel?"

"She has set her heart upon going to school," said Mrs. Grafton.

" Well, we must have her go, if such a thing is possible."

" Boy," called Mr. Grafton, quite loudly; "give those horses ten ears of corn apiece;" and a voice came back from the depths of the stable, imitating as well as it could the rough tones of a man:

"All right, sir; just as you say."

CHAPTER V.

LEAVING HOME.

HE days come and go. Life is but a chain of events following each other in uninterrupted succession. We are hurried forward by the march of time, whether we will or no, and as we look backward upon the path we have trod and the way we have come, we are forced to acknowledge that a power greater than that of our own will has been imposed upon us. The thing we intended did not come to pass.

Thus was it with the Graftons; the summer came and went. Their hopes and expectations, as with others, rose and fell with the varying tide of experiences forced upon them. They did what they could, and having done this, they were still at the mercy of circumstances over which they had not the slightest control Every cloud that rose in the west made them feel their entire dependence on the elemental forces which might, within an hour, deprive them of ability to pay the indebtedness which hung, like a heavy weight, upon their minds. Every moment of waking consciousness was burdened, and even the dreams of the midnight hour took on the sombre hue of possible disappointment and defeat.

Love sweetened the load. A little love, a little hope, with confidence in the rectitude of intent, can sweeten the life of even the veriest slave. With these, life is a pleasure and each day a new-found opportunity.

Mr. Grafton's harvest had not failed him. Despite his fears and the exigencies of his position, he had been successful, and although obliged to make sale of his crops to meet his pressing obligations, and at a lower rate than he felt sure could be later obtained, he yet had been able to meet the demands made upon him. The immediate

Mary and Her Mother at the Institute.

pressure had been removed, and for the present he was
safe.

The Graftons sympathized deeply with their daughter's desire to attend some institution of learning, which
they hoped might afford an opportunity for enlightenment, and a glimpse into that broader and higher life of
the mind, which once beheld and comprehended, lifts its
votaries to a position from which they survey the tangled
web of life with an equanimity and confidence felt only by
those who have learned that the mind of man is, indeed
and in truth, a kingdom.

"Mary," said Mrs. Grafton one day, "I have a plan
in mind for you."

"And what is it, mother?"

"It is this: we cannot pay your expenses at school
this year, certainly; next year may be no better than this,
and yet I feel that the attempt ought to be made. Now I
have thought that possibly a place might be found for you
in Dr. McFarland's Institute in Topeka, provided you
could be able to pay your way by work in the household;
you know this is a boarding-school and there must be a
good deal of work to be done. What do you think of this?
Would you be willing to undertake it?"

"Why I certainly would if you approved of the plan."

"As to that I could not tell," said Mrs. Grafton, "unless I could view for myself the surroundings and see what
would be required of you. Of course, as a member of Dr.
McFarland's household, you would be reasonably safe, but
I could not tell whether the position you would be called
upon to take would be of any advantage to you or not."

"I certainly could advance in my studies there."

"Yes, but there are other things to be thought of,"
said Mrs. Grafton. "I have talked this matter over with
your father and we are both of the opinion that the only
way to settle it definitely, will be by our going to Topeka
and making the necessary enquiries."

"It is nearly time for the fall term to commence, is n't it?" said Mary.

"Yes, and if we go we must start not later than next week."

Youth is hopeful and expectant; it looks forward to the future with pleasure. Mary was anxious to make the attempt, and it was decided that Mrs. Grafton and her daughter should, on the following week, go to Topeka and see what could be done.

The few days which intervened were busy with preparation in the Grafton household. Somehow it became known that Mary was to go away to school and that she was expecting to attend Dr. McFarland's aristocratic Institute for Young Ladies. Mrs. Grafton did not voluntarily speak of it, but in the country, unless one refuses to answer the usual civil enquiries of neighors, it is almost impossible to keep anything long a secret. Being repeated from one to another, the story grew to such proportions. that the real facts regarding the attempt of the poor farmer's daughter to obtain educational advantages and her willingness to do menial work to secure them, were distorted and made to represent the acts of foolish people who desired to ape the manners of those above them in the social scale.

It became at once the topic of general comment; Busteed remarking that pride always went before a fall, and that Grafton was only making a fool of that girl of his. She would get notions that would spoil her and make trouble for the family. He had known, he said, of one such case before; the folks were well-meaning people enough and thought everything of Lucy, and sent her off to the city, and in a little while, maybe a year or two, she was walking the streets, a painted harlot.

Mr. Ellery, the Presbyterian minister, rather guardedly took an opposing view. Mary was a bright girl, and he felt sure would give a good account of herself. That she should desire an education, he thought very commendable, and if she was resolved upon obtaining it, her parents were doing right in assisting her, at some sacrifice, to gratify her ambition. He was acquainted with Dr. Mc-Farland, he said, and would give Mary a letter of intro-duction, which might be of some service.

The appointed day soon arrived, and Mr. Grafton drove to the station with his family. Little Charlie was too young to fully comprehend what was meant by his sister's departure.

"You will come back pretty soon, won't you, sister," he said.

"Yes, dear," said Mary, "I hope so;" and for the first time the full meaning of leaving her home came suddenly upon her. She had been occupied with the preparations connected with the departure ; her mother had been con-stantly by her side, and knowing that she was to accom-pany her on the journey, she had not fully realized that the ties, which were with her so strong, were so soon to be even temporarily sundered. The tears filled her eyes, and for the moment she was sorry the journey had been under-taken.

"Ma, don't let Mary go!" said the child; "she will cry all the time if you do!"

"O, no she won't! Mary knows there is much to do, and that nothing of value is ever gained without some sacrifice," said the mother.

Before leaving the wagon and just as they came into the town, Mr. Grafton said: "Mary there is one rule, which if you will follow will, I think, be to you a sure guide; it is this: Never do anything which you think your father and mother would not approve."

"O, father!" said she; "you know I would not do that!"

"I know you would not now," said he; "but the fu-ture may change you. We cannot tell what may be in store for you."

As Mr. Grafton said this, he took his daughter's hand in his and said: "Do you promise, Mary ?"

"Yes," said she, slowly, looking straight into his eyes; "I will!"

Mr. Grafton drove his wagon up to the depot, helped out his family and, when he had hitched his team, came into the station-house to wait for the train, which was shortly due.

The arrival and departure of trains at country stations forms a connecting link between the gay outside world and the dull and rather monotonous existence lived by dwellers in country villages. Most of the inhabitants occasionally congregated at this time to catch a glimpse of the rapidly-moving train, the strange faces, and to take note who among them is going away or returning from abroad.

Mr. Ellery was there with his letter of introduction, as he had promised; this he gave to Mrs. Grafton and, wishing them a pleasant journey, he withdrew.

"Uncle Bill" Weldon was also present; his shop was near at hand and he was often at the depot for a few minutes at train time. "It's as good as a show," he often remarked. "A fellow can't pound all the time, and I don't believe I lose anything by taking a breathing spell, once in a while."

Watching his opportunity, he said to Mary, unheard by others: "Don't you ever forget the old folks, Mary; just remember that you won't never have any friends equal to them if you live to be as old as Methuselah!"

The train came thundering along and, amid hearty good-byes and hurried hand-shakes, they were off.

Arrived in Topeka, they went at once to a quiet hotel, which had been recommended to Mrs. Grafton.

The "Institute" was at some distance from the center of the city; taking the street-cars they soon came to the place; it was a large, rambling edifice, with spacious grounds. With some trepidation Mrs. Grafton told the pale and rather thin girl, who answered her summons, that she wished to speak to Dr. McFarland, and they were shown into a large reception-room adjoining the hallway. The room was large and the ceiling lofty; it was tastefully furnished with old-fashioned and somewhat worn furniture, the walls were hung with portraits and paintings, a large piano occupied one corner, upon it was a vase filled with rare flowers; some statuettes posed upon brackets, and from an elevated position a full-sized bust of some ponderous worthy looked down upon them. They had just glanced about the room when the door softly opened and an elderly gentleman in slippers, advanced to meet them. Mrs. Grafton rose, saying: "Dr. McFarland, I suppose?" to which he bowed assent; "I have a letter of introduction," said she, "from Mr. Ellery, of Plainville."

"Ah!" said he; "pray be seated!"

As he was reading the letter Mrs. Grafton took a rapid inventory of his features, but without being able to determine much regarding his character. He was of about the average height and size; his face was quite full, with puffy cheeks, rather inclining to red in color, denoting a lack of sufficient exercise, and, as she thought, a possible high temper. Before she had fully made up her mind as to the kind of a man the doctor might be, having finished the letter and now knowing the character of the case in hand, his manner underwent a slight change from the rather stately air with which he began the interview.

"I do not know, Mrs. Grafton," said he, "that we have any vacancy in the line which it seems you are thinking of. We have a great many applications of this kind, and really I must say, that so far, they have given us more trouble than any we have to deal with. No doubt your daughter would expect all the advantages we could give her, and as a necessary result of this expectation, would not be very profitable as a helper."

"My daughter would certainly strive to please, and is so anxious to attend school that she would be willing to work pretty hard to secure a position which would enable her to pursue her studies," said Mrs. Grafton.

"You are aware, Mrs. Grafton, that if your daughter should take the position of helper, that she could not associate upon terms of equality with the young ladies of the house. That she could only receive instruction in the studies taken by the day scholars who do not room in the house, and that her position would be far from pleasant."

"And what are those studies?" said Mrs. Grafton.

"They are confined to the higher English studies and the languages," said the doctor. "Perhaps I should have sooner stated that the whole direction of these household matters is in the hands of Mrs. McFarland. Should you think it worth while, after what I have told you, I will summon her."

"I should like to see Mrs. McFarland," said Mrs. Grafton.

The doctor withdrew and they were left again to their reflections and a survey of the room in which they sat. Just as Mary was trying to make up her mind which one of the ancient Greek philosophers was represented by the big bust, the door again opened.

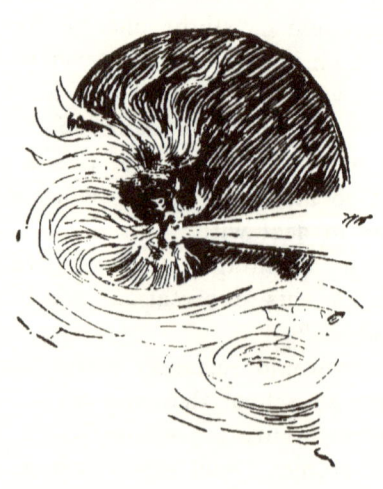

"Taking a book from the table Mary began turning the leaves"

CHAPTER VI.

FACING A FROWNING WORLD.

MRS. McFARLAND was apparently about fifty years of age, spare, slight and nervous. As she advanced to meet Mrs. Grafton and her daughter, for she it was who came in—that lady's attention was strangely attracted by the short, bobbing curls with which each side of her face was furnished. They shook and danced in such a way as to give a stranger a very good idea of the energetic, nervous and quite business-like lady who wore them.

"Mr. McFarland tells me," said she, "that your daughter wishes to assist us in the work of the house, as a means of defraying her expenses."

"That was what we came for," said Mrs. Grafton; "you are Mrs. McFarland, I suppose?"

"Yes; you will excuse me, I suppose I should have introduced myself. What kind of work has she been accustomed to do, and would she be willing to apply herself to, do you think?"

"She has been accustomed to the usual housework done upon a farm and I think would be found faithful," said the mother.

Mary sat silently, looking first at one of the ladies and then at the other, and felt her heart sinking within her. How near and dear her mother seemed to her, now that she seemed likely, temporarily, to lose her. The very tones of her voice, as she talked with Mrs. McFarland, seemed changed. She wondered that she had not before noted how soft and gentle was her manner and expression. She shrank as Mrs. McFarland glanced keenly at her while she talked. Could she endure the life at the school, which did not now

seem so attractive as she pictured it ? She could not tell;
but of this she felt assured : it must now be attempted.

Meantime the ladies had progressed so far in the nego-
tiations that at Mrs. Grafton's request they went out of the
room to inspect the house, that the mother might fully
inform herself regarding the duties which would be required
of her daughter and that she might see for herself the room
she would occupy and the persons she might expect to
associate with.

Mary was left alone, and again the feelings of doubt
and discouragement came over her. This was what it was
to leave home and go among strangers ! How silent it was
and how close the air in the room ! "Ah, but this will never
do !" she thought, and taking a volume from the table she
began turning the leaves, and as she became somewhat
interested in its contents, courage returned and she again
mentally resolved to bravely bear her part in what she now
felt must be the struggle of life just opening before her.

Mrs. Grafton was gone some time. When she returned
the preliminaries had been arranged, and it was agreed
that Mary should begin, in the morning, her round of duties.

They returned at once to the hotel, where Mrs. Grafton
explained to her daughter fully the situation at the Institute
and what her duties would be. Mrs. McFarland had insisted
that Mary should do what she had termed "kitchen work."
She held out a faint hope that after Mary had proved herself both willing and trusty, that possibly she might be able
to give her a more agreeable position, but she was very
politic and made few promises. Mary was to be allowed
the evenings for study, but the day would be entirely taken
up by work, with the exception of the hours occupied by
recitations.

The prospect was not very encouraging, but it was all
there was, and was the best that could be done. They had
not expected much, and yet they had hoped for more.

The next morning Mrs. Grafton accompanied her
daughter to the Institute, gave her a little money, charging

MARY GRAFTON (Λ... I...)

her to come immediately home if she desired at any time to leave, and with many kisses and parting injunctions, left her for the first time among strangers.

The journey home was monotonous and tiresome ; the child whom she had borne, watched over and tenderly cared for had been left behind and her separate life begun ! Somehow, Mrs. Grafton could not help feeling as though returning from a funeral.

Arrived at Plainville, she found Mr. Grafton and Charlie awaiting her. Although she had been absent only for a day or two, it had been a lonesome, dreary time for them, and Charlie, especially, was overjoyed at her return.

Mr. Grafton had a few purchases to make, and they went at once to the store of Mr. Brown, who, as usual, was ready to engage in conversation, which he had found, led to trade and subsequent profit.

"And so you left Mary at Topeka ? " said he.

" Yes," said he ; " I did ! "

" Was n't you sorry to leave her among strangers ? "

" Why yes, I was ; indeed, I was obliged to talk as cheerfully as possible, or we should both have broken down; Mary never left me before ; but we both thought it best that she should remain."

" Yes, I s'pose it's all right, but I should think you would want to keep her to home ; and then, it must be expensive to keep her there, ain't it ? "

" We have made arrangements which will reduce the expense," said Mrs. Grafton ; "but the cost of the trip, books, incidentals, clothing and the like are still, for us, quite heavy."

" Mrs, Grafton felt almost guilty, in the thought that she was concealing the fact that Mary was only a "kitchen girl" at the Institute and was hardly considered a scholar, and yet, mother-like, she could not bear to relate the particulars ; it was no body's business, she thought.

"Quite a number of young folks is talking of going away to school, now," said Mr. Baker; "and they say John Busteed is going, right off."

"John Busteed!" said Mrs. Grafton, with some astonishment; "what has induced him to think of such a thing?"

"Why, it is kinder curious, considerin' that he never would go to school here; but they have a new kind of college now-a-days to teach business, they say, and it's to one of them he is talking of going, I believe; there is a business college there, ain't there?"

"Why, I believe so," said Mrs. Grafton.

Why this announcement should affect Mrs. Grafton, she could not tell; she told herself that this was no concern of hers; that what John did or did not do, could not be a matter of interest to her; and yet she could not bear to think of his ever being in the same city with Mary. Slight as was the occasion, she felt troubled at the thought. She knew, as did every one in the vicinity, of his evil ways, and somehow could not shake off the thought that his going to Topeka was in some way connected with his knowledge of Mary's present residence.

Life with the Grafton's passed soberly along. Letters from Mary were eagerly looked for and read. She was making progress, she wrote, and although her situation was not altogher what she would have chosen, still she made no complaint, spoke eagerly of the pleasure she hoped for, when permitted to return, and desired them to dismiss all anxious fears regarding herself.

John Busteed had gone to Topeka. He was said to be attending the commercial college there, but vague rumors from time to time reached Plainville of rioutous doings and sundry escapades at Kansas City and elsewhere, which were received much as a matter of course. His father was not a man to talk much of his affairs, but expressions from him at different times were reported, from which it was gathered that the son was causing his father to expend what were considered large sums in his maintenance.

One day Mrs. Jones, a neighbor of the Graftons, "ran in" for a little visit, to talk, as she said, "just a minute."

"I thought I ought to tell you," said she, "what they are saying about Mary. John Busteed has writ home that she ain't going to that fine school at all; that she is just working out; says she is just a hired girl there. Says he is acquainted with some of the girls that goes there, and they are high-flyers, too, I guess, if all I hear is true. You see my boy Dick got it from Ben Thompson, up to town, and John writes to him telling what fine times he's a having. He says he goes to the play about every night, and he can go with the best of 'em. I don't believe it, of course, but some of the things they hint about is just awful! He says that the girls get permission to go to visit friends in the city, after school hours, and then don't go, you know, but go off for buggy rides and to the theatre, and dear knows what all. I thought I ought to tell you, you are always so careful about Mary, and so particular. And John says money and fine clothes is all any of 'em cares for, and that enough of them will carry any fellow through, if he is careful to keep straight in the right places. You see, John's father gave him letters, when he went away, to some of the big-bugs he knows there, and that gave him a chance to go to their houses, and he says he knows when to put on the right kind of a face. Says he goes to church, some of the time, nice as a pin, and he writ something about Mary, too. I thought I ought to tell you."

CHAPTER VII.

LIFE'S TRIALS.

RS. JONES was a clever, good-hearted soul, and really intended to do the Graftons a favor by repeating the stories in circulation, which she had heard; still, Mrs. Grafton could not listen to the vulgar and scandalous tales without a feeling of personal injury arising within her breast. Mary's name—her daughter's name—had been lightly used, and although the closing inquiry failed to draw out any direct charge against her fair name or standing at school, yet the poisonous breath of suspicion had been suffered to fall upon her, and this was enough to awaken in the mind of the mother an unrest and concern to which she had heretofore been a stranger. Mary had been reared and most carefully nurtured at home, her every thought and wish as open as the day; her mother had been her constant companion, and between the two had grown up that perfect confidence which the wise mother has found to be a source of control unequaled. Mrs. Grafton had felt that her daughter's every thought was known to her, and in this knowledge she had trusted. Mary was safe; she knew it must be so, and yet—and yet! Ah! the anguish of doubt. What should she do?

Whoever has, in youth, been religiously instructed, turns for help, in moments of distress, to that great Hope, within the veil. Years may pass, and creeds decay. Philosophy may teach and have her claims allowed. Doubt and deceit may have done their work; and yet, in the supreme moments of life the spirit of man rises by a demand of its own nature, instinctively, to its source!

"Feeding the Stock in Winter."

Thus it was with Mrs Grafton, after her kind-hearted, but garrulous, neighbor had taken her departure She walked from room to room and back again, in the little cottage, and all the thought that formed itself in her mind was : "God help us ! God help us !"

Presently she became calmer and, realizing that active exertion was, under the circumstances, best for her, she hurriedly began the preparations for the evening meal.

Mr. Grafton was engaged in moving a fence from one location to another, upon the farm, and as the weather was mild, little Charlie was with him, riding upon the wagon from one point to another. Mr. Grafton liked to have the little fellow with him and talked to him as though he were interested with himself in the progress of the work in hand ; and indeed he was ; at least Charlie felt himself to be of great importance. Did n't he hold the horses while his father was loading up, and did he not drive one load almost all the way alone ?

But now the work of the day was done, and Mrs. Grafton saw them drive into the yard, near the stable. Mr. Grafton remained to care for the team, but Charlie came running in, eager to tell his mother of his efficiency in helping his father with the work.

"Oh, mother, we got it all over !" said he.

Mrs. Grafton replied cheerfully, but very soberly, to the little fellow. Child-like, he instantly divined that something was wrong.

"Mamma," said he, looking sharply at her, " you have been crying !"

"No," said she rather doubtfully ; "I don't think I have cried any !"

"I guess you have," said the child ; "for your eyes are just as shiny as they can be !"

Mrs. Grafton caught the little fellow in her arms, and pressed him to her heart. Giving him a kiss, she said : "Now, go and tell papa supper is most ready !".

Seated at the table, Mrs. Grafton told her husband what Mrs. Jones had said. His countenance fell. and the dark lines which at times disfigured his face were plainly apparent.

"Is everything turning against us?" said he.

Mrs Grafton had had time for reflection, and was now disposed to look more composedly upon the matter than at first.

"Why, no indeed, George!" said she; we have n't heard a word from Mary, you know, and so we can say we know nothing that should trouble us."

"That's just it," said he; "we don't know anything about what may be going on at Topeka, and that's what we ought to know. You ought to go at once and see Mary, and I have n't a dollar to send you with."

"I know it, George; but I have been thinking the matter over and my confidence in Mary is not yet weakened. She will not deceive us; and if we write, she will answer truthfully. I should like to go, but that with us is not to be thought of; still, I feel confident it is all for the best. Don't you know how Mary promised you, when she went away, to do nothing which she knew we would not approve? Surely, you have not lost faith in her, so soon?

"No," said he; "I have n't, but in the life of a young girl these things are so terribly important that one can't help feeling anxious. Well, we must write at once and tell her all that is being said, and of our anxiety, and ask her to tell us all about the Institute. It is all we can do. Poverty holds us as in a vise."

Supper ended, Mr. Grafton went out at once to do the usual evening work upon the farm. Hurrying through this, he came at once into the house and sat down to write. A long letter was soon finished, and saddling a horse, he went at once to Plainville, that the letter might go upon the early morning train. The town was but a few miles away, and yet it was very late before he returned.

The winter passed slowly away. Upon a prairie farm it is impossible for a farmer to profitably employ himself, except in feeding or fattening animals, and with most it

is simply a period of expense and weary waiting for the opening of a new season. Without the capital necessary to engage in stock-raising, the business of cropping is almost of necessity a failure. Mr. Grafton had only barely escaped financial ruin the previous season, and now that another year had dawned and another spring begun, he saw only a repetition of the past in store for the future. His affairs were not in quite so good trim as they had been the previous year. Some losses had occured, slight in themselves, yet to him they proved quite serious. Almost without money, a few dollars must yet be sent to the dear girl, so bravely and patiently struggling against the social slights and ostracism of her position, in the hope of a better and brighter day.

As the spring advanced, poor old Jim, the faithful horse, who, like his master, had struggled on, honestly endeavoring to meet the demands upon his time and strength, but unlike him, without hope in the future, suddenly fell sick, and it was plain his days of service were over. Mr. Grafton did what he could,—summoned a kind-hearted neighbor, who was supposed to be wise in horse-flesh, to his assistance;—but the wise man shook his head: "It's no use," he said; "you can't do anything for him; it's a bad case of lung fever, and in his enfeebled condition and considering his age, he'll die."

But Grafton would not have it so. "He has done his best for me," he said. "He never failed me, and at least he shall not want for care."

The neighbor took his departure, but Mr. Grafton went at once to work. Mrs. Grafton put the wash-boiler upon the kitchen stove, water was heated, and together they watched and worked through the livelong night. As the light began to show in the east, the faithful beast stretched himself upon the stable floor and, with a parting struggle, was gone.

"He is dead," said Mr. Grafton; and as he spoke the tears, which he had endeavored to hold in check, refused longer to be controlled. Mrs. Grafton wept aloud. "To think," said she; "that the poor, faithful fellow never can have any remuneration for all his toil for us, is too bad! too bad! Life is so hard—so ruthless and so cruel!"

Spring found the Graftons compelled to practice the closest and most pinching economy to provide even for the daily returning wants of the body. To add to the gravity of their situation, the payment of the interest on the mortgage upon the farm, which had been deferred, was now demanded. The agent of the loan company at the county seat wrote that the company had instructed him to make a collection, at once, of all amounts due, and that no further time would be given.

In consultation with his wife, Mr. Grafton had almost determined to give up the effort to retain the farm. He felt that without a great change in his affairs took place, he must shortly be compelled to do so, and the thought occured to him that he might be able to make an arrangement with some one who would be willing to take the farm, subject to the mortgage.

Mrs. Grafton was loath to give it up, and yet she could offer no plan which seemed likely to succeed in holding it. " If we give it up, where shall we go and what shall we do?" said she.

CHAPTER VIII.

BRANCHTON.

HAT something should be done, was plain. Money must be had and payments made, and it was finally decided, after much careful thought, that the better course would be for Mr. Grafton to go to Branchton, the county seat, which was distant some thirty miles, and ascertain what could be done; it being plain that either the farm must be given up or more money raised upon it.

The farm upon which the Graftons lived consisted of a quarter section, or one-hundred and sixty acres, of good land. The house was a small and inexpensive cottage; the stables and other out-buildings, scarcely worthy the name, being cheap structures, intended at the time of construction as only temporary make-shifts, which might answer until better could be erected. As is usual under such circumstances, however, it had been found impossible to replace them, and they had been patched and mended from year to year, with a new board here and there, slight additions made and changes effected, with but little substantial improvement. The farm was an average Kansas homestead, and was valued at some three or four thousand dollars. Upon this there was a mortgage of one thousand; this, having been placed some years before the opening of our story, bore interest at the rate of ten per cent. per annum, and called for an annual tribute of one hundred dollars. Mr. Grafton had been told that he could secure a larger loan upon the farm, by agents of the different loan com-

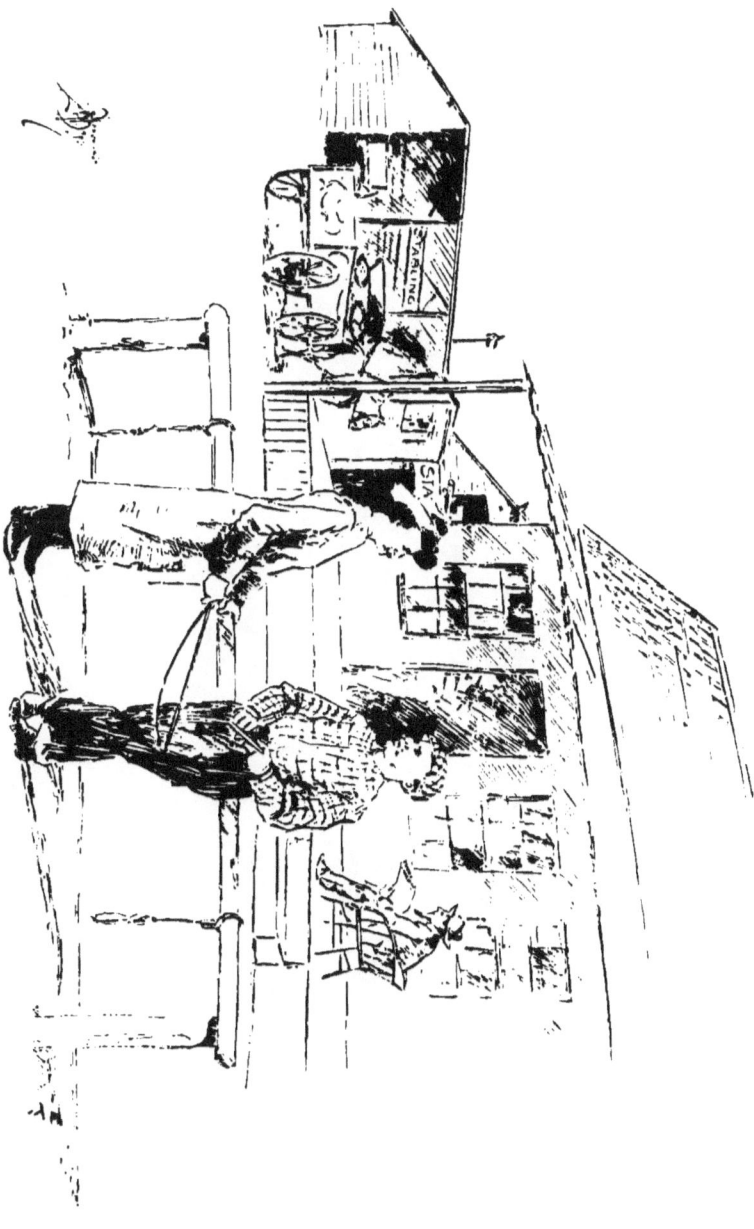

"Fifty Cents Per Day; You Care for Your Own Team."

panies, but he well knew that if he found it impossible to
pay the one he now carried, that to add to the burden made
it certain that the farm must be given up. But now necessity forced him to immediate action. Either the farm must
be sold or a new and larger loan secured. It was impossible
otherwise to pay the interest upon the mortgage now long
over-due.

Bright and early one morning, Mr. Grafton harnessed
his horse to the farm wagon, and placing therein feed for
his team, a couple of loaves of bread and some boiled ham
for himself, with blankets for his bed, drove slowly down
the lane and out upon the highway towards Branchton.
As he turned for a last look at the place he called home, he
saw his wife and little boy watching him from where they
stood, just outside and near the corner of the house; he
waived a hasty adieu and the next instant an intervening
tree shut off the view, and he was alone. As he drove
slowly along, his reflections were strangely mixed. Must
he lose the farm? And what then? He was not likely
to have enough left to enable him to engage in business of
any kind, and although he felt himself competent to act as
clerk or assistant, still he knew that, almost without exception, employers desired young men, and disliked to employ
middle-aged or old men as assistants. Just what could be
done, he could not say; the future was not encouraging,
and yet, when he contrasted his position with that of others,
he felt cause for thankfulness; how happy was his home?
was ever man more blessed than he? Something must
happen to his advantage, he felt sure !

It is only the made-up stories that end with everybody
happy and contented. The comedy of errors which we call
life ends with the tragedy of death ! Disguise it as we may,
the grave is the goal which all are certain to reach, and the
author who would sketch the happenings of actual residence
upon this earth, without other motive than to set down the
realities of existence, must content himself with a recital of
many things which he could wish were not true.

Thirty miles is a fair day's travel for a farmer's heavy team, and it was late in the afternoon as Mr. Grafton rode into Branchton. As he drove up to a stable, a man came out and accosted him with, " Want to stop ?"

"Yes, I guess so !" said Mr. Grafton. "What do you charge for a pair of horses to hay "

"Fifty cents a day ; you care for your own team."

"And a chance to sleep in the hay ?" said the farmer.

" Oh yes, they mostly do," said the man. " If you are going to stop, drive into the wagon yard; I'll open the gate ;" and suiting the action to the word, he swung open the heavy gate, and Mr. Grafton drove into the enclosure, where a number of farm wagons had already preceded him. Unharnessing his team, he led them to the trough in the yard, gave the horses what water they wanted, and placed them in the stalls which the hostler pointed out. When he had fed and cared for the team, washed at the pump in the stable yard and eaten of the bread and meat in the wagon, the day was spent and evening approached. The streets were brilliantly lighted, and invited him forth. Giving a parting look at his horses, he saw that each had eaten his corn and was busily engaged in munching hay. "There! old fellows," said he; "I guess you are all right, and I'll take a turn through the town."

Sauntering carelessly down the street, jostled by people of all classes and conditions, he could not but wonder at the eager air pervading the whole. Each seemed intent on something important; even the little knot of men gathered about the story-teller at the corner were anxious and ex- pectant, awaiting the denouement supposed to lie hidden at the end. The minds of all appeared occupied with the happenings or business of the moment; reflection, there was none. All were influenced and moved upon by the doings of others, and although to Grafton this had been a familiar sight in years gone by; yet, as he had now been for a number of years comparatively secluded, living as he did upon a farm, the difference in manner of thought and life between the farmer and townsman was the more forcibly impressed upon him. The saying of the wise man came again, with added force: "Iron sharpeneth iron; so a man sharpeneth the countenance of his friend!" Yes, that was true; but was it best for the man? Was man a mere hu- man fox whose sole aim in life was compassed by the effort to obtain advantage which other foxes should repel?

As he wandered down the street his ears were saluted by the sound of a drum in the distance; as he approached, he found that a detachment of the despised Salvation Army was conducting a service upon the street. A crowd sur- rounded them, composed of all kinds of people. The leader was exhorting all to flee from what she described as "the wrath to come." With earnest and somewhat incoherent words, she appealed to her hearers. All listened respect- fully. She told of nothing new; no charm of manner invested her words with power; evidently she was uneducated, and in personal appearance inferior, and yet hundreds hung upon her speech. Why was it? Grafton was not what is termed a religious man, he did not believe the iron-bound creed which she appeared to teach, and yet he felt the power of her earnest utterances. What was it that attracted him? Ah! thought he; these people own the bond of human brotherhood; no desire for gain influences their action; despised and rejected of men, they yet seek to serve.

Deep down in the nature of every man there exists a chord of sympathy, which responds to the slightest manifestation of genuine interest in his welfare. All own its power. It exists; the heart of man does beat in sympathy with that of his fellow, and upon this hangs the hope of humanity. And this bond of brotherhood, of sympathy, depends upon no external aid. It is not the creature of custom, or of man-made, or priestly law; it is a natural force inherent in the nature of man and beast. Cattle herding upon the open plain, join in defense; even hogs do the same when summoned by the cries of a fellow. A crowd of men will not see a weakling abused at the hands of a stranger; and wrong, fully exposed, is half cured.

By means of the printed page, the public press, and that inter-communication, which in our day is constantly increasing, men are brought more and more into the relations of brotherhood, their wants and wishes are made known, and that community of feeling produced which is slowly revolutionizing the world, and which will continue to operate with added and increasing force until the kingdoms of this world shall become the kingdoms of righteousness, justice and peace.

The Salvationists took up their line of march, singing as they went, a boisterous song, but one removed from the ridiculous. Grafton turned away and sought the stable; looking in upon his faithful friends and finding them still contentedly eating their hay, he got his blankets from the wagon and ascended to the hay-loft; stepping over first one and then another, who had already composed themselves for the night, he wrapped himself in the blankets as best he could, and soon was lost in sleep.

Early the next morning he was astir and attending to the wants of his team. A hasty toilet at the pump, more bread and meat from the wagon, and he was ready for the business of the day. As soon as the office of the loan agent was opened for business, he was there. Having a slight acquaintance with Mr. James, the agent, that gentleman accosted him with, " Hello, Grafton ; got my note, did you?"

" Yes, I received the notice, and have come for the purpose of making some arrangement."

" Ready to pay the interest?"

"No," said he ; "I am unable to pay it to-day."

" Well, what are you going to do about it? You know my orders were peremptory!"

"I suppose," said Mr. Grafton, "that if nothing else could be done, a new and larger loan might be made?"

"Yes, and unless you have the money, I expect that will be the only way you can do."

" I would sell the farm if I could get anything near what it was worth," said Mr. Grafton, rather ruefully.

"Well, now, that's the thing you just can't do!" said Mr. James, very positively.

"No sale for land, eh?"

"O, Lord, no! ain't been a regular *bona fide* sale of a farm, I don't know the day when."

"Why, I occasionally see notices of transfers in the county papers," said the farmer.

"Oh, well, you know how that is, I 'spose. They are just turned over; same as if you had already got as heavy a mortgage as could be placed on your farm, and could n't pay the interest, then sometimes the company, to save expense of foreclosing, gives the holder a trifle to make clear title; but you are in a pretty fair shape to what a great many are. I can get you sixteen, and may be eighteen hundred, on your place; then you can pay off the old mortgage and have something left."

"My farm is worth near four thousand dollars!"

"Yes, if you could get it!"

"What's the reason I can't get somewhere near what it's worth?

"When so many are being transferred at about the face of the mortgage, what would be the need of a buyer paying more? You see, money is so blamed scarce that men can't get it to meet obligations. That brings everything right down to bed-rock."

"Then there is no way of obtaining money except by borrowing at high rates of interest? Grain does n't really bring as much as it costs to raise it."

"That's about the only show for money, and grain brings no more, because the demand is light; there's too much of it raised."

Papa We've Got Home.

CHAPTER IX.

THE LAWYER.

OW can there be too much wheat raised, when the price of flour remains so high and so many in the large cities lack bread?" said Grafton.

"Oh, well, I'm not going to get into a discussion with you on political economy. I know well enough that, morally speaking, something is out of joint, but I'm no reformer. My business is to make a living and something over, and whatever passes current in a business way is good enough for me; I can't change the general run of things, if I was to die for it. So I've pretty much concluded to let 'em slide, and if business in general is run on a wrong basis, why I'm not to blame for it."

"Who is to blame?"

"Oh, everybody, I reckon; and as what is everybody's business is nobody's business, nobody feels specially concerned."

"Now, Mr. James," said the farmer, "you are a practical man, a shrewd man, and a lawyer, and have often, no doubt, considered the fact that those who produce the wealth of the world get but a small share of it; that, in fact, as things go, the man who honestly spends his life in producing the real wealth of the world stands no chance of retaining in his own hands more than a very small share of what is rightfully his. Schemes and plans of one sort and another, mostly under the protection of law, take from him here a slice and there a portion, until he is only allowed to retain, after all exchanges are made, barely enough to live upon; and, as you know, while the original producer of all values,—the laborer,—is, by means of invention and improvement, annually producing more and more of the good things of life, the amount taken from each producer is

increasing in a far greater ratio. Now what I want to ask
you is not whether you think all this morally right—for
you agree that it cannot be—but whether you think there
is absolutely no remedy?"

"That's a mighty big question!"

"Yes, I know it, but I want to know what you think?"

"Well, if the present manner of doing the business of
the world is wrong, there ought to be a remedy, had n't
there?"

"Yes."

"Well, I am an optimist; I believe in the final triumph
of right?"

"Then you do not believe there can be a wrong without a remedy?"

"See here, Grafton, it occurs to me that you are getting
me into an argument, after all!"

"Oh, well, it's yet early and you have no other cus-
tomer just now, and as you are a man of affairs and a keen
business man, I would just like to know what you think on
this question?" said Mr. Grafton.

"Question: why are you pulling the whole cook-shop
on me;—capital and labor, God and mammon?"

"No; I simply ask you whether, in your judgment,
there is any remedy for a condition of affairs which you
acknowledge does not square with equal and exact justice
to man?"

"Well, Grafton, I can tell you this that, there is not
the slightest chance in God's world for any improvement
until what we call the upper classes get woke up and move
in this matter. Mankind is moved from above. Mental
force and improvement operates from above, downward.
It don't go the other way. I expect you look on the laborer
and producer as practically enslaved,—and, in a certain
sense, he is; for whoever is in a position where the profits
of his labor are taken from him, is the slave of the parties
who get the benefit of his labors. Really, that is the
essence of slavery; to have the profits of your labor

taken from you without your being able to help yourself.
Suppose that we admit that the producer of all values,—the
laborer,—*is* a slave; now I just want to tell you that, since
the beginning of the world, slaves never have freed themselves, and they never will. There is only one instance
where they are said to have done it, and the evidence on
that is all *ex parte;* it's just their account of it. The He-
brews got away from Pharoah and the Egyptians, *borrowea*
all their jewelry, stole right and left, and decamped—run
away. I don't know much about that case; they say God
helped them; sent them dry shod through the Red Sea, and
drowned the Egyptians who pursued. I don't know much
about that, but if God actually performed miracles and set
aside the laws of nature for their benefit, that's all right;
they had to win; but it is safe to say that no other set of
toilers will free themselves until more miracles are performed; I'm not looking for anything of that sort, and I
don't believe you are. You 've read history, you know how
that runs; there's no instance to the contrary; slaves,
toilers, laborers, have never freed themselves, where it was
to the interest of the masters to retain their hold. The
French Revolution is the only instance where the lower
classes ever got the upper hand, and that was only an
insurrection; it was soon put down, and they gladly welcomed an Emperor who used the whole French nation as a
plaything. Now, Grafton, I expect you 've an idea that the
working people of the country, because they have a majority
in numbers and the right to vote, are going to free themselves from the exactions of capital. Well, now, they 'll
never do it, and yet I don't say that they ought n't to."

"You have n't answered my question yet," said Grafton;
"you admit the wrong; is there a remedy?"

"Why I told you that I thought that finally **there**
would be!"

"Well, what is it?"

"Why, of course I can only give you my opinion; I am
sure, though, that the laborer can never lift himself; that

some power exterior to himself must do it, if it is ever done."

"Is there any power that will do it?"

"Yes, I think there is. Public opinion, the general average judgment of society, is such a power; it really governs us, and if I mistake not, this power is being exerted in the direction of a change, but it proceeds entirely from what are sometimes called the upper classes, the thinkers, the educators. What the laborer himself thinks exerts no appreciable influence upon the mass of society. As long as the preachers tell the people that the powers that be are ordained of God; that they must not resist evil and that they must bear all things, hoping for a reward in another world, there'll be no change in present methods. The churches form the great bulwark of the present system, and for the most part they pay a good deal of attention to the heaviest-paying pews. But these questions, although as old as man, are comparatively new to the mass of thinkers in this country; still, I think I can see a change taking place."

"Now, I have answered your question; what are you going to do about the mortgage?"

"It seems that there is no other course open to me except to make a new one," said the farmer.

"No, that's all. It will take a few days to get the business fixed up, and you just sign an application for a loan now, and you and your wife come up in about a week and make out the mortgage, and I will have everything all straight. I will try and get you eighteen hundred on it. I know the place well, and can get the appraisers necessary, right here in town. It is possible that I can't get but sixteen hundred on it, but you sign an application for eighteen, and I'll do the best I can for you."

"I need some money to-day," said the farmer, rather regretfully; and did not know but what I might borrow it.

"How much do you want?"

"I ought to have fifty dollars. I brought up my wagon, and need to take some things back."

"Well," said the lawyer; "you just sign this application and I can get it for you."

"We will make out a note for the fifty dollars, on thirty days, and I expect the discount will be about two dollars."

"Why, James, that will be at the rate of four per cent. per month, and I only want it for a week, you know," said Grafton.

"Yes, I know; but that's about the only way you'll get the money; that public opinion we were talking about has n't had a great deal of effect on the loaning of money yet."

Seeing that nothing else could be done, Mr. Grafton signed the application, obtained the money and began making his little purchases, preparatory to leaving for home.

As the evening shadows began to appear, Mrs. Grafton and Charlie began to look for the return of the absent one.

"I know he will come soon, Charlie; he told us he would n't be gone but one night," said Mrs. Grafton.

Charlie was constantly running out to the "big road" to look, and no sooner did he return from one of these expeditions than he was seized with a desire to go again. "May be I could see him now, if I were there," he would say.

Mrs. Grafton could see Charlie, from the house, as he stood at the roadside, looking anxiously into the distance, and at last he seemed intent upon something: she called to him:

"Do you see him, Charlie?"

"Somebody is coming," said he; "I can't see if it is him."

Mrs. Grafton could resist no longer, and joined her child at the roadside. A wagon was approaching, but the fading light of the summer evening prevented them from determining whether it was the one they looked for or not.

"Listen!" said the mother; "I believe that is our wagon; I can tell the rattle of its wheels."

Reassured by the sound, Mrs. Grafton took the hand of her child, and together they approached the slowly-moving wagon. Mr. Grafton saw them coming, and called out pleasantly: "Couldn't you wait any longer?"

"Oh, mamma! it's him," said Charlie; "let's run;" and tugging at his mother's hand, he actually induced her to run the few steps which intervened between them and the returning husband and father.

The wagon was stopped, and although it was but a short distance to the house, both climbed up into the rough wagon beside the driver.

"Why, Emily," said Mr. Grafton, as he placed his arm around her, "I believe you are glad to see me!"

"Oh," said she, "you men know nothing of the lonesome, weary times that come so often to a woman on a farm. So many women spend their lives in waiting, hoping, trusting! Work is their only relief."

"Ah! you are downhearted again; you have health and the love of your family; just think of our Mary; perhaps she will be famous some day,—who knows! there is n't such another girl in the world—for us."

The horses had now drawn the wagon in front of the little stable, and come to a halt. Charlie clambered out and called to his father:

"Papa, we 've got home!"

But the occupants of the wagon for the moment showed no disposition to alight.

It is a little remarkable that the tender passion, which forms the staple of most works of fiction, appears to the average reader as interesting only when it concerns the loves of men and maids. The supposition that husbands and wives may and do love each other, is of course admissible in print, but strange as it may seem, when the lover's tender wooings have resulted in matrimony, sentiment seems to have received a most fatal wound in the house of its friends, and the writer who should so far forget himself and his readers as to devote space to the love of husband and wife, would most surely be considered as having violated all the proprieties at once. And yet, who for a moment believes that the sincere affection of youth, strengthened by confidence and trust, which has not been misplaced, is inferior to the vaporings of deceptive passion? The man and woman who have a common interest in a little grave upon the wind-swept prairie, have, in that unutterable sorrow, a bond far stronger than all the whispered nothings ever uttered by man or listened to by maid.

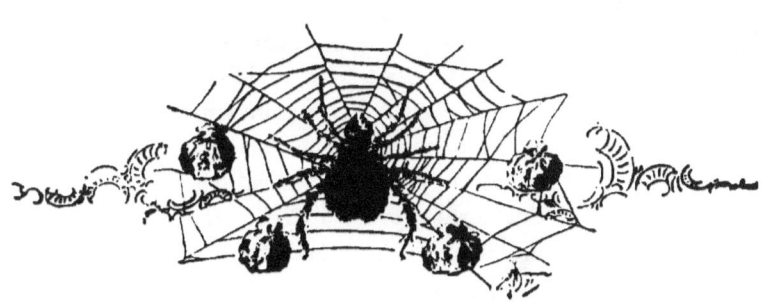

CHAPTER X.

QUESTIONS AND ANSWERS.

ICKEY Jones was in town, and brought me out a letter from Mary," said Mrs. Grafton; "you shall see it when you go in. She says that Mrs. McFarland has sent her, a few times, to take her place as teacher of one of the lower classes, among the "day scholars," and that she had begun to feel as though she had made one step toward a somewhat better position, when some of the parents of the little girls complained to Dr. McFarland that they did not send their children to the institute to be taught by a "hired girl" and that if a change was not made they should take their daughters from the school."

"Human nature has some awful mean streaks, hasn't it?" said Mr. Grafton. "Now just think of our poor Mary struggling against the social slights, which mean so much to a young girl; working hard in the kitchen, that she may have an opportunity to do something more to her taste in the future, and then, when the door appears to be opened, only a trifle, to have those people so eager to close it again in her face. It couldn't have been that they found any fault with her teaching, for she was fully prepared to teach a primary class long ago; and then, she has one of the sweetest dispositions in the world, and her desire to teach would have made her exert herself to please her little scholars. The only reason was that some of the pupils knew that Mary had been employed in the kitchen. But that was enough. Life is a fight, even for a girl. Animals

Uncle Jabez and Grafton.

all join in keeping the underlings down, and human nature differs but little from brute nature."

"And so Mary was relieved of the responsibility of teaching, I suppose?"

"Yes, Mrs. McFarland told Mary all about it, and really seemed to feel badly for her; and she said, too, that those people were very foolish, for, for the little girls, Mary was a much better teacher than she would have been, herself; that Mary had more patience with them and was better adapted to teaching."

"The summer vacation is at hand, and Mary must come home for a visit, at any rate," said Mr. Grafton.

"Why, can we afford it, do you think?"

"No, indeed, we can't afford anything, but we must have her come, whether we can or not. We have got to give up the farm, sooner or later, and I am for cutting the thing short. In fact, all we can do is to mortgage the place for all we can get, sell off stock and crops, and—"

"And what then?" said Mrs. Grafton.

"Oh, I don't know what, but that much is clear, for we can't continue to raise crops and sell them for less than it costs to raise them. They were only talking of paying ten cents a bushel for new oats up at Branchton, and it will cost anybody eighteen to grow them, if all the items of expense are counted up."

"All that may be true," said Mrs. Grafton, regretfully; "but I can't bear the thoughts of giving up this farm, just as the trees which we have planted begin to make it look so home-like and so pretty."

"Well, mother, we can't settle everything by sitting here in the wagon all night ; Charlie has almost got the horses loose from the wagon ; poor fellows, they are tired ; they are not used to the road, and thirty miles have in them a great many steps."

A few days later found the Graftons in Branchton ; Mrs. Grafton came along to sign the mortgage, and Charlie, because he could not be left. Driving up to a boardinghouse, or second-rate hotel, Mrs. Grafton was left, but Charlie would go with his father to the stable, that he might see as much of the town as possible.

Mr. James office was soon reached ; that gentleman was in.

" Hello, Grafton," said he; "come back for another lecture ?"

" No, I came on other business, but I'm always ready to talk to a man from whom I can hope to gain any information."

" Well, according to the best of my recollection, you got me to talking pretty' lively when you were here last; fact is, I don't believe I ever spoke out quite so plain before. But then, what I said is all true enough."

" You are surprised that you told the truth; is that it?" said Grafton, laughing.

" Oh, well, it is n't usual for men to say just what they think, you know."

" The men usually say what they *don't* think, eh?"

"At it again, I see," said the lawyer. " But then, you know as well as any man that men generally are a set of damned moral cowards. Plenty of fellows that will fight you at the drop of a hat, that don't dare vow an opinion that has n't been approved by public sentiment. They say that the voice of the people is the voice of God. Nonsense! You can see that it has n't been, through the most of the world's history It chose Barabas, rather than Christ, long ago, and has kept it up ever since; kept on killing its Christs and elevating its Barabases. History is only a record of wars, that the men most honored have always been the greatest robbers and murderers. And that is public opinion! That is what rules us now, and that is the sort of stuff we are told is the Voice of God! The truth is, public opinion is made; it's manufactured, and it always has been, and never was it more under the control of the ruling power, than to-day. The great newspapers of the country make public opinion; you know that, and you probably suspect that they advocate what they do for pecuniary reasons, only you don't suspect it half hard enough. It is all done for pay, in one way or other. Of course there are slight exceptions to this, but they are not worth noting. Now that's the way public opinion is made; you know it—and then to say that the voice of the majority, made in this way, is entitled to respect, is too funny;" and the lawyer laughed with a hard, metallic sound.

"Say, Grafton," said he; "I don't know what makes me talk so freely to you, unless it's because I know, or think I do, your opinions and feel like shocking you. Some influence appears to make me talk, anyhow."

"You say the public opinion is controlled by the ,ruling power'," said Grafton; "and when I was here before you told me, if I remember right, that the churches formed the main support of the present order of things."

"Oh, well, you see there is a power behind that throne greater than the throne itself. Mammon is the god that is really worshipped. Not by all; some of the old-maid members of the church are pure gold; they live right up to preaching, but the most of 'em keep the Jesus that they really worship right down in their breeches pocket, or they wish that they had him there."

"Look here, James," said the farmer, warmly, "you are a little too fast and too bitter. You are allowing your feelings against some deacon or other, to run away with your judgment and your memory. Now I am pretty confident that when we had our talk the other day that you admitted that there was a remedy for present economic troubles, in public opinion, and that public opinion is changing for the better; now you berate public opinion, tell how it is made and say that it isn't worth minding."

"I suppose you think you have me on the hip now," said the lawyer, mockingly; "but it's the honest fact that both views are right and both are entirely reconcilable. In the laws of nature we see force everywhere triumphant; there is no pity, no morality. The survival of the fittest

is the rule. Cunning and strength succeed in the natural
world and in all the operations of nature, now, as they
always have. The pig that steals the most swill becomes
the best hog and the progenitor of the future herd. The
plant that crowds other plants out of existence, occupies
the ground. Morally, all this appears to be wrong and
reprehensible to the last degree, but it is the way of the
world. Still, running through all the course of nature,
we can see that there has been an enormous advance.
The remains of prehistoric plants and animals, when compared with those which exist to-day, are only remarkable
for their size and hideousness. We see that, through the
untold myriads of years which have elapsed, that, although
selfishness and disregard of the rights of other organizations have prevailed, to the utter exclusion of what we
regard as justice, still, some principle which is above and
beyond our grasp, has secured an advance. There has been
a steady upward movement. The world in which we live
has improved, and is improving. True, great periods of
time are necessary in order to note great advances, but
they have been made. The means used—complete selfishness on the part of all organizations engaged in the struggle, and utter disregard of the question of right, judged by
the moral standard—can only excite our aversion and
contempt, and yet we see that, through it all, there has
been in operation a power which has controlled everything—and for good. There is something which man
hasn't been able to measure, or weigh, or understand, and
that something includes a design which is being advanced,
and yet that advance is being secured by the use of what
must seem to us the most horrible and cruel means!"

"Well, now it is just so in mental advancement; in
the life of men. The most horrible things take place;
things which we cry out against, which we ought to cry
out against, and yet we see that these very things which
excite our horror or our disgust, finally are controlled for
the advancement of the race."

"The Jews crucified Christ; without this there could have been no Christian religion. It was necessary. Public opinion sanctioned it. Public opinion brought it about; and this very public opinion was wrong then, as for the most part it always has been wrong, and yet it was a necessary agent in the transaction, although it was on the wrong side. The power of public opinion induces change, mostly from wrong motives, and should be withstood by the conscientious, and yet we cannot shut our eyes to the fact that there is a power which we cannot control, which is above and beyond the power of man to control, and this power is pushing the race onward and upward through the course of life."

"There! I haven't been talking but a few minutes, only"—taking out his watch—"a few minutes, and yet I have given you a pretty good dose. I suppose you've come up on that mortgage business?"

"Say, Grafton, you are a good listener!"

"I am always interested to hear a man talk, when he is saying what he really believes. Yes, I came on the mortgage business."

"Well, I couldn't get you but sixteen hundred on your place."

"Well, I left that matter in your hands, entirely. Really, I couldn't do otherwise."

"All right; I suppose your wife is here. I see you have the baby with you. Well, you bring her around; we will fix up the papers."

Grafton soon returned with his wife, she was introduced to the lawyer, signed her name mechanically and, with Charlie, returned to the hotel.

"That makes it all snug, Grafton; I sha'n't charge you anything for the appraisers, although it's usual to do so. I know they didn't have to go out to the farm, but it's usual to charge, all the same. Now let's see—beginning to figure on the table—there is the face of the note, that's $1,600. Then out of that will come the old mortgage of

$1,000, then there was $100 interest long past due, I'll have to charge you two per cent. per month on that; money is worth that now; it was due four months ago, making $8. Then I'll have to charge you $25 for releasing the old mortgage. Then the interest for one year in advance, that at nine per cent. will be $144. Fixing up the abstract of title will be $5 more. Then the note for $50 will make a total of $1,332. Take that from $1,600 and we have $268. Run my figures over, Grafton, and see if I am right."

"I have," said he; "if all the items have to go in, the figuring is correct."

"All the items go in? Of course they do! I didn't charge you for appraising, and that's usually quite an item."

"The item of $25 for the release of the old mortgage is all right, is it?"

"Of course!"

"Who gets that?"

"Why I am the agent of the company, you know!"

"That's the usual charge, Grafton; I have done this business on the square and made no unusual charge."

"I expect that's true," said the farmer; "anybody in your line would have done the same. Make out your check for the money and we will close up the trade."

Taking his check, Grafton walked out of the office and down the street where the farmers' wagons bringing wheat usually stood waiting for a buyer; curiosity induced him to examine the quality of the wheat and hear the price offered by the buyers. Among the sellers was an old German farmer, who could speak but little English; his wheat had among it traces of a worm which sometimes fastens itself upon wheat in the open bins of the country, where it has become wet. It is not of much damage to wheat, as it can only attack that which has been softened. A few grains in the German's load only had been affected, and yet the buyer was expatiating loudly on the damage this particular load would do if placed in the elevator with other wheat. He wouldn't have it in his elevator for $100. He had a feed-mill, however, in connection with his other business, and could grind the stuff for feed, and would give twenty-five cents a bushel for it,—the price of good wheat being sixty cents.

The old German seemed dazed and hardly knew what to do. As the buyer stepped away for a moment a friend came up and said: "Two blocks away there is a man who has a fanning mill; drive your wheat down there; put it through the fanning-mill; you can have my wagon to use long enough for that; get a friend to drive it up here and he can sell your wheat for sixty cents."

The German nodded and drove away.

As Grafton was leaving town some time after, he went through the same street and happened along just as the old German, having made the exchange of wagons and sold his wheat, was now on his way home.

"Who bought your wheat?" said the buyer to the old man.

"You did!" said he, in broken English,; "we put it in
another wagon and cleaned it up and you gave sixty cents
for it."

The man was furious with rage. To "beat a granger"
was great fun, but to have the "granger" succeed in getting
an advantage over him was so great a departure from the
usual way that he scarcely knew what to say.

As usual, however, when nothing else can be thought
of, oaths come handy to the average man, and these poured
forth. The old German smiled peacefully, and whipping up
his horse, was soon out of sight.

The Graftons had an acquaintance who lived a few
miles out of Branchton, on the road to Plainville, and as it
was now quite late in the afternoon they resolved to make
him a short visit and stay over night, going home in the
morning.

"Uncle" Jabez Smith was a man of marked force of
character, who, although of genial manner and happy disposition, still contrived to make whoever spent any time in
his company feel that he "had views" which he considered
important. The families had been acquainted in Ohio, so
when the Graftons drove up to the Smith homestead, they
were warmly welcomed. "Uncle" Jabez and "Aunt" Sarah
both came out at once, and the old man, the better to show
his friendship and the warmth of his welcome, began at
once to unhitch the Grafton horses from the wagon.

"Get out, George!" said he; "hain't seen ye for a long
time. We can talk everything all over and back agi'n."

Mrs. Grafton and Charlie soon followed Aunt Sarah
into the house, while the "men folks" looked at stock and
talked of crops and prospects until it was too dark to see,
when an adjournment was had to the house.

"What do you think of the Farmers' Alliance that is
taking such a hold, Uncle Jabez?" said Grafton.

"Why it ought to be a good thing, George, it ought to
be; the principles is all right, *ef* they would live up to 'em.
But there it is; mebbe they will; and mebbe they won't.

'To judge by what's past, the prospect ain't any too encour aging. Smart and designin' men will set the whole caboodle to quarrelin' about some fool thing or other that reely is of no importance at all. Likes as not they will all be a wantin' to cut each other's throats about the blame southern niggers a votin' when their own votes is contracted for, months before election and the goods delivered regular. And the fools don't know enough to know they are voted by the wire-pullers. Why their own votes is always used against their interests right along, and then for 'em to be afraid the niggers votes ain't counted, is just too funny. And there ain't one of 'em that dares to vote counter to what the lawyers of his party tells him is the straight thing, and I don't believe there is a single one of them jack-leg lawyers up to town that can't go into an Alliance meetin' or convention and set 'em to fightin' one another like all rip in one hour's time. Now if it can be done, it stands to reason it will be. Farmers has got a heap to learn before they get down to business. Then, see how jealous they be! Why, if a farmer gets a nomernation for some office, his own neighbors will say he is stuck up and like's not, not vote for him. They would rather vote for some lawyer or professional man that can put on style."

"I know," said Grafton, "that has been the way, but don't you think they will learn after a while to stand by one another and let the political tricksters alone? It is only a short time since the Grange was first organized and farmers began to think of working together. Of course, they would be expected to make mistakes and failures at first. Now, you know how it is with a young colt when it first tries to stand. How many times it will throw itself down before it finally makes a success of it! If you saw this for the first time, and without previous instruction, you would say: 'that thing can never stand on those pipe-stem legs;' and yet it does, because there is a natural force behind it. Now don't you think the necessities of the farmer will finally induce him to stand, too?"

"Well, I dun know," said Uncle Jabez, doubtfully "colts mostly does stand up after tryin' a while, but farmers and laborers never has yet."

" But in the first settlement of our country, our people were all farmers, and they humbled the power of even Great Britian and secured their independence."

"Oh shucks," said Uncle Jabez, "what'd the farmers a done without Patrick Henry, the Adamses, Jefferson, Dr. Franklin, Hamilton, Morris, Paine, and the rest of the law-yers, and doctors, and preachers that furnished the brain-power of the whole thing? Why, they never would have made a declaration, let alone gaining their independence!"

" Well, but Uncle Jabez, don't you know there has been a great advance in general education," said Grafton, un-willing to be thus summarily put down, "and the farmer of to-day is away ahead of the farmer of a hundred years ago!"

" Well, now don't you fool yourself on that; the ad-vance has not been with the farmer,—in fact the farmer has almost stood still, and the other classes has all the fruits of victory in their hands. It will be a heap easier for the big-bugs to manage the crowd now, than it was before. Them Revolutionary farmers would a been tolerable hard to manage; they had spunk and stamina and would a held out for an idee. Now-a-days, what with the big newspapers and all the lawyers and means of information in the hands of the farmers' opposers, it'll be just as easy to manage them as can be. Why, what every man lives on is his thoughts, and when he isn't man enough to have thoughts he has prejudices, and that's more powerful still, and what with the rotten politics of our time and the Grand Army sentiment, and hate of the other crowd, all completely in the hands of the men that intend to keep the farmer in his place, or worse, why he just ain't got no show; he'll stop where he is until the powers that be want him to rise, and I hain't seen no sign of it yet, have you?"

" I can't help but think," said Grafton, "that you fail to give the rising spirit of independent thought enough prominence. I know there is a change in the air."

"Independent thought!" snorted Uncle Jabez, "whose got the independent thought? Not the farmers! They don't dare say what they think; fact is, the most of 'em don't think, they just suck whatever some shiny coat sees fit to give 'em. Why, if an average farmer happened to go up to the county seat with an independent thought in his head, a couple of them court-house hangers-on would make him so ashamed of it in five minutes' talk, that he'd go home, and the next day be usin' the same arguments on his neighbors, that the court-house fellers gave him. But say it's time to go to bed, and we can't stay up all night a talkin'."

"I expect you miss your daughter, don't ye?" said Uncle Jabez to Mrs. Grafton.

"Yes, indeed! I little thought I should miss her as much as I have. Mary is a good girl, and wonderfully thoughtful for one of her age. She was really more of a companion to me than a daughter. But she is coming home now in a few days for a visit, at any rate."

"I know you will enjoy that," said Aunt Sarah. "A mother's relation to a daughter is wonderfully close. A father seldom sympathizes fully with his son, but most mothers do with their daughters."

It was now quite late, and as the desire to converse began to wane, the Graftons were shown to their room, and sleep soon possessed the household.

Before the sun rose the following morning, the good people were astir. Mrs. Grafton was assisting Aunt Sarah in the preparation of the morning meal, and Uncle Jabez had made Mr. Grafton take an excursion to the "near field" to see a wonderful crop of corn that he was raising, after a new method.

Breakfast over, the friends separated with mutual ejaculations of "come over often, now!" and "*you* come over!" and "see't you do, now!"

As the Graftons drove slowly along, they began to talk of their situation. They must now leave the farm. There was no longer any hope of retaining it. Mrs. Grafton was depressed at the thought, but strange as it may seem, Mr. Grafton felt relieved. He surely could earn a living, and the farm had been such a struggle to hold, and the living it had afforded him lacked all the advantages which he told himself his family ought to enjoy. Surely, they would not in future fare worse than they had in past!

About noon they began to approach their home. As they came in sight of neighbor Jones' house, which they would pass on their way, some one came down the path to the road, as though she would speak with them.

"Why, that can't be Mrs. Jones!" said Mrs. Grafton. "I wonder who it is?"

"Maybe," said her husband, "it's the school miss."

Charlie had been asleep in the bottom of the wagon for some time, but as they began to near home he had awakened, and now at the thought of seeing some one he knew, he had roused himself and was looking eagerly at the approaching figure. As she came nearer the sunbonnet was thrown partly back from the face, and at the same instant Charlie screamed excitedly:

"It's my sister! it's my sister!"

"It is Mary!" said both the parents at once. The ready tears came at once to Mrs. Grafton's eyes; for the moment she was completely overcome. Charlie had clambered out of the wagon, his sister held him in her arms and covered his face with kisses; her face was wreathed with smiles, she laughed excitedly, and all the time the tears were freely flowing down her cheeks.

Mr. Grafton, alone, retained any semblance of self-possession.

"Why, Mary!" said he; "how came you here?"

"Why, Mr. Ellery, You Talk Like a Free Thinker; I Thought You Preached Christ and Free Salvation."

CHAPTER XI.

MARY AT HOME.

ACATION was announced one week sooner than we had been expecting," said Mary, "and I wanted to give you a surprise, so I came at once. I had carefully saved the money you left me, mother, to pay my fare. I came to Plainville yesterday. Neighbor Jones was in town and I came with him. Oh, dear! I am so glad to see you, and you look so natural and so good!"

And how Charlie has grown! My! but you will be a big boy soon, and then you won't love me as you do now."

Charlie was very certain that such a result of growth was not to be thought of; while Mary climbed into the farm wagon and was most affectionately welcomed by both father and mother, and as they slowly proceeded on the homeward way, questions were asked and answered without number, and mutual expressions of joy at meeting were, again and again, exchanged.

The parents looked with wonder and admiration upon their daughter. To them she seemed like a dream. Was this the child that but the other day had been delivered into their keeping, whose very beginning had been with them, whose childish prattle still lingered in their ears? Could it be? Were they not dreaming? Their child, so well-remembered, was a chubby little flaxen-haired midget, with childish ways. This was a woman, whose abundant brown hair and soulful hazel eyes were accompanied by that inde-finable something which gave evidence of a mind of high resolve within.

Yes, Mary had come, their daughter was with them now, but for the first time there came over them a realization of the truth of the fatherhood of God: that each soul bears first relation to the great First Cause, that all alike are afloat upon an unknown sea and that existence, fate, destiny and the experiences of life, which make or mar our futures, come to each soul in silence and alone. Form what relationship we may, the *I* within us must walk alone!

They were soon at home. Mrs. Grafton busied herself with the preparations for the noonday meal. Pleasure beamed in her every look and motion. They were again united; this was their first reunion; how happy they were! how Mary had improved! ah, well! she was now eighteen; it was to be expected that she would have changed somewhat; but she had not expected quite so great a transformation in so short a time. And that glorious creature was his daughter! Why, how strange it seemed. How happy she was! Ah! the good God had been kind to her! she thought.

Mary and Charlie, hand in hand, ran from place to place to look at all the well-remembered pets. Would old Shep know her? Indeed, he did! How the trees had grown, and even the garden must be visited and the chickens called and fed. Seated about the table once more, they could scarcely eat. Thoughts too sacred for utterance filled their minds, and but for Charlie's prattle, conversation would have been stilled for very excess of joy. The first questions had been asked and answered; the deeper thoughts were struggling within.

Dinner over, Mr. Grafton sat a while, but he could not talk freely as he had been wont to do. His eyes followed his wife and daughter as they performed the ever-recurring tasks of the household, and his mind reverted to the story of the ancient, condemned to spend his time in constantly rolling up the hill a stone, which as constantly rolled down again. Women did have a hard time of it! Of that he was convinced. How faithful and unselfish most of them were! If beloved and happy in their homes, they always were! Were they not? Could he think of any who were not? And before him passed in review, one from another, the various households of his acquaintance. He could recall no exception to the rule. This was not true of men. No! Men were not thus controlled; with them the home, with its joys and sorrows, was but an incident of life. To the true womanly woman, it was life itself.

Rousing himself from his reverie, he went out, aimlessly at first; the day was a broken one and now far spent, but not many steps had been taken before work was presented which needed to be done, and this led to more. Shortly he found himself busily employed and interested in the completion of what had long been neglected. But the ever busy mind would not be still. The work of the farm: was not that, too, a rolling up the hill of a stone which by all the forces of nature was forced again to the bottom? No! the scene was changed, the hills were not the same, the landscape varied from hour to hour; the summer's sun and the winter's cold, the bursting bud and the falling leaf, secured an indefinite variety. The kaleidoscope might be old and worn, but the views were never quite the same.

The four walls of a kitchen—ah! there was little coloring there! The same stew-pan and coffee-pot constantly in view, until, perchance, worn and defaced, they succumb to the inevitable! And then—well, others were brought to share the same fate.

Ah! women did need to be loved and cherished! That was the contract! This was the promise on the part of her master! Master? Yes, man was the master, and the life of the wife was at his mercy.

Should this be so? Was it just?

He could not tell. Women were not happy, though, who looked down upon their husbands. Indeed, did they not desire to look up to them? Was ever woman truly mated who did not fully esteem and reverence her mate? To despise him, was to inflict untold horrors upon the future of the soul confided to her care. That was sure.

The loved wife and mother was the happiest individual of the whole human race. Yes, that was true; she found liberty in love and happiness in duty, and yet, for it all she was dependent upon another. This had been the unvarying history of the race. Happy marriage had but few conditions, but those conditions must most inflexibly be met.

The unmarried were not to be considered; unmarried men and women were alike in their social and natural rights. All this was quite apart from the question of marriage, the creation of homes and the uplifting of the race. Every child possessed the right to be well-born. If not well-born it was defrauded.

Whatever defrauded the future child of its birth-right was most inexpressibly wicked, and would most surely be revenged! Could anything worse be conceived?

And what of Mary's future? She was now a woman; so far the direction of her life had been in the hands of her parents. She would yet be guided by them. What should they do?

Poverty never seemed so crushing in its weight before. The prayer of Agur came up before him. Give me not poverty, "lest I be poor and steal, and take the name of my God in vain!"

Yes, one felt like questioning the fortune that denied him the right to "provide things needful" for his family. And now was the time; Mary's destiny would soon be fixed for life—and those who might come after her? Ah! how far-reaching the responsibility of life! Did the dear God load man with such a responsibility and then deny him power to act in accordance with the dictates of his reason and his judgment? Was there a God? And where did he dwell? And what were the evidences of his existence? Did not all the operations of nature proceed without regard to man, and was he not the mere sport of circumstance, a leaf from the tree of life, afloat upon the ocean of existence for a brief moment, soon to sink into the depths of unknown and unknowable nothingness—that bourne from whence no traveler returns?

How soon does the wisest reach the limit of his knowledge! Faith and Hope buoy him up, but what are faith and hope which do not rest upon knowledge?

Grafton had been busy with his thoughts, as he worked in the garden, and had not noticed the approaching footsteps of his daughter, who now stood beside him.

"Father!" said she, "why do you stay out here?"

"Why, daughter, don't you know that 'men must work and women must weep'?"

"Oh, yes; but not always; life is n't all working and weeping. We 've been having a happy time in the house. Charlie and I have been playing pranks, and mother laughed like a girl at our folly, and we want you to come in."

"It is nearly time now," said he, "to do the evening chores; it will soon be night."

"Well, we will all help, won't we, Charlie?"

Looking up from his task, Mr. Grafton saw that his wife and little son were near at hand, coming from the house.

"We could n't let Mary get away from us," said the mother, with an evident attempt at gaiety; "she has been bringing back the old times in the house, and the children have had such a romp!"

" Yes, and mother played, too," said Charlie.

" Becoming young again, are you, Emily?"

" Well, George," said she, "we never had an eighteen-year-old daughter come home to visit us, before. And do you know, I'm almost afraid of her, she makes me think so much of your sister, Ellen, as she was at Mary's age. Two or three times I have called her Ellen, and I'm afraid I've lost the little Mary that used to cling to my apron."

"Ah, mother !" said Mary, putting her arm about her mother's waist, "you haven't lost your daughter's love. Come father, throw down that old hoe and let us go and feed the stock and see the pigs eat their corn, as we used to do !"

Willing hands made light the evening work, and when done, all gathered upon the porch and in the fading light, discussed the family hopes and fears.

Mrs. McFarland had intimated to Mary that some changes would be made in the arrangement of classes at the Institute, during the vacation, and that she might be enabled to offer a position as teacher of some of the under classes for the ensuing year. This would release her from work in the kitchen and allow her to continue her studies in some of the higher branches. The lady was disposed to be very "thrifty" in the arrangement, however, and had not hesitated to convey the impression to Mary that she ought to thank her stars for the opportunity of becoming a teacher, and that she must not think of receiving pay for her services.

" If this is done," said Mary, "and I am engaged, Madame Emory, who has been receiving $40 per month, will be discharged, and I am so sorry for her, as she needs the position and the pay."

" Perhaps," said Mr. Grafton, "if she is discharged she can obtain another situation, for it seems to me you ought to continue at the Institute."

" But how can I get clothing to wear?" said Mary. " I 've worn threadbare my little stock, and I could not have gotten through the last year if Mrs. McFarland had not given me a nice dress of hers that was spoiled for her in the making."

"It seems to me," said Mr. Grafton, "that there is an opportunity for you at the Institute that you must avail yourself of, and as opportunities come so seldom, that you must write and tell Mrs. McFarland that you accept; as for the clothing, we will sell the last cow, if need be, to get it. At present, this will not be necessary."

Mrs. Grafton joined in the opinion that this was the course that met her approval, although she dreaded to allow Mary again to leave her.

"But what will you do? Must you leave the farm?" said Mary, mournfully.

"Yes," said Mr. Grafton, with determination, "we shall be obliged soon to give it up, and I think that we will not remain longer upon it than next spring. I can, by closing out what we have here, get enough to start us in a very small way upon a claim in the western part of the state. Perhaps I may be able to make a new farm that will be valuable at some time in the future. We shall get on in some fashion, never fear."

"I did n't know, said Mary, "until I went away, how terribly hard women can be toward each other. They seem to acknowledge among themselves, that they occupy an inferior position and so when they have a semblance of authority over others, they tyrannize. Mrs. McFarland meant to be just, and yet she was terribly hard and cruel to the kitchen girls and chamber maids, of whom there were three or four. She did not seem to think that they had any rights or privileges and all her little power appeared to be put forth to crush any aspirations which they might have. Young girls, even if of foreign birth and ignorant, have hopes and expectations, and yet, so far as could be judged by her actions, Mrs. McFarland did not acknowledge their right to think of anything higher than peeling potatoes or washing dishes. There must be truth in the Bible account of the subordinate position assigned to women, for they seemed to recognize it themselves. Cursed themselves, they endeavor quite generally to keep from rising, those whom they consider as occupying a lower position."

"Life is a riddle at best," said Mr. Grafton, "and yet there is nothing more sure than that injustice perpetuates itself. Slaves made the meanest over-seers." After a moment's silence, he said:

"I think, now that you are here, Mary, to keep your mother company for the summer, that as soon as we are through with the harvest, I will go on a prospecting tour and see what can be done in the way of finding a new location, and when that is determined on, will make the change, while we yet have a few dollars to help ourselves with. For if we remain where we are until spring, we shall come out 'spring poor,' and unable to make any change whatever."

Affairs at the Grafton homestead moved gently along. Mary was both guest and member of the family. Mother and daughter were constantly together, and the mutual exchange of confidence was uninterrupted. Together they performed the tasks of the day, and together they received the occasional calls and congratulations of well-wishers.

At a church "festival" which the Graftons attended at Plainville, shortly after Mary's arrival home, Mr. Ellery, the minister, was the first to congratulate Mrs. Grafton upon having so charming a daughter.

"I thought," said he, "that she would improve her opportunities, and it is apparent that she has done so. She will make a grand woman if the promise of her youth is kept."

Mr. Busteed, who was present, had overheard the eulogies of the preacher, and shortly after, finding him separated from the Graftons, took him to task for the expression of his views.

"Don't you know," said he, "that Grafton is financially busted; that he has got to leave his farm; that he is mort-

gaged out, and that it's all brought about by his extravagant management, sending that girl off to an expensive
school, and the like."

"Well, Mr. Busteed," said the preacher, quite decid-
edly, "if he had not sent her, he would have failed in the
most important duty that will probably come to him while
he lives."

"But isn't a man's first duty to care for his family
and provide for their wants."

"Yes, but you ought to know that it is written that
'man shall not live by bread alone.' Life, Mr. Busteed, is
a problem, a preparation for something to come, or, it is a
riddle that no man can read. Now, this being the main
business of a true life,—the enlargement of the powers of
the mind, of the soul,—is absolutely the only way to make
that preparation; to increase the future capital."

"Why, Mr. Ellery, you talk like a free-thinker! I
thought you preached Christ and free Salvation?"

"So I do! so I do!" said he, with a twinkle of the eye.
"But I want Christ to have something that's worth saving
for His trouble."

Mr. Busteed was not very well versed in theology, or,
indeed, in anything but the getting of money, and he
moved away from the preacher with a vague idea that
Mr. Ellery was becoming radical, or in some way departing
from the orthodox standards.

Mr. Busteed was a church member for much the same
reason as that which induced him to insure his property.
Having paid the premium and placed the policies in his
safe, the matter was dismissed from his mind. Somebody
else was carrying his risks and he did not propose to
trouble himself further in relation to the matter. In
religion, "Jesus paid it all" came very near expressing his
creed. To be sure, a man ought not to be guilty of "out-
breaking" sin, but men, in his opinion, are very fallible
creatures. In total depravity he firmly believed,—man
was bad by nature; entirely so, and as he couldn't make

himself better if he tried, he "let out the job," as he, him-self, expressed it, and in his view, his duty consisted only in occasionally interviewing his Agent, who had the whole matter in charge. As for himself, being "diligent in busi-ness" was the duty which, in his opinion, overshadowed all others. Thus equipped and prepared, he was able, not only to deal harshly with those who came into his power, but to justify himself with what he termed "religion," and woe to the luckless wight who failed not only in paying notes, but in "believing," as well; for such, the world had no room.

Mr. Busteed did not fail to note that at the festival, Mary Grafton was the observed of all observers. Mary had always been a favorite, but to the general favor with which she had been received was now added somewhat of curiosity in viewing the girl who was struggling, not for social recognition, dress and the triumphs of so-called society, but rather for education and intellectual advance-ment. Easily, she was the queen of the evening, and to Busteed the fact was an enigma. He could not solve it. She wasn't as pretty as doll-faced Jenny Harris, and her dress was plain; jewelry, she had none; her people were poor, with prospects of future poverty in store.

Moving uneasily away, Busteed came in contact with Grafton, slightly irritated,—why, he knew not; he would have passed without speaking, but this he could not well do without appearing to offer rudeness to an old acquaint-ance. He did not want to do that.

"Well, Grafton," said he, "they tell me that you are going to leave your farm?"

"Yes, that is my intention; in fact I shall be obliged to do so."

"Obliged? Why, you will go of your own free will, won't you?"

"No! circumstances will compel me."

"Well, you are responsible for the circumstances, aint you?"

"The reason why I shall leave the farm," said Grafton, "is because I can not raise money enough, by cropping, to pay interest on money at a high rate of interest, at the low prices of my products, and between these two the necessity arises. These two items tell the whole story."

"Well, Grafton, farming must be profitable generally, or so many would not remain in the business. Half our people in this country are farmers, and it must be that they are satisfied or they would quit a business that didn't pay."

"You forget, Busteed, that opportunity is lacking for general change. It can't be done! Look at the reports in the papers of the horrible conditions of the coal-miners in many places. You say, if they don't like their business, 'let them quit;' but they can't. Men do not easily change the habits of a life! Thousands of women and girls are stitching their lives away for a few cents a day. You say, 'if their work doesn't suit, let them quit'. But it is impossible. Men and women, in the mass, are bound by their surroundings. The peons of Mexico might emigrate and the factory operatives might stop their wasting toil, if it were possible, but in the mass, and in general, it is not. Conditions are made for most men, and most men are dissatisfied, in part at least, but environment is too powerful to allow radical change. Men who know that they are in the frying-pan, fear the fire."

"Then, according to your view, most folks are being fried for their fat?"

"Substantially, that's true!

"Well, who's a doing the frying?" said Busteed, rather hotly.

"I will answer you as Horace Greeley did an inquirer a good many years ago, when he told his questioner that the great difference between the wealthy and prosperous and the poor and impoverished, was brought about by the fact that one class paid interest on money and the other received it."

"Well, if interest is such a power, why shouldn't men save, and shortly they could begin to loan?"

"We were talking about people at large, the general public, not special cases. Now, if everybody undertook loaning, who would they loan to?"

"Oh, shucks," said Busteed, with a disgusted air; "let every fellow look out for himself and do the best he can, that's my plan."

"Yes," said Grafton, "that's the way they do in hell!"

Both men had, by this time, become somewhat heated by their controversy, and realizing that the place was not suitable to a discussion, they separated, each somewhat disgusted with the other.

The festival soon came to an end. Not so, with its consequences.

Mr. Busteed felt somewhat aggrieved at what he considered the rather lax views of Mr. Ellery, and openly questioned whether it might not be time to make a change in the pastorate. Indeed, he did not hesitate to charge the good man with advocating unsound views upon the "atonement," and, said he, "that is a mighty important matter, and we can't afford to allow anybody to preach unsound doctrine, when it won't cost any more to have the matter straight."

Thus bad begun, while worse remained behind. Within a day or two, Mr. Grafton heard it reported that he and Busteed had "almost fit" at the festival ; that Busteed had said that he would fry the fat out of Grafton, and that Grafton had told Busteed to go to hell..

"The Result Was Appalling."

CHAPTER VII.

MR. ELLERY IN TROUBLE.

NOT only was all Plainville very much interested in the questions which appeared to have arisen at the festival, but the surrounding country, as well, took them up. No person could be found who was not ready to express an opinion or back it up, if need be, with arguments more or less weighty. The controversy very soon took the shape which might have been seen from the first, and the two sides, which are necessary to a quarrel of any sort, resolved themselves into those who attacked and those who defended Mr. Ellery.

Busteed led the attack; Mr. Ellery had previously shown signs of independence, but at the festival he had openly opposed him, and as he furnished the larger share of the preacher's support, this, in his opinion, was rank ingratitude and deserved fitting punishment. The officers and more prominent members of the church sympathized with Mr. Ellery, but felt called upon by the exigencies of the situation to act with Busteed, and Mr. Ellery shortly found himself in the queer position of one who was openly defended, with one or two exceptions only, by those outside of his flock. All treated him with deference and no one attempted argument with him, but wherever two or three were gathered together the matter in dispute was sure to be introduced and discussed, generally with much heat and feeling. Gradually, too, the subject under discussion, as is often the case, underwent change as discussion proceeded. Busteed had charged Mr. Ellery with giving utterance to unsound doctrine and proposed his dismissal upon that ground, although it was very generally felt that his real reason was the fact that Mr. Ellery was disposed to free himself from the rather irksome control exercised by Busteed over the affairs of the church. This had been the original cause, but in the discussions which followed it was shown that the preacher had taken sides with Grafton and against Busteed. That he had upheld the idea that the farmer and his family were entitled to the good things of life and society, as well as those who only absorbed what others had created. He had thus become, in the eyes of the farmers, their champion. Discussion proceeded upon the new base and would have shortly left Mr. Ellery entirely out of the question, had not something occurred which again made him a prominent figure.

Mr. Ellery possessed a very modest turn-out, in the shape of a horse and buggy. The horse was fat and sleek, but somewhat the worse for many years of wear; still the preacher and his wife contrived to extract a deal of comfort from the possession of these means of locomotion.

One morning, while the controversy was at its height, when Mr. Ellery went to the stable to feed his horse, he was horrified to find that some miscreant had entered the stable during the previous night and sheared the old horse's mane and the hair from his tail completely and smoothly. In addition, the wretch had, with white paint, traced on the sides of the poor beast, broad strips of white, evidently in-tended to represent ribs; about his eyes an enormous pair of spectacles had been painted in white, by the same villain-ous hand.

The result was appalling! Deeply injured as he was, Mr. Ellery could not forbear laughing at the odd expression produced in the looks of the poor beast by the spectacles. For the moment he was almost stunned by the sense of personal injury involved in the indignity thus thrust upon him; the next instant he hurried into the house to acquaint his wife with the new phase which the argument against him had taken.

Mrs. Ellery could see nothing to laugh at in the mournful condition of the poor beast, and at once set to work to see if the paint would rub off. But it had "been done in oil," though evidently not by one of the old masters. They

MR. ELLERY.

could not remove the paint, and as anything which would remove it would probably remove the hair also, they were at a standstill regarding further procedure.

After breakfast the parson went over to "Uncle" Bill Weldon's blacksmith shop. Uncle Bill had shod the horse from time to time, and, like most blacksmiths, having picked up a knowledge of many things useful to the keepers of horses, Mr. Ellery had gradually come to consider him the proper person to consult whenever anything ailed his horse. Something ailed him now—that was clear. He went for advice:

"Mr. Weldon," said he, "I want you to go over and see my horse!"

"Sartin, sartin," said Uncle Bill; "what 'pears to be the matter with him?"

On the way the preacher related the whole shameful story.

"That's John Busteed!" said the blacksmith; "I've heard him poke fun at the old hoss, and I remember some time ago of his making spectacles with chalk over an old horse's eyes. Them specs was soon rubbed off, but the idee is the same, and there ain't another one in the place that would have thought of harming your horse, but him. He's the feller."

After viewing the horse, Weldon prevailed upon Mr. Ellery to turn him over to his care.

"I'll scrape off what I can," said he, "with a right sharp knife and then I'll go over him careful with benzine, and I can clean him off, I guess, quite natural; the mane and tail, however, is cleaned off quite on-natural. It'll take some time, and lots of it, to fix them."

Weldon was one of Mr. Ellery's partisans; and the opportunity of showing up the miserable character of "the opposition" was altogether too good a one to be allowed to pass unimproved. Before the morning had passed, and while Mr. Weldon was engaged in scraping the paint from the horse's sides, most male inhabitants of the village had

viewed the animal and expressed an opinion as to the author
of the deed. None thought the elder Busteed privy to the
transaction, but all felt that the insult to the worthy owner,
which insult each partisan took home to himself, had been
the result of the objections raised by Busteed to Mr. Ellery.

"The idee is," said one, rather more intemperate in his
speech than the rest, "that no body has a right to do any
thing or say any thing contrary to the wishes of the fellows
with money. Old Busteed and the fellows that work with
him fix money matters around here pretty much as they
like, and now he's trying to say what the preacher shall
think. Must be something he's afraid of, for just as soon
as Mr. Ellery had but a word of encouragement for Grafton's
idees, Busteed is determined to get rid of him."

The shearing of the parson's horse aroused a depth of
feeling among all classes of people in the vicinity almost
unprecedented, and discussions involving the rights of
thought and property and the control which one man might
rightfully exercise over another were every where rife.

It so happened at the time of these occurrences that the
Farmers' Alliance was being organized in the vicinity of
Plainville, and to the questions which had taken their rise,
as the reader has seen, in the discussions between Messrs.
Grafton, Ellery and Busteed, were added the general subject
of the relations of capital and labor, as exemplified by the
Alliance and the right of the producer of wealth to an
equitable share of his own production.

Feeling ran high ; no one escaped, and a disposition
was manifested to question much which had heretofore
passed without challenge.

Mr. Grafton made his trip into the western part of the
state, as he had announced. Instead of going, as he had
intended, by wagon, upon reflection he had changed his
plan and taken the cars. A few days' sojourn in a western
county was sufficient. It was apparent that all the difficulties which surrounded the farmer in the vicinity of Plainville
were in full force, or would soon come into play in the

western counties, and that to these difficulties would be added a greater uncertainty in cropping, which he did not care to test. "Uncle Sam's" desirable farms were all taken in Kansas; that was sure!

He had fully made up his mind to leave the farm before he was compelled to do so, and while the opportunity for disposing of his equities yet remained.

Being in Plainville one day he thought he would ask Mr. Busteed if he could tell him how he could make the change. He did not expect much help from Busteed, but as he was familiar with all the business transactions of the vicinity, it occurred to him that some hint of advantage might possibly be obtained.

Enquiring for Mr. Busteed, he was told that he was in his office. Entering, he found Mr. Busteed, in company with a farmer with whom he was well acquainted.

"I don't want to intrude," said Grafton, politely, "but I just called to ask if you could put me onto a way of trading my farm?"

"No intrusion, Grafton, sit down!" said Busteed, quite pleasantly; "I would do anything I could for you, in reason, though I don't expect you would give me credit for it, if I did. Fact is, Grafton, you are not disposed to give me any show for my life. I expect one of these days the Farmers' Alliance will order me before it for trial. I understand that you are a prominent member, and I would n't be surprised to have you turn up as one of the judges to try my case"— and the money-loaner laughed as though he had said something quite witty.

"You seem to think you ought to be tried," said Grafton.

"Oh, come now! don't be so sharp! don't you see how good-natured I am? I believe in everybody having a fair show, and then if they don't take advantage of their opportunities, why I don't know what more can be done; people can't be like little birds and have their victuals just pushed down their throats. Some of you folks that talk so much of the government doing this and that, appear to want the

government to feed those who won't hunt worms; now I am
satisfied to hunt for my worms!"

"That may be all right for you," said Grafton, "but
how do you suppose it suits the worms you catch?"

"Can't seem to please you at all to-day," said Busteed,
"and I am sure I don't know of any chance to trade your
farm, just now. Might be a' chance this fall, if there is any
immigration comes in, and we raise a good crop. I should
just like to know now, Grafton, why we can't get along? I
am sure I have the kindest feelings in the world for you,
and yet you seem to think I am a horrible kind of a man.
What's the reason?"

"Oh, you enlarge on the feeling. Men who think as
you do are too common to consider horrible, but the difference in mode of thought between your class of men and the
class of men being rapidly created by the Alliance, is
radical. Now we believe that no man should possess property or have anything which he did not either earn or
recive in exchange for some valuable consideration, or as a
free gift."

"Why, I believe that! You can't shut me out on such
a rule as that! Fact is, that is a rule of law, as I understand it."

"Well, now," said Grafton, "let us test this rule. A
man buys lottery tickets in, let us suppose, an honestly-
conducted lottery; the drawing takes place and he draws a
blank; now for the money that he had paid for his ticket
did he receive a valuable consideration—was the exchange
between the buyer of the ticket and the seller, an equitable
one that should be upheld by the law?"

"By no means!" said Busteed, very cheerfully; "the
man who bought the ticket is swindled, because his chance
of gain is so remote the law very properly steps in and
prevents lotteries, as opposed to public policy, even if honestly conducted, on the ground that the general public
must necessarily lose large amounts of its money, with no
return. The lottery company gets the money of the public,

without returning a valuable consideration. The law holds that the thousandth part of a chance to win is no chance at all, and prevents the swindle, because the company fails to return the valuable consideration which must be given to constitute an equitable exchange. Oh, I am solid on that! Prove 'no consideration' and you can knock any contract cold."

"Seven-eighths of our farmers are living on mortgaged farms," said Grafton; "the mortgage is made to secure the return of the money borrowed; interest is paid in addition. Now, you know that under present circumstances, the givers of these mortgages have no more chance of paying off their mortgages than the holders of lottery tickets have of drawing fortunes. A few may be able to pay and a few may draw prizes, but generally speaking, it will be impossible, and you money-loaners know it. Now let us see how it works in actual practice. There is Charles Bagley, a steady, hard-working man, with a small family, who has been in debt and struggling along for four years. *He has had to have money, and has paid your bank the highest rates for it; in order to get money, he has sometimes paid large premiums, in addition to the interest. Then, he has bought teams and machinery, often paying a premium above cash price, in order to buy 'on time'—the only way he could buy. He began farming with only a capital of a few hundred dollars. He bought a quarter-section farm for $1800, worked hard on it for four years, spent no idle time and fooled away no money, except to your bank for interest. At the end of the four years the place is sold for $3800, owing to the advance in land caused by the big crops of wheat raised those years. Charley pays up his notes and finds he has n't puite as much left, after four years' hard work, as he began with. And further, he has kept a book-account which shows that he has paid in premiums and for interest, for the use of money, between twenty-two and

---

* Actual record of a case, and literally true.

twenty-three hundred dollars in four years. At the end of
the time he is cleaned out and turned adrift; now, what has
he got for the more than two thousand dollars of interest
which he has paid? The 'machine' has taken from him
this money, the result of his toil; what did it return him as
an equivalent? Did he really get anything?

"Why, he must have thought he was getting something, or he would n't have paid the money!"

"Of course he was fooled," said Grafton, "but it's clear
now that he really got nothing. He might as well have
played against a faro bank. Charley's money is gone from
him; your bank has got the most of it; what's the 'consideration' you gave him, and where is it? Charley's case
is a little more pronounced than a good many others, because he went through the flint-mill so quick, and we all
know the facts, but if we figure right down close, we find
that most farmers are on the same road and certain to land
in the same net. The fact is, in all these transactions there
has been no equitable consideration returned for the huge
amounts they have paid as interest and, as you say, if an
equitable consideration is lacking, the business is in the
nature of a fraud. It is a skin game. We have become so
familiar, however, with this way of doing business, and it
has been practiced so long, that we can not blame the parties
who fail to see the wrongfulness of it. People are led by
their interest until they are completely blinded. Society is
to blame, the church is to blame, but no individual, no set
of individuals, no class of men, can be charged with this
wrong. And yet the law upholds it. Society would hold
up its hands in holy horror if the law-makers should protect
and enforce the demands of card-gamblers, and yet the results of their demands would be no worse for the victims
than is the case under the present system. True, it is quite
respectable to be on the winning side, in this game; the
churches uphold it, but that really shows nothing. I suppose that there is no form of injustice between man and
man worse than chattel slavery, but that was upheld by the

churches, and those who would abolish it were denied all social recognition, not so very long ago. So you see, Mr. Busteed, that there is a radical difference between our ideas of right and wrong, to start out with. Now, I suppose you would not say that a man ought always to have all he earns?'

"Why," said Busteed, "if a man was always to get all he earned, how could it pay any man to hire another?"

"That's not the point at all! never mind that bridge until you come to it;—the question is: ought a man to have all he earns? I say, 'yes.' You say 'no,' and seek for a plan to take from him some portion of his earnings. That is the spirit which resulted in slavery. You propose to toll his earnings by some financial arrangement; it makes no difference how it is accomplished, if you take from him the profits of his labor, you enslave him."

It is not probable that Mr. Busteed had ever given serious consideration to the thoughts presented by Grafton before, but as he happened to be in good humor, he had determined to remain on good terms with Grafton in any event so he curbed, for the moment, any feeling of resentment he may have felt, saying:

"Well, it's plain we don't look at things alike, but our interests in the long run ought to be the same. Whatever is for the best interests of the community ought to please us both."

"Oh, yes," said Grafton, "the only question is as to what is really for the best interests of people generally!"

As Grafton came out of the office he saw gathered a knot of men eagerly discussing something which they apparently regarded as quite important. As he was passing, Weldon, who made one of the gathering, called to him:

"Say, George, look here!"

"What is it?" said he.

"Why it is this," said Weldon; "I have got a clue, so that I know positively that John Busteed sheared and painted the preacher's horse, and I thought I'd get your idea of what we'd ought to do about it."

" What's your clue ? "

" Well, let me tell you, John was seen to drive out of town in his buggy, and he threw, when he thought no one was looking, an old paint can and brush over the bank into the creek ; it did n't happen to strike the water, and some boys who were there brought it in. The paint left in the can matches that on the horse; it is not exactly white."

"Well," said Grafton, "it looks as though you had him there ! "

" Why, of course ; but what had we better do ? "

" Well what's wanted is, first, to make the parson's loss good. I should say that if half a dozen should go to old man Busteed and put the case right at him, that he would get the preacher another horse."

Vainly Trying to Sell His Potatoes.

CHAPTER XIII.

CARE AND COUNSEL.

INCE the events recorded in the last chapter a year has passed.

Mr. Ellery was yet in Plainville. The clumsy effort made to disgrace him produced the opposite effect from what had been intended, and made every well-disposed inhabitant of the town his friend; and even Mr. Busteed, after the disclosures implicating his son had been made public, was prevented from advocating his removal by the feeling, that for the present at least, his opposition must cease.

As Grafton had proposed, a self-appointed committee waited upon Mr. Busteed and told him plainly that in their opinion he ought to get the preacher another horse. Quite a stormy scene ensued, in which Busteed denied and scouted the evidence which they presented, but finally agreed to send Mr. Ellery's horse to one of his farms, at a distance, and to *lend* him another until such time as the ill-used beast should be fit to be seen in public. The change had been made by the committee at once, and although a year had passed, no thought of the old horse's return was expressed.

Mary was again at home, albeit the home had been removed. Changed somewhat she was, with added charms of mind and person, and with it all an increase of that air of rapt abandonment of self to high living and thinking which so seldom comes to the young and lovely, but when given to comely form and winning ways, the world is assured that nature has set her seal upon a masterpiece whose living and breathing soul shall carry with it a lesson of sweetness and of light.

Grafton had struggled along as best he could. Since the time of the second mortgage he had only looked forward to being able to make some arrangement by which he might be able to receive for the farm some reasonable portion of what he considered its value, over the amount of the mortgage.

The knowledge that they were about to be obliged to leave their home weighed heavily upon Mrs. Grafton. She had been much attached to the farm; it was her home; withdrawn from the world, here she felt at ease. To lose the home was to be obliged again to begin an unequal struggle. If they left the farm, life in town or village was a necessity, and with this she had been familiar in other years. Grafton cared little for appearances or for the thoughts of others; self-centered, he depended upon his own opinion of himself: if his own conduct met the rather critical examination which he gave it, it mattered little to him what others might think. With his wife it was different. More sensitive naturally, she had also been more exposed to social slights, which, although consisting only of a shrug of the shoulders, a drawing away of the skirts or a cool "looking over," has for the sensitive and shrinking woman, more terror than rough words and blows to men of nerve.

During the past year she had brooded upon the change which she felt must come. The fear of coming want, which is the motive-power of much of the world's activity, which impels the hardy mariner to brave the danger of the seas, which nerves the arm of the mechanic and speeds the steps of the ploughman upon the windy plain, is also weighing upon the mind of the lonely woman in the farm-house kitchen, as she wearily makes her accustomed rounds.

Mrs. Grafton's health, never robust, began gradually to fail. She had reached that age when the powers of life begin to wane. Depressed in mind by the necessities of their position, fearful of the future, her heart sank within

her as she contemplated the coming on of age which in
her mind's eye was accompanied by deprivation and poverty. Mary had been to her both daughter and companion,
and upon the lofty spirit of her child she had gradually
come to lean. For the future their lives were separated;
she would not have it otherwise; it must be so! Mary
must advance! how—she knew not; but it was clear to her
woman's intuitive thought, that for Mary there was, there
must be, a future which should take hold upon those
higher and ennobling fields which her life had failed to
reach. She gloried in that looking forward which she felt
she could not share and on which she could exert no further influence. Struggle against the feeling as she would,
the thought impressed itself upon her, more and more,
that her work in life was done. Her little son clung to
her as though, to his child-like and simple vision had
been revealed the loss of that gentle spirit to whom he had
never gone for love and sympathy in his childish troubles
without receiving that comfort and consolation which, to
a child, is like to nothing short of the everlasting Arm
of the Father. Her husband strove to awaken anew the
thoughts and hopes of younger and happier days. To his
caresses she returned a mild and languid recognition, but
the, work and the struggles of life had worn upon her
physical frame; failing health left its impress upon her,
and melancholy seemed to mark her for its own. As her
family gathered about her, each intent upon her happiness,
she exerted herself to appear pleased at every attention
and satisfied with their presence; but they could not rouse
her from the mental condition which physical weakness
had fastened upon her. When Mary sat by her side and
held her hand she seemed supremely content, and at such
times was manifested that wonderful and mysterious pro-
cess by which there seems to take place a transfusion of
spirit. With Mary's hand in hers, they were one again;
one spirit possessed them! One thought animated them!
The mother lived anew in her daughter. What she had

dared in the bright dreams of youth, her child should realize! In her weakness, time and physical sense fled away, and the windows of the soul were opened. The universe was an open book before her, peace held her in its embrace and the white-winged angels of glorious thought ascended and descended before her eyes.

But these moments of exaltation were but temporary; pain called her back, and then it was that no touch was like Mary's, no soothing word like the murmured tones of her whom the gentle invalid curiously began to regard as her other and perfected self!

The family gradually began to see that in the gentle and unasserting mother, had existed almost unknown and unnoticed, an ambition and a hope of social success and these pleasant surroundings which so largely make up a woman's world, which had continued to live and exert their influence, to be at last rudely dispelled by the loss of home and, in her eyes, all possible means of accomplishing the secret desire of her heart.

To Grafton it was in the nature of a revelation; for himself he had not cared for wealth or the refinement of dress or fashion. That his wife had in her weakness betrayed the well-concealed hopes of her life for a well-appointed and generous household, now shattered and destroyed by their loss of their home, which it was clear she had thought might afford at least the stepping-stone to the realization of her hopes, was occasion for surprise and self-reproach. Had he done all he could? Might he not have been able to obtain for her, what it now seemed she so much desired? But as he carefully scanned the record of the past, he could not see that in aught he had failed: he had done what he could; if another could have done more it would be another who should be judged, and not himself.

For the most of the year which was now past, he had continued to work the farm, but his wife's failing health and his own discouragement had prevented his being very

successful in its conduct. Towards the close of the year
he had been able to exchange his claim upon the farm for
a small house with a few acres of land, in the outskirts of
the village of Plainville; and after selling a portion of his
stock, had removed his family to the new home, where
Mary had found them on her return from her second year
in Topeka. As a teacher she had been eminently successful, and during the latter half of the year had been receiving a moderate compensation for her services. At the
close she had been given a handsome present by the Mc-
Farlands, the Institute being now in a flourishing condition; and had received an urgent request to return at an
increased salary for another year. And this had been her
intention previous to her visit home. Her mother's
condition, however, forbade: she could not leave her; nor
did she desire to do so. The education which she had
received at home and in which she had schooled herself,
included her own advancement only as a means to an end.
She desired to know, and to lift herself, that she might be
able to assist in some way in the great work of life. How
this was to be accomplished and in what way she should
be able to serve, she had felt that she was yet too young to
determine. The lesson, so seldom learned, that happiness
is not grasped by self-seeking, she had instinctively
grasped. She had not learned it. It came to her from a
child, and the earliest and most grateful recollection of
her youth had been that of denying herself for the dear
mother who now followed with wistful eyes her every step
and motion. To be able to minister to her comfort was
her chiefest pleasure. Of duty and the requirements of
natural or religious law, she did not think. Love conquers
all, and is the law of that true life which is to be!

Since it became plain that he was to lose his home,
Grafton had given much thought to the cause which had
involved himself and neighbors in what appeared to them
an almost universal ruin. Many were losing their homes,
and all were finding their means of subsistence gradually

slipping away from their control. His previous reading had enabled him to mentally grasp the principles and causes which he saw in operation around him, and he began an inquiry which, when he had reached a conclusion, ended only in a resolve to do what he could to make known certain evils and their causes, as the best and only means within his reach toward remedying the conditions which he felt sure were destroying the happiness of the great middle class, to which he belonged.

Among other means of information, he sought the opinion of those in authority, as to the causes and means to be employed in remedying the evils which all fair-minded men began to acknowledge as existing. With Senator Plumb he had a very slight acquaintance, but as he was a public servant, he felt that duty required him to answer questions of great public moment, when called upon for his opinion. Accordingly he wrote the senator, asking him for his opinion as to the course which the farmers and people of Kansas should pursue. He received the following letter:*

UNITED STATES SENATE, WASHINGTON, D. C.
GEORGE GRAFTON, Esq., Plainville Kansas.
Dear Sir:—I have before me your favor of the —.

* * * * * * * * *

While I have given very much thought to the question you suggest, I can not go into it very deeply in the space of an ordinary letter, and in fact I would not undertake, even if I had ample time, to formulate a remedy for the present condition of things. No remedy can be devised which will bring relief to everybody. At the very best, a considerable number of those who are heavily mortgaged must succumb. It is difficult to apportion the responsibility for the trouble. The contraction of the currency, which has been going on for the last three or four years especially, is responsible for part of it. This has had to do with the decline in values of farm products, notably, in cattle; but the farmers themselves have powerfully con-

---

* The original letter, written by the late Senator Plumb, is in the author's possession.

tributed to the decline in the prices of farm products by their plan of raising only those things which were designed for a market away from home, and by the reliance upon outside sources for the things which they could have produced, and many of which they did produce, at home.

Very few Kansas farmers raise their own bread, still fewer provide themselves with meat or fruit, while the seeds, the soap and a great number of minor things, which, twenty-five years ago, were all produced at home, are now universally supplied from outside. The result is that the farmer not only is wholly dependent on outside markets for what he sells and also for what he buys, but he pays for the outward and inward transportation of articles which he ought to produce at home and on which he now pays a tax to the railroads and the middle-men, which greatly diminishes his own profits and, in most cases, in fact, eats into his own capital. The effect upon the price of what he raises is still worse because, as he insists on selling everything at Kansas City, Chicago and other distant markets, he puts the question of price more fully under the control of those who purchase at those points. To all these things have been added high taxes, some extravagance in living, and in fact a general departure from those minor economies which have been the characteristic and the necessity, in fact, of the business of farming. It is impossible to go into this matter in detail with the time at hand, but you will readily see the objective of my statement. As I have before stated, no remedy can produce immediate effect. There must be, I think, a complete reversal of the practices of which I have spoken. There must be a greater diversification of industry upon the farm. It is not going to be possible much longer to ship grain to Liverpool, or to any point outside the United States. The further it is shipped, the greater tax the farmer pays for his transportation, but there is still a more conclusive reason why the foreign market cannot be the reliance of the Kansas farmer. The wheat of India is already crowding us out of the Liverpool market. Large areas of virgin soil have been brought under cultivation in Africa and elsewhere, the product of which will come in competition with the wheat, corn and pork of the United States, and I am quite sure that within five years India wheat will be selling in New York. The farmer, therefore,

must raise those things which he can sell at home,—the
butter, eggs, cheese, fruit, vegetables, and so on, and above
all things, he must live as nearly within himself as possible:—that is to say, off of the productions of his own soil,
and thereby keep as nearly as possible out of that line of
production which compels him to submit to the exactions of
railroads and middle-men, and makes him depend upon the
varying fortunes of speculation for market and for prices.

I have written the foregoing somewhat hastily and no
doubt crudely, but I hope there is enough in it to put you
on inquiry if you have not already given the subject
thought, and I shall be glad to hear what you have to say
in reply. I am, very truly yours, P. B. PLUMB.

Grafton received the senator's letter with another, at
Plainville, and took them from the office just as he had
vainly endeavored to sell a few bushels of potatoes which he
had taken to the stores for sale. He had taken only five
bushels of extra fine ones, and a few pounds of butter, with
quite a large basket of eggs.

Mr. Baker would take the eggs; he could ship them to
Kansas City—if Grafton would take goods from his shelves
in payment—at eight cents per dozen. He really did not
care for them and only took them as an accommodation to
his customers. His only profit was in the goods for which
they were to be exchanged. Butter he could not ship at
any price, as most of the villagers made their own; he did
buy a little at from five to eight cents, but at present he was
overstocked and would be glad to take four cents per pound
from any one who would take all he had. Busteed, who
happened into the store, bought a bushel of the potatoes,
paying twenty-five cents for them, saying that, although he
had plenty in his garden he would rather buy a bushel than
to dig them himself or hunt up any one else to do it for him.

Four bushels of potatoes remained in the wagon; ex-
changing the eggs for groceries which Grafton thought
might be useful and taking the butter for which there was
no sale, he slowly drove back to his home. Putting his
horses in the stable he sat down to read the senator's letter.
That he was disgusted, our readers will readily believe.

Having read it once through, he again read it, this time carefully and critically.

"At the very best a very considerable number must succumb!"

Yes, most farmers would.

"Farmers had contributed to the result by raising only those things designed for markets away from home."

But what could they sell at home?

"Very few Kansas farmers raise their own bread, meat and fruit."

What did the senator mean? Most raised all.

"The farmer insists on selling every thing at Kansas City, Chicago and other distant markets."

But where else could he sell the beef, pork and grain, which was all he could sell at all?

No remedy but to cease producing the only things which could be sold, cease patronizing railroads, and "live within himself?"

Opening the other letter, it proved to be from the editor of a widely-circulated journal whose writings he had often admired. It was as follows:

CHICAGO, ILL., —— ——

MR. GRAFTON.

My Dear Sir:—I thank you for the kindly and fraternal tone of your letter and I am pleased to be brought in personal relations with one so entirely in earnest as yourself.

*   *   *   *   *   *   *   *   *

I believe with you that the farmers are destined to boss things ultimately; but before that happy time arrives we must turn a lot of mountains upside down. I never appreciated the magnitude of the task that confronts us as fully as I do to-day. The monopoly foe has as yet only wiggled its little finger, comparatively speaking. It has not begun to show forth its tremendous resources, for there has been no call for them. It is on top, and has the people by the neck. Just wait until *demos* begins to get turbulent and you will see monopoly's mailed hand come forth. We fellows who are on the watch-towers and see these things can, however, by no means seek a quiet place and wait for the storm to roll by. Our capacity to apprehend the work and peril only truly comes to us when we are enlisted for the war, and could not escape our duty, if we would. We can see all the toil and danger that is before, but our mission has possessed us, and even the thought of shirking becomes impossible. We must march right along at the head of the column until we keel over for good, and our persistence in doing will be the same, whether we close our eyes in victory or defeat, and know our fate before-hand. Yours very truly,

LESTER C. HUBBARD.

"Half Crazed He Wandered Down the Street."

CHAPTER XIV.

LIBERTY FOR THE TOILERS.

S Grafton finished reading Hubbard's letter it dropped from his hand. What a radical difference, thought he, is there in men! With the senator, common men were mere pawns upon the chess-board of life, to be used and then forgotten. They could "succumb,"—what ever that might mean. What did he intend it to mean? Why, simply, that they might drop out of sight as mere inconvenient and disagreeable reminders of practices, customs and laws which he knew to be wrong, but which he had no stomach to oppose. Absorbed in his ambitious schemes, he had no time to waste upon former friends who had become mere under-dogs in the fight of life. "A very considerable number must succumb." But Hubbard's letter was a breezy call to the conflict. The good fight must be fought! Giant wrong must be opposed! *Men* would assert themselves; cowards might succumb, if they would! As for himself, he knew which side he would take; whether winning or losing, he would do what he could!

But the next instant his thought reverted to his own condition and to that of his family. How hopeless it was! The wife of his youth in a decline, with no prospect of improvement. His children deprived of those opportunities which he had always intended should be theirs. Poverty, disease and probable death at his door, and he as helpless as an infant in the presence of these enemies. For the moment desperation seized him! Thoughts of suicide crossed his mind! No, that would not do. That would simply be an abandonment of his family to their fate and a desertion of his post. Fate had placed him where he was,

He had always endeavored, in the changes of life, to do what seemed at the time for the best. And this was the result !

Half crazed, the man staggered to his feet; scarcely knowing what he did, he walked aimlessly down the street, a tumult of emotions raging within him. He had gone but a little way when, raising his eyes, he saw Mr. Ellery approaching; he would have avoided him if it had been possible, without seeming rudeness, to do it. The next instant they met.

"You look troubled, friend Grafton," said the preacher.

"Well, I am troubled, and so it's quite likely that I show it."

"I dislike very much to enquire into the cause of your trouble, Mr. Grafton, but can I assist you in any way ?"

"Oh, I presume not; my trouble is too deep for immediate help from any source. My wife is seriously ill, and, in the presence of increasing poverty, my complete helplessness almost maddens me," said Grafton, as he looked desperately away and across the fields.

Mr. Ellery scarcely knew what to reply; he appeared sympathetically troubled, but for the moment made no answer, and Grafton continued : "The worst of it is, I can trace not only my own financial condition, but that of most of our farmers to the doings of men and operation of laws which it is possible to change,—which ought to be changed! I see the deviltry of man so plainly in all this, that it raises my ire."

"But do you think you can change the conditions which surround you ?" asked the preacher.

"Personally, I am powerless, but if I can induce others to act with me, something may be done. In short, I believe that the farmers of this state can help themselves ; and self-help is the only help which is of value."

"Let us sit down," said Mr. Ellery; "I have no particular business on hand just now and possibly we may both gain something by talking these things over ;" and, stepping one side to a convenient place, he sat down, and Grafton was practically forced to do the same.

"I understand," said the preacher, "that most of the farmers have joined the Alliance and that you are a prominent member. I don't believe I understand just what they intend to do. I can see that conditions are not favorable to the farmers, but just how to remedy the trouble is not clear to my mind," and he turned enquiringly toward the farmer.

"Well," said Grafton, "it is plain that debt and the payment of interest, both public and private, is at the bottom of all the trouble. From my reading of history I can see that this has always been the cause of the downfall of nations and peoples, and has universally resulted in the poverty and misery of the producing classes, and until something is now done to change the causes in operation, the effects will continue. The amount paid as interest on money in this state is far in excess of the value of all the people have to sell, after the expenses of living are deducted. The excess is great; in fact there is really no surplus if the people are decently cared for and the children educated, while the payments of interest run high up into the millions. So you see the subtance of the people is being absorbed and the average farmer is constantly encroaching upon his capital. The end is sure, although it may be somewhat delayed. Even in the case of the railroads, of which many of our farmers grievously complain, any one who will examine into the matter can easily see that it is the heavy interest charge on bonds and watered stock that prevents the reduction of fares and freights. Then, too, the interest to be obtained on bonds and watered stock is the reason for the creation for this class of investments. Usury is at the bottom of it all. You know what the Bible has to say of that, and that the result must be ruinous."

"But do you really think that the taking of interest on money is to blame for the present condition of the farmers?" said Mr. Ellery.

"Why, there can be no doubt of its being one of the greatest causes," said Grafton; "just go back to the fifth chapter of Nehemiah, and the first thirteen verses of that chapter give us a perfect picture of the doings of the present. The loaning of money upon usury—and you will note that one per cent., or the hundredth part, was usury then—the taking of mortgages, foreclosures, evictions, and the misery of the people is pictured as plainly as the difference in forms of language used will allow. The prophet cursed it then, and if we had a decent prophet, he would curse it now."

Mr. Ellery moved rather uneasily in his seat, but said nothing, and Grafton went on:

"Now let me show you how it is with the farmers, not only in this state, but throughout the Union:

"A friend of mine, an old Kansan, but born and reared in the Keystone State, visited the home of his boyhood, in Pennsylvania, last summer. Meeting a former play-mate, now a wealty man and proprietor of half the little town, he said to him:

"'You are in the banking and loaning business, you tell me; what rates do you obtain for money here?'

"'Well,' said the capitalist, 'we loan money at low rates; I have known of much money being loaned at four per cent.—fact is, I have loaned at that, myself, when everything was all right.'

"'But,' said the Kansan, 'why don't you come out to Kansas, where you could get two or three times as much interest? Our farmers in —— county pay a nominal rate of eight to ten per cent., but when commissions and premiums are all footed up, it is often from twelve to sixteen that they really pay.'

"Relating this to me, the Kansan said: 'My friend would make no answer, but instead said, 'take a ride with me this afternoon, I want to show you my new fast stepper and we will take a spin out among the farms.'

" In due time my old school-mate drove up to the house where I was stopping, in a splendid 'rig' with a horse which even Bonner might admire. Seating myself beside him, we were soon among the highly-cultivated fields of —— county. Driving along the 'ridge' road, he stopped for a moment that we might admire the scenery. Spread out in the sunlight, below and upon our right was a glorious sight, an 'intervale' farm, in the highest state of cultivation. Clean-kept fields, divided by straight lines of well-built stone walls, some of them being whitewashed, that, by the contrast of green fields and white fences, the beauty of the scene might be enhanced. Blooded cattle of beautiful proportions cropped the rich grass in one of the enclosures. A well-built mansion, embowered in trees and shrubbery, was upon one side and near by, the 'bank barn', built of stone in the most substantial manner, added its solidity and air of stability and prosperity to the view.

" 'There!' said my school-mate, 'ain't that a pretty sight ; can you beat that in Kansas?'

" I was obliged to confess that we could not. But, said I, who owns this farm ?

" 'This morning,' said he, ' I did not answer your question, and I have brought you out here to emphasize what I say. You remember Jim ——, son of old —— ——, the big farmer of by-gone years ? "

" I nodded, and he went on : 'Well, Jim married Nancy ——, a fine, buxom girl, and his father gave him this farm as his patrimony and started him out in life. They seemed to be as happy as larks for a time ; finally Nancy fell sick, and there was a year or two of poor crops. Jim ' got behind,' and came to me for a loan, and, to make a long story short, I let him have $1,000, twenty-three years ago, at four per cent. This amount was afterwards added to at the same rate and, to cut the story short, I 'll just tell you that now, after twenty-three years of a struggle, Jim and Nancy are out in Chatauqua county, Kansas, with a houseful of children, trying to make a new start. I own

the farm; Jim just left it—abandoned it—I did not foreclose
on him—but he just could n't pay, and had to go.'

" ' Now, you see the reason why I don't care to go to
Kansas to loan money at higher rates, I can get the land at
four per cent., but I don't want it, it won't pay the cost of
the farmer's living in any decent fashion and four per cent.
beside, and there are no better farms in America than these.
I own more of them—I wish I did n't—and so I surely don't
want Kansas mortgages. It is a dead sure thing at the
rates you mention, but I have my notions and don't care to
invest.'

" Now you see how it is with us: it is impossible for
the average farmer to succeed in business who desires to
obtain the advantages and refinements of life in the Nineteenth century for his family. Now, as a matter of fact,
there never has been any profit, taking a series of years
together, in the business of Western farming, except in the
rise in value of land, but that has now reached its limit.
So, Senator Plumb is right as to the fact, shameful though
it is. I forgot to tell you that I have just received a letter
from Senator Plumb, in which he says that large numbers
of farmers must succumb under present conditions."

"Well," said Mr. Ellery, "if he is right and there is
no hope, why do you continue the struggle?"

"Suppose I give it up, what then? And what of others?
What of my children? What of the community? Considering these things, I have made up my mind to resist.
Just think of it! Busteed told me the other day, substantially, that I lived too extravagantly, that my daughter,
whom I have hoped to educate, should 'work out'—that is,
become a servant to some one like himself, probably. Of
course she must work, as she always has; but that my
child should become the servant of a class of people who are
unscrupulous enough to seize upon the little earnings of
the poor, is enough to raise the devil in me. Just think of
it: we, that is, 'the lower classes,' are to study 'economy,'
we are to live on what we can not sell, and spend our lives

groveling for dollars. Too many of us ape the rich, we are told; we are too finely attired; a piano or an organ is found in too many of our homes. We should wear homespun; our hard-worked wives and mothers should have yet other burdens added to their labors. Music and the refinements of society are not for us. The Nineteenth century is not for us, we are to live in the Eighteenth; our daughters are to be brought up to household service—the service of the rich. The rich have absorbed the wealth created by us, and now we are to fall down and worship them! I tell you, Mr. Ellery, I 'll never do it! Never!! Never!!! "

During the delivery of this, Grafton had become somewhat excited, and Mr. Ellery hardly knew what answer to make, if any. He finally managed to ask:

" But, Mr. Grafton, what can be done? "

" When ever our people become thoroughly aroused and are ready to help themselves, help can be obtained. We can get it from the only place it can possibly come from—ourselves. Most of our people have been looking to the general government for relief. Well, now, no help will ever come from that source until we do something for ourselves here in our own state; and we can do much. The power of corrupt politicians and corrupt voters in the great cities can be, and will be, used against us to such an extent that our success in obtaining possession of the general government is, at the very best, a long way off. In the Western states we can rule, when ever we get together; and finally, after much wrangling, we are going to do that. Then, we can help ourselves by the passage of State laws. We can stop the machine that is dragging us to death. If we are successful in this State, other states will follow our example, and then Congress and the President will hear us; then they will be willing to listen to our complaint; now, our enemies have their ears, and in fact control them. So long as we are willing to allow them to fleece us, they will, in one way or another, keep that control of the general

government which enables them, under our present laws, to
continue their trade of blood-sucking."

"You speak very strongly of these matters; I suppose,
though, you have studied the subject and given it more
thought than I have," said Mr. Ellery.

"I have given it a good deal of thought, and yet I have
no new plan, no patent scheme for saving the country; my
only plan is simply this : A return to the juster laws and
purer practices of our fathers. When I was a boy in Ohio,
my father lived on a farm in what was then considered a new
country. People were poor all about us, it is true, but they
all had their homes,—there were then no mortgaged farms,
debts were comparatively few, and people lived without that
terrible load of care and anxiety which comes from debt and
the payment of interest money. And people were not only
comparatively happy, but they were in the line of mental
advancement; in fact, those early days were prolific in the
production of men of resource and character. These were
precisely the surroundings which produced such men as
Washington, Jackson, William Henry Harrison, Clay,
Douglas, Lincoln, and all the rest of the band of patriots
who made America what it was up to the time when our
late War was made the excuse for loading every thing and
every body with debt. As soon as our people became burdened with that, the energies of the common people—from
whom our saviours have come in the past, and from whom
they are to come in the future—have been directed to this
miserable weight and clog of debt. Now it is impossible to
produce *men;* the people are engaged in producing *dollars.*
Debt makes slaves and cowards;—always has and always
will. Not only is the material improvement of our people
put a stop to, but mentally they must be debased if present
laws and customs are to continue."

"Well, but Mr. Grafton, does not what is called the
'land question' cut quite a figure here? In the days you
speak of land was comparatively free ; does not this tell the
story?" said Mr. Ellery.

"Of course that has much to do with the matter, there can be no doubt of that; but men lose their homes almost entirely through the operation of monetary laws and customs, Mr. Ellery. Go back to the fifth chapter of Nehemiah and you will see that loan, mortgage and usury came first, then, the loss of the land and home. It has always been so, in every age. No people, no nation, ever lost its homes in any other way, peaceably. And next to the family, a home belonging to the family is the most important thing in the creation of strong, intelligent, resourceful men and women, in all the world. Now, if we can get rid of debt in the future and make it possible for families to own homes which can not be taken from them, unless they wish to sell them outright, we shall come back to the conditions which surrounded the people in the earlier and better days of the American republic "

"That sounds very well, Mr. Grafton, but do you think it possible ?"

"Certainly it is possible ; any thing is possible to men who are willing to do and dare. In this case we shall only be required to take away by law certain special privileges enjoyed by the dealers in money, and the thing is done. That's all. The power of State law is sufficient to do that, and if we have in our State government a set of men possessing half the spirit which animated the Continental Congress, it would be done, and quickly, too. But if we have not this spirit, if we are too fearful and cowardly, then the people now controlling our government are right in their treatment of us, for we are despicable creatures and less than men, fit only for that slavery which waits for us not far in the future."

"But, Mr. Grafton, you speak of State laws,—what laws would you have ?"

"Well, the first thing necessary would be a stay law, putting a stop, say for two years, to the foreclosure of real estate mortgages and the payment of interest upon them."

"Would that be just?"

"Certainly ; the security would remain; the debt would not be repudiated. It would simply give the holder time to make the best use of property in his hands."

"But wouldn't the courts hold that this would be unconstitutional, as interfering with contracts?"

"Courts hold their sessions in pursuance of and under the direction of law. Otherwise they have no force. Let the Legislature pass laws directing the methods of foreclosure to be practiced in the courts. A practical and constitutional stay can, in this way, be secured, which will afford relief. But, anyhow, the public good is the supreme law, or should be. Laws should be made to protect the majority of the people, not to allow a few to rob them. No doubt our State government of the future will have occasion for resolution, courage and "sand," but with the right kind of men in the Legislature all we need can be obtained."

"Well, what next?"

"Then abolish all laws for the collection of voluntary debts to be incurred in the future. If possible, put this in the State constitution, then it will be out of the reach of the courts. That is the proper place for it: properly, a constitution is simply a bill of rights. If there are no laws for the collection of voluntary debts, debt-making will not be encouraged and the debt-makers will soon discover that more money must be put in circulation, so that all deals can be settled at the time by the payment of cash. That will convert them,—nothing else ever will. This legislation will do away with seven-eighths of our court expenses and three-quarters of our lawyers. No doubt, the lawyers would fight any thing tending to relieve the people from the burdens which they impose and the privileges they assert.

"The third step would be one which will allow the people to get away from the control of the money-loaners. *Liberty* is what we are after. All our measures look to the abolition of special privilege; special privilege of the fund holder ; special privilege of the creditor; special privileges of the lawyers; special privileges of the money-managers. Abolish these and make every family secure in its home, and Society will be rejuvenated, reformed, Christianized, saved! Then we will have the conditions prevailing in this country in its infancy, when men were free. At the present time we have in this State probably a thousand different kinds of warrants. The State issues them, so do the counties, the municipalities and the school-districts; and each of these issues them upon different funds. All bear interest, and most of them are at a discount. The people lose the discount and pay the interest, and the money-shavers gain both and lock up the warrants, which might serve as a medium of exchange. Now, suppose that in lieu of all these different kinds of warrants the State issues only one kind, made receivable for taxes anywhere in the State, bearing no interest, and engraved in the highest style of the art, in sums of 25 cents, 50 cents, $1, $2, $5 and $10. These warrants to be issued by the State Treasurer to each county, municipality and district, in amount equal to its tax-levy, properly certified to him. The State Auditor's office to be made a clearing-house for the settlement of balances between said counties, municipalities and districts. Under these circumstances, warrants bearing no interest and made receivable for taxes anywhere in the State, would circulate anywhere in the State at par, as they did in our Colonial days. Then, public improvements, for which the State is suffering, can be constructed, paid for in warrants, and every idle man in the State set at work. It can be easily shown that such warrants have, in the past, and will, in the future, circulate freely, and at par. In that event it will be easy to obtain what legal-tender money we may need for the payment of interest, everybody will be employed and real prosperity will be assured."

" I must say," said Mr. Ellery, " that you interest me greatly. If these things can be done, they ought to be done, and if they ought to be done they can be, if people are sufficiently awakened and aroused. But is that all?"

" The fourth step should be one making occupied homes, up to a certain moderate valuation, free from all taxation and from seizure and sale for debt contracted after the passage of the law. But, Mr. Ellery, I must return home. I left there a while ago, scarcely knowing where I was going. Now I must go; I will leave you, however, a copy of a constitutional amendment which I think favorably of; you can look it over at your leisure. You will see, if you investigate the subject, that its provisions do not apply to the great properties in the State, nor to the business portions of the cities, to mines or other natural opportunities not available as homes for the people. It is only for the benefit of those owning and occupying homes. At present it would not affect ten per cent. in value, of the property of the State. There is plenty of property, now escaping taxation, to bear all the expenses of government. I am convinced that the passage of this amendment would so increase the demand for land to be converted into free homes, that even land monopolists, finding ready sale for land, which now they cannot dispose of, would be led to favor it. Then, too, they would know that increased taxation upon unoccupied land held for speculation, which would result from the exemption of homes, must finally make future land speculation uproductive and unprofitable. This would induce them to sell, so that altogether all classes would find the amendment drawn in their interest. Shall be glad of your criticism upon it. We shall be glad to have you call on us, Mr. Ellery; now I must go." Handing the preacher a printed slip, he walked away in the direction of his home.*

---

*The printed slip given Mr. Ellery read as follows:

PROPOSED CONSTITUTIONAL AMENDMENT.

SECTION 1.—Real estate, or land, and all usual improvements, to the value of a sum not to exceed .... dollars held, used and occupied in good faith as a homestead by any usual and private family the head of which family shall be a citizen of the United States and the State of Kansas, is hereby forever exempted from all taxation of every kind and character in this State. Provided, that all lands and natural opportunities used or needed for public use or business,—as certain limited and restricted areas in towns and cities, all mines, forests, waterfalls, or other natural opportunities not available for cultivation or as dwelling places be and the same are hereby expressly exempted from the provisions of this article.

SECTION 1.—The right of every family described in Section One of this article to the exclusive possession of a homestead, held, used and occupied as described in said Section One and valued at a sum not exceeding.............................dollars shall not be abridged or denied by reason of any contract, agreement, mortgage or other instrument or promise whatsoever, verbal or written, made or executed by the possessors of said homestead after this article shall have been adopted in proper form by the people of this State.

SECTION 3.—The Legislature shall have power to enact all laws necessary to carry into effect the due intent and meaning of the provisions of this article.

CHAPTER XV.

SORROW.

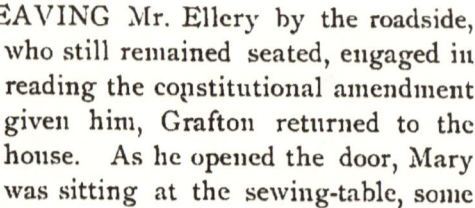

EAVING Mr. Ellery by the roadside, who still remained seated, engaged in reading the constitutional amendment given him, Grafton returned to the house. As he opened the door, Mary was sitting at the sewing-table, some unfinished work was upon her lap, her head was resting upon the table in front, while Charlie stood at her side. As her father entered, she raised her head and began to wipe her eyes with her handkerchief; evidently she had been weeping.

"Is mother worse to-day?" said Grafton.

"Oh, I don't know that she is any worse, but it is plain that she is no better," said the daughter, as the tears began again to flow; "she is sleeping now; the doctor was here a little while ago, but he says it's of no use for him to come; that she doesn't need medicine."

"When will mamma be well?" said Charlie; "it's so still in the house, and sister can't play with me, and she's been crying, and I don't want my mother sick," and the little fellow began to snivel, while Mary was endeavoring to calm herself, that she might the more readily comfort the child.

Grafton did not answer. Sitting down, he rested his elbows upon his knees, and with his head in his hands, he abandoned himself to the gloomiest reflections.

Brushing away the tears, Mary began tidying up the room; bringing a pail of water from the pump, she bathed her swollen eyes, and proceeded to arrange for the evening meal.

Heedless of what was going on around him, Grafton still continued in the characteristic attitude of despair which he had assumed. His thoughts ran back to the days of his

youth. In the bright dreams of the future, which came to him then, he could detect no likeness to the sober realities of the life he had lived. Was life only a struggle, to end in nothing? Was hope only an *ignis fatuus* to lure us on? Was man born to be cheated, or to cheat himself with vain hopes and idle illusions? One way there was, out of the darkness. The ideal held up before the mind of the true man was a perfect one; it took hold on higher things. A spark from the Infinite Light possessed him. It was impossible that he should be content with sordid and imperfect things. Sordid and imperfect men might be content. Human hogs might increase in fatness and grunt with satisfaction in their styes, but the life which should endure took no note of swill. To increase in knowledge one must be dissatisfied with ignorance. Intelligent discontent was the origin of all mental progress. Mind was necessary to a man, and the mind which grew must be fed. To a hog, swill was the chief concern. But the hog soon came to an end.

" Father," said Mary' " supper is ready ! "

Grafton roused himself from his reverie and, mechanically, the family gathered around the table.

" Mother is sleeping yet, and I thought it best not to wake her," said the daughter.

' I really do not care for any thing to eat, but I suppose it is best to go through the motions at about the regular time," said Grafton. " Charlie wants his supper, don't you boy ? "

Charlie made no audible reply. His mouth was full, and he contented himself with replying by a nod of the head and a look of the eyes, quite readily understood.

Grafton and his daughter ate but little; occasionally a furtive glance was exchanged, but very little was said. The mind of each was burdened by sorrowful thoughts of the wife and mother. What of her future? Would she recover and be to them as she had been? Was her mind to continue to wander? Had they, in fact, already lost the gentle soul whose smile and quiet word of approval outweighed the plaudits of all beside? They could not tell! Hope struggled with despair. Uncertainty weighed upon their minds and left them in the control of that cankering care which corrodes and rusts every material treasure possessed by man.

The dishes had been cleared away. Mary was busy with her needle, and still the invalid slept. Grafton sat reading by the evening lamp, when a knock was heard at the door. Mary opened, and Mr. and Mrs. Ellery were seen standing without. A most cordial invitation to enter from both father and daughter being given, they were soon seated in the one " living room " of the little cottage.

Mrs. Ellery's first enquiry was for the invalid, and as Mary replied, explaining as well as she could her symptoms and the condition of her mind, Mr. Ellery engaged Grafton in conversation, remarking that he had long intended and wished to call, but confessed that he scarcely knew what to say. His desire was to comfort and console, but, said he, · " Mr. Grafton, you must take the will for the deed! "

" There is so much," said Grafton, "that passes all understanding! "

" One can understand that trials and troubles may bring a final reward in some cases, but how is it with my poor wife? Is her life, which was always so careful and conscientious, now to end in a mere blank? Is it to be a struggle, ending in nothing? "

Even at the worst, my friend," said the preacher, " you must remember your children are to live. You can not say that your lives are without fruit, which gives no promise for the future!"

"Ah, well!" said Grafton, "that simply carries the struggle along. Another youth of promise may end in defeat, as her's seems to have done."

"All roads, Mr. Grafton, lead to the end of the world; and, considered without relation to what may take place beyond, no transaction of this is fully explainable. But, with a future existence in view, which shall be a continuation of this, all is clear. Doubt is removed only by action. For every man there is a duty. He cannot know all reasons and understand all mysteries. Whatever appears to a man to be truth, that must he follow or be condemned. But he must follow! Conviction must be converted into conduct! Action must result; and if action square with his highest conception of truth, all will be well. Of one thing I would, if I could, convince every man, and that is, that the Great Power which controls the forces of nature is friendly and favorable to man."

While Mr. Ellery continued talking, the ladies adjourned to the little bed-room which opened out of the room in which they sat. Mrs. Grafton was now awake; she knew Mrs. Ellery, and spoke pleasantly to her.

" Where is Charlie ? " said she.

" I put him to bed long ago, mother," said Mary.

" He was crying, a while ago, I heard him just as I went to sleep, and he wanted me. Poor dear! I fear he will do without me soon; Mary, you will not leave him, will you?"

"Ah, mother!" said Mary, "you must not talk of leaving us! If you would only think so, you could recover and bring happiness to us all!"

" Do you not think,,' said Mrs. Ellery, "that it is your duty to try to get well?"

" No; I have struggled all my life, I have done what I could, I am tired and weary. Rest! Rest!! I must rest!

Mary was unwearied in her attentions, and Mrs. Ellery assisted her as well as she could, but the invalid relapsed

into a somnolent condition, but half awake, and answered
their further enquiries with only a monosyllable now and
then.   After a short interval Mrs. Ellery rose and, with her
husband, took leave of the sorrowing household.

"Grafton," said Mr. Ellery, as he took his hand in
parting, "if there is anything I can assist you in, you will
let me know, won't you?"

Life at the Grafton cottage had lost its charm.   Charlie
was fretful and querulous at times, apparently without cause.
He wanted this or that—until he got it—and was contented
with nothing long.   Sister must help him find the ball
which he had lost, or assist in his game of marbles; and,
unwearied as she was in his behalf, when not attending
upon her mother's wants or engaged in the daily round of
household cares which now absorbed much of her time, yet
it seemed impossible for him to be the contented, happy
child of the past.   That his mother was ill was occasion for
sorrow with him, when in her presence, but, grown familiar
with her absence from the kitchen, where her waking hours
had mostly been spent, he soon forgot it all, or so it seemed;
and yet he was unhappy; why, he could not tell.

Whoever has seen a fretful, crying infant, in its over-
tasked and discouraged mother's arms, taken from her who
should have been its chief joy and source of comfort, by the
possessor of even-tempered vigorous health, and seen the
quivering lip, the fretful sob and the injured air of the child
quickly disappear and give place to the happy smile and
exultant crow, can well believe that little mortals, at least,
are dependent upon the mental states of those with whom
they are associated.   And are we not taught by the occurrences of our every-day life, that children of a larger growth
and maturer years are also dependent upon those with whom
they come in contact for the color of their thoughts?

Mrs. Grafton had gradually become weaker and still
weaker, as time passed on.   She did not complain, but had
apparently abandoned all hope of relief at mortal hands.
At times her mind wandered, and the poor, tired, discour-

aged woman became again, in thought, a little child. Again she trod the joyous paths of youth, wandered beside the running brook her childhood knew, and gathered the flowers which, in imagination, she saw. Seated upon her bed, although heart-broken in their anguish, Grafton and his daughter were forced to join in thought with her.

"Ah, there is such a beauty! Mary, help me to get it; it is there near you!"

"Here, mother, it is!" said Mary; and, although the hand which touched her mother's contained no visible thing, the want of the moment was filled.

"See! is n't it lovely! look at the beautiful colors! Ah, how nice to be here!"

As the thin, wan face of the rapidly-aging woman was lighted up by what should have been a smile, but which only served to show the distraction of a mind diseased, bitter tears filled the eyes of the beholders. But she saw them not. Occupied with the conceit, her mind took no note of things as they were, she only saw what her disordered brain bade her observe. Suddenly, perhaps, the scene with her would change and hysterical tears flow from unnatural eyes. For the moment nothing could allay her fears. Then, as suddenly as it came, the paroxysm would depart, to be followed by a new fancy which her family were called upon to share. During these trying times there was no relief to the anxious watchers. Her eyes constantly stared, with a dreadful look, which did not change. Whether distressed by fear or overcome with simulated joy, the eyes which so long had shone with the mild radiance of approval and love, now glared with a light from which reason had departed. The joyless hours flew wearily by. Day was as night, and night as day. Wearied at last, nature gave up the contest and sleep came, to quell, for a time, the anxieties of the family.

These terrible scenes left the afflicted soul each time weaker than before. Succeeded as they were by seasons of comparative rest and quiet, which yet brought no hope, no ray of returning comfort to the invalid, she gradually sank and came nearer and nearer to the end of the life to which she did not cling and for which she had ceased to care.

The doctor came occasionally and talked learnedly of anæmia and of hysterical conditions. He brought in consultation a brother physician from Branchton, who advised that, upon the return of the paroxysms, large doses of opium be administered, or if this should fail, that chloroform be used to quiet the sufferer; but neither Grafton nor his daughter would listen to this. They would not, and could not hear to the thought of thus destroying sensation, in the being they loved so well.

" She is not violent," said Mary, " and I will not do otherwise than I know she would wish me to do. I know she would not approve, and I cannot give my consent."

Mr. and Mrs. Ellery, as well as other friends, were constant in their efforts for the sufferer. But there was little to be done, except to sit and watch at the bed-side of her who was gradually fading away. Generally, she was quiet and rational, and for the most part complained only of weariness. Death, she longed for, and spoke only of it as a relief. She would soon be at rest. The weakness of the body had infected the mind; she cared little for any thing. Her life, she felt, had been lived. For herself, she no longer participated in the thoughts of those about her. But, for her child, the mother-heart within her still welled up with entreaty and prayer for her boy: " God pity him; he would be so lonely without her!" Calmly she spoke of her rapidly-approaching death, and urged again and again that Mary would remember the charge she left with her.

" He will need a mother, Mary," said she, " and you must be one to him."

" You have been a good daughter, Mary; you never failed me; I know you will not in this;—and your father, Mary; he will need your care; our home has been happy; he will miss me, and sorrow in silence. Be a true woman,

Mary, and I feel that somewhere, and somehow, we shall all be again united. Kiss me, daughter!"

With streaming eyes and heaving breast, the daughter clasped the worn and wasted form of the dear mother to her heart.

Again and again was this repeated, and still she remained with them. Nature still refused to loose the silver cord. As she gradually became weaker the paroxysms were also less and less violent. Often had Grafton and his daughter prayed with tearful earnestness that she might be permitted to die, if die she must, in peace, with all her powers of mind unimpaired and in possession, at the last, of all those faculties which had so endeared her to them.

The turn of the tide came at last. The violence of her disease had finally expended its force. Though so worn and wasted as to bring the bitterest tears to the eyes of her husband,—who so well remembered the light-hearted and beautiful girl, who, years before, had trustingly given her hand to him,—she yet was sane. The eyes which looked lovingly into his, were the same which had answered to his glance through all the years of their pilgrimage.

Hope suddenly filled his heart. She would now recover! Life had still a charm for him. In the twinkling of an eye his thought had taken in the prospect of future years. He would slave for her, if need be; she should not be denied the advantages which he felt so lovely and gentle a soul had earned of right. For her he would dare any and all things. How precious she seemed! And, as he bent over her, their lips met in an ecstacy of love.

"George," said she, feebly, "I am going to leave you! You have been a good husband to me—you never deceived me—you—you always loved me—God bless and keep you."

He would have interrupted her with gentle remonstrance, but suddenly the unwelcome truth was forced upon his mind, struck his new-found joy ruthlessly to earth, and pressed the chalice of bitter despair to his lips.

"Call Mary!" feebly said the dying woman.

Mary had gone but a moment; she was in the adjoining room. Grafton hurriedly called her; she came at once. The mother looked lovingly at her; essayed to lift her hand for a last farewell; the light of life departed from her eyes, the dear head fell wearily, and she was dead.

CHAPTER XVI.

GRIEF.

ORDS cannot portray the agony and distress which overwhelmed the minds of George Grafton and his daughter at the loss of wife and mother. The thought of her death had been terrible; it was a spectre which of late had been a constant guest at their home, but the realization of the worst, left them with nothing to oppose, save the blackness of darkness which now shrouded their every thought. The spectre of coming evil is still a spectre; it may be escaped; it is not fully comprehended, and, like a terrible dream, its influence may be shaken off, in part, by the resolute; but bereavement and the ruthlessness of death strike the afflicted with a chilling force, against which no resolution of the mind or argument of the intellect can avail.

The ancient Persians worshipped fire as a symbol of deity. Taken from, it does not decrease. It apparently destroys all things, and yet is, itself, never consumed. Capable of infinite division, its character never changes, and while it may be transplanted to the uttermost parts, yet it ceases and determines if a suitable dwelling place be not provided. And may it not be, indeed, a type and sign of the Infinite Light? But from mortal man ever goes up the cry, when from the altar of his affections the fire of life has departed: "Whence? and Whither?"

Where, now, is the ruddy gleam which so lately cheered the heart and delighted the sense? The fire that has gone out; where is it?

Gradually they begin to feel that duty to the living required them to cease useless repining, and an effort was made to assume again the duties and responsibilities of life; and this was made the more necessary by Charlie's youthful insensibility and lack of comprehension. As the form of his mother had been lowered into her grave he, for the first time apparently, fully realized his loss and appeared overwhelmed at what to him seemed the heartlessness of utter abandonment. His cry: "Don't let my mother be put in the ground," had brought tears to the eyes of the most careless and indifferent looker-on.

Standing at the grave, George Grafton supported the form of his daughter and held the hand of his boy. He stood erect, no sound escaping his lips; tears streamed from his eyes and coursed down his face, and although his vision took in the occurrences about him, he yet was occupied with the thought, which at that trying moment was turned into conviction: "We shall meet again!"

The burial had occurred just at set of sun, and as Grafton stood at the grave-side, his little family clinging to him in an agony of grief, the spirit of the man sustained him: looking up, for the moment he was comforted, just as the rays of the departing sun struggled from behind the cloud which here obscured its brightness. And as its last beams shone full upon him, conviction was borne in upon him and fashioned itself in the thought: "My love, you are not lost!"

But the exaltation of the moment soon departed. At the poor little home every thing brought his loss to mind and stirred the grief which filled his heart. Days followed in which he abandoned himself to the luxury of grief.

But now the time had come when he must bestir himself and provide for the wants of his children. Charlie's boyish fancies and easy forgetfulness had been a source of trial to both father and daughter. He soon wished to be amused, and his active little muscles ached at thought of further inaction. That he should so soon be able to laugh struck them with wonder and amazement, as something almost akin to sacrilege. But nature always triumphs! Little by little they began to see that the healthy activity of the boy called them from the selfish indulgence in a sorrow which could not save and which if further indulged would dishonor the wishes of her whom they mourned. Sorrowfully the thread of life was taken up, and work again begun.

Mr. Ellery was among the first to call. He attempted no word of consolation, but the grasp of his hand and the look of his eye told all that was worth the telling.

"As you know," said he to Mary, "I am a member of the school-board, and I have had a conference with my associates in which we have agreed to offer you a position in the Plainville schools. Will you accept?"

As Mary hesitated, making for the moment no reply, he continued:

"No doubt you feel at this time very little inclination to engage in any occupation, but your own good sense will tell you that employment of some kind is an absolute necessity to your own mental well-being."

"Your offer is most kindly made," said Mr. Grafton, "but I scarcely see how she could accept it, on account of the difficulties in the way."

"I have thought of them," said Mr. Ellery, cheerfully, "and think that all can be arranged satisfactorily. You, my friend, are well fitted for some kinds of employment to which you might turn your attention, provided you were not tied to this little homestead. Mrs. Ellery and myself have talked the matter over and she is anxious to have Mary and Charlie make their home with us. We have no children, and, as much of my time is employed in my study, or in the duties of my position, she is sometimes lonely. Mary was always a favorite of hers, and would be to her a most acceptable companion. The little fellow could have a home with us, and go with his sister to school. Of course, we are poor, and have little to give, but the necessary expense of living would be reduced for Mary and the boy at our house. We have quite a large house, and but two inhabitants."

"I am very grateful to you for your offer," said Grafton, " but I fear that you may be drawing too heavily upon your generosity and that you do not fully count the cost in such a complete change as this must bring about in your household."

" On the contrary," said Mr. Ellery, " my wife will consider it a favor to herself. Being alone so much, she fears she may become morbid and selfish, and looks forward to the arrangement with the greatest pleasure. She has long looked upon Mary as a daughter and I feel sure that if you will give the plan encouragement she will be able to bring arguments to bear which will silence all objections."

So far Mary had not spoken. Evidently her mind was engaged in revolving the advantages and disadvantages of the proposed plan. Both Mr Ellery and her father had spoken, and now both looked to her for an expression of opinion.

" I do not see how it can be," she said. " You would have no home, father. I could not bear the thought of thus completely breaking up what was once so happy a home."

Tears came to her eyes, and for a moment she was unable to proceed. Grafton, himself, could not resist the infection, and a silence fell on all, broken only by the ill-concealed sobs, which Mary could not entirely suppress.

Mr. Ellery prudently withdrew, with the intention of sending his wife to still further urge the matter

After Mr. Ellery had taken his leave, Mary gave way to her feelings completely, while Grafton sat, with his head resting in his hands, for the moment irresolute and broken-hearted. The wild grief of his daughter, which had now broken forth afresh at thought of the final breaking-up of the family, strangely affected him and completely unmanned him.

" Oh, my mother! my mother! Why were you torn from us? Why could I not have been taken instead?" she wailed. Tears and sobs and broken ejaculations followed.

Gradually she became calmer, and endeavored to restrain herself.

Seeing that the violence of her grief had, for the time, expended its force, Grafton took his hat and went out.

Charlie was engaged near the house in driving little sticks into the ground, in the form of a circle. As his father came out the door, he called to him :

"Say, pa, come and see my little corral!"

Grafton walked slowly toward the boy, saying, as he drew near: "Yes, I see the corral, but where are your cattle?"

"Why, don't you see them over there?" pointing, as he spoke, to half a dozen queer-shaped pieces of corn-cob, into which he had carefully stuck short splinters to represent legs; shorter sticks, stuck into one end, representing horns; at least, that was the explanation offered. One of the "cattle," which Charlie said was "old Crumple," was possessed of crooked little sticks, representing the old cow's crooked and ungainly horns.

The ridiculous little "cattle" made Grafton laugh, before he knew it.

"How do you tell which end is the head?" said he.

"Oh, you just stick on the horns, and that makes the head; the other end is n't."

Grafton laughed again, and, although he had made no sound, and his laugh was only a larger smile, he instantly checked himself with a feeling that he had done an unseemly thing.

"Come Charlie," said he, "let us go up to town and see what there may be in the post-office for us!"

The home of the Graftons was, as has been stated, just in the outskirts of the village of Plainville, and as it was only about a quarter of a mile to the post-office, the walk was not unsuited to the little fellow's abilities.

As he walked along, the clear, bracing air and the childish talk of his boy gradually produced their effect upon the mind of the man, and although he replied to the boy and kept up a desultory sort of a conversation with him, his mind was really engaged in turning over the proposition made by Mr. Ellery, and the conclusion which he quickly reached,—if, indeed, it had not been reached before,—was that, for Mary, the offer was exceptionally advantageous. Mrs. Ellery was a cultivated woman of equable temperament and a most charitable disposition, and, although he had at first thought that the plan might have been proposed solely as a sort of semi-charity to an afflicted family, further reflection satisfied him that the arrangement with a young woman of Mary's capabilities and generous disposition might prove as much of a help to the Ellerys as to her-self.

Arrived at the post-office, he sat down to read some letters which were given him. Charlie sat on a nail-keg by his side, engaged in noting the peculiari-ties of Mr. Baker's various customers.

Grafton had been one of the earliest or-ganizers among the farmers, of the Alli-ance. Having taken an active part, he had gradually come to be considered as one of the fathers of the or-

ganization and had been elected by that body as "lec
turer." Holding this position, he had been called upon to
deliver addresses at different places, but of late, on account
of his wife's illness and death, he had not been able to
leave home. Two of the letters were from places at a distance, urging him to once more take up the work.

He had barely finished reading his letters and was
folding up the last one he had read, when Mr. Greene, the
state president of the farmers' organization, came hurriedly
into the store.

"Hello, Grafton," said he; "I've just come from your
house!"

"Why, so have I," said he.

"Well, I missed you on the way, somehow, I suppose."

"When did you come in?"

"Why, just a little while ago, on the last train, and I
bolted right down to your house, which a boy showed me.
Your daughter said she thought you were here, and so it
proved. Say, Grafton, I've got some work for you," said he.

CHAPTER XVII.

BREAKING UP.

ELL, what is it ?" said Grafton.

"Well, it is rather a long
story to tell all the whys
and wherefores, but to cut it
short, the executive board has come to
the conclusion to take a forward step
and make an organized effort to secure
what we have been 'resoluting' about
so long. Resolutions cut no figure
whatever, except to draw the attention
and fix the thoughts of men upon a
definite method ; and, as a matter of fact, most resolutions
don't even do that. An average crowd is satisfied with
swelling periods and eloquent words, which may be only
used to deceive. Now we have come to the conclusion that
we have got through with the 'Whereases' and 'Be it re-
solveds' and have got to do something. Some of our men
want to resolute some more and are most afraid of doing
something, but the time never will come, I guess, when all
men can see exactly alike. Anyhow, the board has made
up its mind to go ahead with a definite plan. It is plain
that we can only get what we want by political action ; by
the election of men who will carry out our wishes, and the
next thing is to elect them. But first we must be agreed as
to what we want them to do when elected. The members
of the board, after a good deal of argument among themselves, have come to an agreement upon a general plan very
near like that proposed in your address, which was published
in some of the papers, as you remember. The next thing
is to carry it out, and a resolution was passed which, in effect, brought me here as a committee of one to induce you
to undertake a mission. You are to visit every County

"Well, Green, I Regard Your Proposition as Favorable"

Alliance in the State, and as many sub-Alliances as possible, deliver an address advocating the proposed plan of campaign, answer objections, and otherwise forward the work the board has undertaken. The board will direct you from time to time regarding minor matters and will see that you are paid for your services. There! that's the whole story."

"Well, that is a mission, sure enough!" said Grafton. "How much time will be employed in all that?"

"Oh, that's hard to tell. You have held the position of State Lecturer, are well known and are just the man for this special business. The board will engage you until the annual meeting, and I make no question that you can then be elected as State Lecturer again and kept constantly at work."

"Well, Greene, that strikes me rather favorobly just at this time; fact is, I am undetermined what course to take. Seems strange, though, that you should come just now."

"Oh no; nothing strange about that. I heard of your recent affliction and thought that now you would be able to leave home. I should have come to see you before if I had n't known that it was impossible for you to leave."

"There is more in this than you know," said Grafton. "Only to-day was an offer made which will place my children in a comfortable home and make it possible for me to leave them with a feeling of security and satisfaction."

"These so-called co-incidents are semetimes wonderful as mere happenings," said Greene. "But somehow I've an idea that affairs move on a regular plan. Each man only sees one act in the play, and can't make head or tail to it; he only reads one chapter in the story and thinks the villian is having too good a time of it, and that the good men and women are not sufficiently appreciated, but my notion is that when we are able to read the book clear through we'll see that things are managed for us."

"Come home with me and we will talk this matter of the mission over," said Grafton. "You can't go back until to-morrow, any way."

"Charlie," said Grafton, "you run on ahead and tell sister that Mr. Greene is coming home with me! We will be along directly."

When Grafton and his friend arrived at the cottage, they were met by Charlie, who came out a little way to meet them.

"Mrs. Ellery is in the house," said he. "She came to see sister."

"I'll not go in just yet," said Mr. Greene. "Charlie will show me his pig first. I see you have some pigs; which one is yours?"

Charlie led the way to the pig-pen, anxious to show Mr. Greene which one he called his, tell him what its name was and describe its peculiarities.

Grafton went at once into the house. As he entered, Mrs. Ellery and Mary were sitting close together; Mrs. Ellery had her arm around Mary, who was actually smiling, although her eyes bore evidence of recent tears.

"I came right down as soon as Mr. Ellery came home and told me that he had been here," said Mrs. Ellery, speaking to Grafton, "and I am so glad I did. I can sympathize with Mary, perfectly; my mother died when I was quite young and, although it is now years ago, it seems but yesterday to me. Mary has promised to come up in the morning to see me, and we can then arrange all the particulars of her coming to us,—that is, if you don't object, Mr. Grafton."

"You don't know how grateful I am to you, Mrs. Ellery, for the offer made," said Grafton, warmly, "but I can't help feeling some misgivings in relation to the matter."

"Yes, of course I should expect it, but we can put it in this way: Mary can have a place in the schools as long as she pleases, no doubt; everybody loves her, and she will then be self-supporting. She can board with us and keep Charlie with her. Should this arrangement come to an end, another can be made, never fear. But I want her near me. Here, everything brings her loss constantly to mind, and it would unfit her for the place which I believe she will yet fill."

As Grafton made no immediate reply, Mrs. Ellery bustled about in a kindly, motherly fashion, putting on "her things," as she prepared to go.

· "Put on your sun-bonnet, Mary, and go a piece with me," said she.

As the ladies stepped out the door, Grafton rose, went into the little kitchen and begun to build a fire in the stove, that it might be ready for Mary, when she returned, to use in getting supper. While he was busy at this, Charlie came in, leading Mr. Greene by the hand, busily engaged, meantime, in giving that gentleman a full account, not only of the pigs, but also of other matters in which he was interested.

Mary soon returned and busied herself with the preparation of the evening meal. Mr. Greene was interested in a book, and comfortably seated in the "living room," while Grafton still remained in the kitchen. Softly closing the door between the rooms, Grafton said to his daughter:

"It seems to me, Mary, that it will be just the thing for you,—at this time, at any rate,—to take up with the offer of the Ellerys."

For the moment she made no reply; indeed, she felt that she could scarcely trust herself to speak, and kept busily at work; presently she said:

"Everything seems to point to the arrangement as the best that can be made." ·

"Well, then," said he, "we will understand that you undertake the school. I will sell off our little stock of movable property and can let you have some money, which you will need. If worst comes to worst, we can at least come back here."

Grafton rejoined his friend in the other room, and before the evening was over it was arranged between them that within two weeks he should report to Mr. Greene, as the president of the executive board, for duty.

The next morning Mr. Greene took his departure, well pleased in having secured the active co-operation of the one man whom he thought fully capable of conducting the work undertaken by the organization of which he was the head.

Having made up his mind, Grafton was not the man to long delay in the execution of his plans, but actively set to work to make the necessary preparations for carrying into effect the plan in view. As soon as breakfast was over and his guest had departed, he went at once to see parties whom he thought might buy the property he was now anxious to sell.

After Mary had finished her morning work she put on a neatly-fitting black dress, combed her luxuriant brown hair with even more than her usual care and, taking Charlie by the hand, set out for the promised call on Mrs. Ellery. As she locked the door of the little cottage and turned away from its silent and melancholy walls, it was with difficulty at first that she could proceed. Thoughts of the past, now gone forever, came over her with great and most depressing force. But she was young and healthful, the morning air was invigorating, and as Charlie, with the thoughtless gaiety of youth, kept up a cheerful and enlivening conversation, in which she was forced to join, she had not gone far until she found her spirits rise and much of that dread weight depart, which so long had pressed, with crushing heaviness, upon her heart. On the way, she met a number of her acquaintances, all of whom greeted her with interest and plain evidence of good-will in their countenances. This could not fail of its effect. The human heart is hungry for sympathy, and without it the half of life is lost.

Meeting "Uncle Bill" he stopped for a moment: "Good morning, Mr. Weldon," said she.

"I am awful glad to see you looking so well this morning," said he. "I believe you are getting prettier all the time!"

Mary blushed, and, with some slight confusion, said: "Now, Mr. Welden, you really are a flatterer. I did't think it of you!"

"Oh, well," said he, "I am an old man and half the time I have a sneaking notion that I'm an old fool, but there is no flattery in that."

As Mary continued her walk the old man turned to look after her, saying to himself as he did so, "She is a pretty woman, that's a fact." Going into his house, which was near by, he told his wife: "That girl of Grafton's is going to make some man's heart ache 'fore long' or I miss my guess."

Arrived at the Ellery's, Mary and Charlie were in the midst of a pleasant chat as Mrs. Ellery, having seen them coming, appeared at the door and drawing Mary's arm within her own, ushered her at once into the sitting-room.

It contained a stranger. A tall, broad-shouldered young man of light complexion and expressive face was engaged in conversation with Mr. Ellery.

"Mr. Maitland," said Mrs. Ellery, "this is my young friend, Mary Grafton; she was not aware that any one was present or, I dare say, she would not have come in."

Mr. Maitland rose with easy grace and politely acknowledged the introduction.

"Mr. Maitland is the son of my old townsman and college class-mate," said Mr. Ellery, "who has just arrived this morning, rather unexpectedly. He is on a pleasure trip, at present, and happened in, as we say. I don't know of anybody, George, that could give me more pleasure by a visit than yourself; unless, indeed, it should be your father himself."

Mrs. Ellery had, by this time, removed Mary's hat. The morning walk and the unexpected meeting with a cultivated stranger had caused the native rose to flush upon her cheek and dispel the pallor which, of late, had prevented its appearance. Mr. Ellery wondered that he had not noticed before, that she was really a beautiful woman. He had thought her an interesting and intelligent girl, pretty, perhaps; but now his eyes were opened and he was surprised.

The look of the stranger clearly showed that he, too, was impressed. He was a gentleman, he did not stare, but his occasional glances betrayed the feeling of interest and admiration, which he could not conceal.

Mr. Ellery's conversation and Mrs. Ellery's officious pleasantries prevented any feeling of embarrassment on Mary's part, while Charlie, unnoticed by all, sat bolt upright on one of Mrs. Ellery's "stuffed chairs" and looked at first one then another. Evidently he didn't understand the situation.

CHAPTER XVIII.

THE STRANGER.

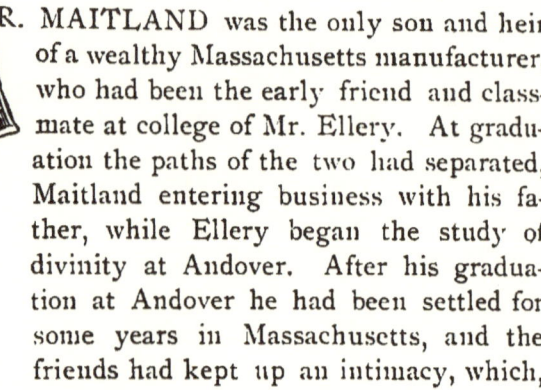

R. MAITLAND was the only son and heir
of a wealthy Massachusetts manufacturer,
who had been the early friend and class-
mate at college of Mr. Ellery. At gradu-
ation the paths of the two had separated,
Maitland entering business with his father, while Ellery began the study of
divinity at Andover. After his gradua-
tion at Andover he had been settled for
some years in Massachusetts, and the
friends had kept up an intimacy, which,
upon Mr. Ellery's return to the West had been interrupted,
and with the exception of the very rare visits of Mr. Ellery
to the old Massachusetts home, had now almost ceased.
The younger Maitland was also an alumnus of the same
college at which his father had passed what he now looked
backward to, as four of his happiest years. At his gradu-
ation he was entirely undetermined regarding the course
of life which he should adopt. He was a generous-hearted
youth who, having never been obliged to exert himself, on
account of his father's growing wealth, had so far pursued
the even tenor of his way without meeting with opposition
sufficient to determine what his real character might yet
prove to be. Possessed of a stalwart frame, he was also
indebted to nature for an equable temper and cheery good
sense. That he was an optimist, looking upon the brighter
side of life, was a matter of course.

Although the elder Maitland had left his son free to
choose the manner of life he would lead, his own high sense
of fealty to the race had induced him, after due reflection,
to take up the study of divinity with the intention of finally
entering the ministry. And this had been accomplished,
and at the time of his visit he had finished his studies and
been licensed as a preacher, although he had never been

"You Poor Little Innocent."

settled as a pastor. During the progress of his studies at Andover doubts had arisen in his mind regarding the doctrines there taught, and he had become somewhat unsettled in his views. Seizing upon this as a favorable opportunity, he had resolved to spend some time in travel before he began the work of his life, regarding which he now felt some misgivings.

This, then, was the man whom we have now introduced to our readers. He had never been in the West, and Kansas and her people were alike new and strange to him.

After a little time spent in general conversation, Mrs. Ellery said:

"Mr. Maitland, will you please excuse us; here in the West we are our own servants, you know, and therefore not entirely the mistresses of our own time; no doubt Mr. Ellery will now have some one who can fully sympathize with him."

No sooner had the ladies got away from the sound of the voices of the two gentlemen, now busily engaged in telling and hearing news from "old Amherst," than Mary said:

"Now, Mrs. Ellery, what made you take me into that room?"

"Why, my dear, Mr. Maitland had just said that the people of the West whom he had seen did not impress him very favorably, and I was anxious to show him that we really had some nice people residing here, and from his manner I fancy that he will now acknowledge that he was too swift in his judgment."

Mary blushed: it was a new experience to her, and for the moment the thought that she had been paraded as a specimen was rather unpleasant. And this must have appeared upon her face, for Mrs. Ellery continued:

"You poor little innocent, don't take it so seriously to heart. You made a good appearance. It was plain to all that you were ignorant of his presence when I ushered you in. If any one is to blame of course it must be myself, but I can't say that I feel that I have sinned. I think, however, that most women take delight in bringing together eligible young people."

The flush upon Mary's face gradually disappeared as she said :

" Don't deceive yourself; Mr. Maitland is a gentleman of wealth and position, and would only feel amusement at the mention of my 'eligibility.'"

" Don't deceive yourself, my dear," said Mrs. Ellery; " I know something of society and of the people whom Mr. Maitland has been accustomed to meet, and I am of a very different opinion ; still, we will not discuss the matter further, now, at any rate, as I must proceed to get my dinner. No matter how nice and refined men may be, I never found one yet that didn't like a good dinner."

Charlie, long ago, had taken himself out into the yard, where, just now, he was trying to minister to the wants of a distracted old hen. The hen, with her little brood about her, had been tied to a stake that she might not wander. Anxiety for the welfare of her downy flock had, however, taken away the little judgment her foolish head contained, and much fluttering had hopelessly involved her. She lay upon her side, the string many times about her, and preventing further motion. Charlie was unable to extricate her, and called loudly : " Oh, Mary, come ! The poor biddy can't get up ! "

Mary ran out the back door and soon had poor biddy upon her feet, with all her brood about her. Giving Charlie a love pat upon the cheek, she charged him not to "get into mischief," and was back again in a moment. Mrs. Ellery had noted the occurrence from the window, and when Mary appeared she said:

"What a dear little mother you are, to be sure!"

For a moment Mary did not understand, and Mrs. Ellery explained:

"Just to see how Charlie depended upon you, and how you managed both him and the poor old hen."

"Why should n't I?" said she.

"To be sure," said she, "it seems easy and natural to you."

Mrs. Ellery did not offer further explanation, but she could not but wonder at what appeared to her as the wonderful adaptability of the young woman beside her. Of generous temper and naturally elevated thought, well-read for her years, she yet was most capable and efficient in the ordinary walks and work of life. In whatever position placed, she yet seemed easily to lead.

As they proceeded with the work of the kitchen, the proposed change was fully discussed, and it was determined that when Mr. Grafton had completed his preparations, that Mary and Charlie should take up their residence with the Ellerys. .

Having assisted Mrs. Ellery up to the time when she was nearly ready to place her dinner upon the table, notwithstanding the entreaties of Mrs. Ellery to stay to dinner, she took Charlie by the hand and soon was at home.

Ushered in to dinner soon after, Mr. Maitland at once inquired for Miss Grafton.

"Oh," said Mrs. Ellery, "she would not stay. I knew she would n't, although, of course, I tried to induce her."

"She is quite pretty," said he.

"So, then, you have changed your opinion," said Mrs. Ellery, playfully; "only a little while ago you were saying that Western people did not impress you favorably."

"Of course," said he, "I spoke hastily, and really without much opportunity to form an opinion."

"I think, George," said Mr. Ellery, "that we understand, in part, at least, why you have spoken as you have. I know that was my impression on first coming to the West. People in Massachusetts pay far more attention to dress and appearances than here, and the average dress and manner of the men of a Western town, in the eyes of a resident of an Eastern city, appear very careless and hurried, while occasionally a prominent and worthy citizen is actually slovenly in both dress and manner. This does not arise from intentional disrespect for the forms of good-breeding, but is simply owing to the newness of the country and its consequent freedom from social mannerisms. Men readily run back to first principles; our own frontiersmen, thrown into contact with Indians, dress like Indians and act like them. Send a dozen college boys on a "camping-out" tour, and they very readily and naturally drop many customs which are quite indispensible at home. And so it has been with us of the West. We have followed the custom of the country, but you will find as much, if not more, sterling character and native ability among Western people as among the better-dressed and more dissembling citizens of the East. This, however, is being rapidly changed, and in our larger towns you will find great efforts made in keeping up appearances, which, after all, are very deceitful."

"No doubt that is true," said Mr. Maitland, "but you have n't told me anything about this Miss Grafton yet."

"No, I have n't; I shall be obliged to turn you over to Mrs. Ellery for full information, although I can say that she is a rather remarkable young person."

"We will call upon Mary to-morrow, or in a day or two, if you wish," said Mrs. Ellery, secretly overjoyed at the turn affairs had taken.

"Why, yes," said he, "if we can do so properly, and without violating the proprieties. I should be pleased to do so."

CHAPTER XIX.

THE STUDENT AND THE FARMER.

R. MAITLAND seemed wonderfully attracted by Kansas scenery and people. The clear sunny days, the lightness of the air, with the consequent slightly-increased respiration and natural invigoration, had for him as they have for all, when first they come under these subtile influences, a nameless charm and fascination not easily resisted.

The people, too, were to him a constant study. While some there were who strove to appear what they were not, for the most part there was an absence of that miserable spirit of dissimulation and pretence which, in larger or smaller measure, appears inseparably connected with the advancement of cultivated and refining influences. With most there was a hearty naturalness which had for him, as it has for all, an attraction which he felt no disposition to resist.

Aided by the natural and womanly tact of Mrs. Ellery, within the first week of his residence in Plainville he had several times met Mary Grafton. Her fresh, young face had first attracted him, but as he came to know her better, this was temporarily forgotten in his growing wonder at the grasp of mind betrayed in casual conversation. Where had she learned the thoughts expressed? Although the cottage contained a good many books, for a cottage, still to him the collection, exposed as it was in the little "living-room," was insignificant and wholly incapable of revealing the mystery. Who had taught her to think? Was she self-taught? And where did thought originate? Could one think only the thoughts of others? Or, in the evolution of interior consciousness, did this comparatively untaught woman

"Well, Mr. Grafton, What Do You Propose To Do About It?"

originate for herself the clear opinions which she so modest-
ly expressed? Or did thought "come" to people from an
exterior source, a supersensory realm whose very existence
was unknown to those favored by its ministrations? But
who could answer? To the deepest questioning of his mind
no answer had ever been returned. Would answer ever
come? Could it be possible that the intense desire of man
to know would, in some far-off sphere, be finally and fully
satisfied; or,—distressing thought—did man but grope in
darkness, forever reaching blindly toward an ideal impossible of attainment?

To Maitland, Mary Grafton was an enigma he could
not solve. She seemed possessed of a two-fold nature.
Seen at her home and in the homely performance of the
duties devolving upon her as daughter and sister, she was
most charmingly natural and helpful. Her very look, as
she sought her father's pleasure or answered the childish
questioning of her little brother was to Maitland an inspiration and a lesson in that divine sympathy which enfolds
the world with the radiance of heaven. Engaged, however,
in serious conversation, the elevation of her thought and the
calm superiority of her manner, utterly lacking in self-
consciousness, evinced the power of an intellect which compelled his respect, although he could not agree with its
conclusions. She certainly differed from the young ladies
of his acquaintance.

The little household was an open book to all who came,
and the very poverty of its surroundings compelled a pub-
licity to which Maitland had heretofore been a stranger.
The little "living-room" with the "lean-to" kitchen and
two tiny bed-rooms made up the establishment. One room
served all the various purposes of parlor, dining-room and
library; between this and the kitchen the door was generally
open, and thus was for the first time presented to the visitor
an opportunity to study a manner of life to which he now
paid close attention. Here were people without what he
had been taught to regard as the comforts and refinements

of life, who yet were happy in each other. Without scho-
lastic attainments, here was an attractive personage who yet
was capable of the most elevated thought.

Plainly, he was becoming interested, and Mrs. Ellery
was correspondingly happy. The visit, which at first was
intended only as a stay of a day or two, on the way to California, gradually lengthened, without apparent intention on
the part of the young preacher of bringing it to a close.

Mr. Ellery's horse and buggy were often seen standing
at the cottage door. Mrs. Ellery, somehow, had so much to
say to Mary concerning the removal, that frequent trips were
necessary, and as the duty of entertaing Mr. Maitland had
in part fallen on her, she contrived to be accompanied by
him on divers and sundry occasions, which the neighbors
remarked, became more and more frequent as time passed on·

Mr. Maitland had met Mr. Grafton a number of times,
but between the two no intimate acquaintance seemed possible;—in fact, a serious constraint had early developed.
The business which Grafton intended undertaking was
often discussed in the hearing of the young man and com-
ments varying with the feelings and sentiments of the
speaker were expressed, so that he had come to believe that,
as Grafton's mission was that of an agitator, intended to
affect political action, it was, no matter how honest the
intention, rather shadowy in its nature. He did not think
it exactly disreputable, but his education and previous training inclined him to think it exceedingly questionable in
character.

In his view, the fortunes of all were in their own hands,
and for people to rebel against what he regarded as the de-
crees of fate or the orderings of Providence, was simply to
find fault with themselves in endeavoring to foist the blame
of results upon laws or customs, when whatever of ill had
resulted was entirely owing to personal shortcoming.
In consonance with this, the only way to remedy whatever
of ill there was in life was for each to bring himself into
right relations with his surroundings. And this was to be

effected mainly by each securing for himself a personal righteousness of character which would insure to all the highest development of which each was capable, and whatever measure of worldly success was intended for the individual. The American form of government was as nearly perfect as it was possible for human effort to construct, and fault-finding with that was almost sacrilegious in character. Thus armed, he considered that Grafton, in undertaking radical change, was rushing in where angels might well feel the need of caution in their movements.

The two men, thus differently constituted, had, in conversation, drifted upon the topics in which Grafton was so deeply interested. Each felt satisfied that he had found out how the other stood, and like mental combatants generally, each had underrated the position of the other.

But they could scarcely refrain from argument.

One day when Maitland was at Grafton's little place, the younger man determining to " have it out " with the elder, said: " I don't think I understand, Mr. Grafton, the position you occupy. Farmers, from the nature of their occupation, have always suffered some privations, though certainly fewer now than ever before; but then, they have many advantages over the dwellers in cities. Cultivators of farms have been happy and contented in the past. Years ago the New England farmer was thought to occupy a most favored position; how is it that I find, now-a-days, so many who are dissatisfied and discontented? Are they not largely to blame for this, themselves?"

" Would you advise a man to cultivate contentment who sees all he holds dear in life slipping away from him?" said Grafton.

" By no means," returned the other; " but do not men have as good, or even a better chance, to hold their own now than in the past?"

" In the revolutionary days," said Grafton. " I suppose you will admit that the people of Boston might very easily have borne the exactions of the stamp act and the tax on tea, if so minded?"

"Doubtless, that is true," said Maitland.

"People in those days were not suffering for the means of living. History shows us that, so far as ordinary affairs were concerned, King George's taxation did not bear heavily upon them. It was the principle involved that roused their ire. The burden they bore was largely a mental one. Liberty was what they desired."

"I presume you are right in that," said Maitland.

"Well, Mr. Maitland, do you think they ought to have submitted?"

"I have always been taught that our fathers were right in what they did then."

"Mr. Maitland," said Grafton, "you know very well that the true man and the true nation must advance. This is the law of life. To cease to advance, is to begin to decline. The common school, the habit of reading, the telegraph, the amazing spread of intelligence and the advance of invention are all pushing the race forward. Intelligent people cannot remain at rest mentally. As with our revolutionary ancestors, so it is to-day; we, too, desire liberty and an opportunity to advance.

"Every intelligent man desires for himself and his family some part in the activities and privileges of the present and the hopes of the future. For the future opportunities of his children he will fight, if need be. In bringing children into the world he has assumed responsibility for their future well-being. No true man can think complacently of their existence as mere beasts of burden. Surrounded by the wonders of the Nineteenth century, it is impossible that those who create the wealth of to-day should be satisfied to be continually defrauded. It was not that the people who threw overboard the tea and overturned the statue of George III. were reduced to poverty, but rather that, having determined to be free, they recognized the fact that between themselves and their oppressors there was an irrepressible conflict impending which could only be prevented by the renunciation on the part of the governing power of unjust taxation.

"So it is to-day—we complain of unjust laws and unjust taxation, as our fathers did; like them, we see where it all must end, and like them, we perceive that between ourselves, who represent the producers of wealth, and those whose desire is simply to absorb without creating, a conflict is impending which will never be settled until each man is free to retain within his own hands the fruits of his own labor—now he is not. In a hundred ways his little earnings are taken from him by indirect and crooked methods, made justifiable by law. And these impositions are constantly increasing; even now it is practically impossible for the ordinary farmer who would give his family any of the advantages and refinements of modern life, who wishes them to take part in the hopes and advancements of the future, to keep out of debt, and when once in debt his financial ruin is assured. So, seeing what the future has in store for us and our families, we have determined to resist."

"But do you think that your condition can be compared to that of the revolutionary fathers?"

"Yes: except in this, that our causes of complaint are far greater than theirs. Then, too, the British ministry,—their government, of which they complained,—was not farther from them than are the monopolizing forces which control our national government from our Western farmers to-day. We are unrepresented in the councils of those who really control the hundred forms of robbery of which we complain."

"Well, Mr. Grafton, what do you propose to do about it? You tell me that the people are unable to control the general government. Do they intend to rebel?"

"If they are ever successful in obtaining relief they must rebel, though armed force is not necessary; they can proceed entirely within the law. They have the ballot.

Heretofore, in all the history of the world, advance has come through blood. But it came. Nothing could prevent it when the time was ripe, for the forces of nature and the purposes of God in the creation of man were, and now are, behind the forward movement. All the forces of nature are concerned in uplifting the race,—the great mass of mankind,—from the plane of the savage to higher and yet higher conditions. Of course, the comfortable classes and those possessed of privilege have always opposed; they have always imagined that they represented civilization and enlightenment; they have despised the innovators who have always arisen from what they term "the lower classes." "Throw down your arms and disperse, you rag-amuffins!" said Captain Pitcairn at Lexington to the poorly-clad American farmers.

"In the past, unjust governments, and consequent economic conditions, could not be changed except by armed rebellion. Now they can. Universal manhood suffrage is a new thing in the world, and by means of it the people who create wealth will be able to manage it. But the change will come in some manner. To suppose that it will not is to think that the progress of the race can be stayed. Only the ignorant rich think that. Everybody else knows that the clock of destiny marks the time of another step in advance. Of course, I know very well that we are despised and derided by the men we oppose. That makes no difference to us. We are upheld by knowledge that our cause is just. That is sufficient for us."

"But I do not understand," said Maitland, "just how you would proceed to bring about these changes. You tell me of the difficulty of obtaining possession of the government, and yet you speak of the ballot as the only weapon you would employ!"

"Usury, Mr. Maitland; usury has been the cause of the downfall of all the nations of the past. You know very well that at the time of the translation of the Bible, in the days of King James, that the word 'usury' meant

any interest on money. This is what is cursed from one
end of the book to the other. And yet not one of your
fashionable preachers dare preach against it. Read Nehemiah, v: 1-13, for a detailed account of mortgage, usury,
foreclosure and eviction among the Jews. You know, too,
that one method, and only one, has ever been used in the
destruction of all the buried nations of antiquity. See how
it was in Rome: the rich loaned the poor money and took
mortgages upon their homes, foreclosed and seized them.
Then the nation perished. A very crafty way of making
slaves of former freemen; but it is sure. Open your eyes,
investigate, and you will see the same schemes already
well under way in America. Very little money circulates
without the payment of interest by several parties on the
same dollar. It is borrowed from the bank, re-deposited
and re-loaned, in some instances, many times. In this way
several business men often pay interest on the dollar in
the hands of the laborer. This is blue ruin itself, if men
only had sense enough to perceive it. Business and labor
are shackled to the banker's car, and yet men are taught
to regard this system, by means of which every community
is made to pay tribute on what the banker owes, as the
sum of human wisdom! And, strange as it may seem, the
average citizen believes this lie and scorns the man who
shows it up!

" In our Colonial days several of the colonies, notably
Virginia and North Carolina, issued scrip receivable for
taxes, which allowed exchanges to be made without the
payment of usury. Jefferson says this scrip never depre-
ciated a farthing in twenty years. When it was made to
bear interest it was locked up,—when it did not, it circulated freely. Really, you will see, if you look carefully for
the evidence, that the prohibition of this scrip by English
law was a chief cause of our revolution. Now, English
influence, operating through our Wall street, is endeavoring to prevent the making of exchanges between man and
man unless tribute is paid many times over on every

dollar used as a tool of trade. This diminishes trade, lessens business, depreciates the value of property, throws men out of employment and stops the wheels of commerce. Debt and the payment of interest constitute the main reason for the increasing wealth of the rich and their growing power over the lives of the poor. This is hateful to us. Intelligent Americans cannot bear the feeling of injustice which arises from this state of affairs—and no man ought to bear it! It is idle to talk of the comfortable position of some subjected to these conditions. That cuts no figure with men who desire to be free! We despise those who only look for generous masters! Laws regarding the rate of interest are quickly nullified by the necessities of the borrower and the avarice of the lender, and the only final and radical cure of the trouble which now threatens our civilization is the abolition of debt. And this is not only possible, but easily arrived at whenever the people are sufficiently aroused to take an active part in securing so desirable a reform.

" One-half of the trap into which the people of Kansas have fallen is provided by Wall street in its control of Congress, but the other side is furnished by the laws of Kansas; and whenever the debt-cursed people of Kansas get up spirit enough to hold their side level, then the 'jaws' will fail to come together and the machine will be out of joint.

" Then congressmen will discover for the first time that something must be done in our behalf, and they never will move until this is done.   Mark that!"

" You propose, then, to nullify the laws of Congress, do you?"

" No; that will not be necessary. We propose to protect our own people by the passage of perfectly constitutional State laws."

" Please tell me what those laws may be?"

"Of course, I can only outline them here; but I will say that four measures enacted into law will bring about the changes we desire.

"First—Laws directing foreclosure and sale of mortgaged real estate, by means of which a stay of proceedings may be had. This will temporarily save our homes.

"Second—A repeal of all laws for the collection of voluntary debts to be incurred in the future. This will, to a great extent, do away with debt, courts and lawyers, and cause future business to be done for cash.

"Third—A system of non-interest-bearing State warrants issued to each county, municipality and school district, made returnable to office of State Auditor, and receivable for taxes anywhere in the State. These warrants, passing from hand to hand in the journey from the recipient to the State Auditor, will enable the people to make many exchanges free from usury, and greatly assist in our escape from the control of the dealers in money.

"Fourth—A homestead exemption, by means of which a homestead in the country or outside the business portion of our towns and cities, valued at a sum not exceeding say, $2,500, will be free from taxation and sale for debt contracted after the passage of the law. In the future, this would absolutely protect the homes of the people.

"These are our 'abolition laws.' They are for the abolition of future debt. No repudiation of existing contracts is intended. In the future, then, business would be mainly done for cash. Small credits would depend upon the honor of the debtor, as is the case to a great extent now; but the business of debt-making and the extortions of usury would come to an end. These proposed laws would abolish the special privileges given to the managers of money, by means of which less than five per cent. of the people are enabled to absorb the little earnings of the laborer and impose upon him and his kind their luxurious support."

"It seems to me," said Maitland, "that in this way you are stirring up strife between those who should be friends. You invoke the assistance of law for the farmers and against business men."

"Business men!" said Grafton, scornfully, now thoroughly aroused; "are managers of trusts, promoters of fraudulent enterprises and absorbers of other men's goods the only people to be called business men, and are they the only people to have the protection of law? And even though what you say were true, is it not clear that these so-called business men have possessed themselves of the law-making power in the past? When was a law passed in our interest? And if one side is to be specially favored, who is most worthy of the protection of law: the producer of wealth, or he who seeks to obtain by shrewdness and chicanery what others have painfully toiled to grow? But we do not desire that either shall be favored; we wish to—and we will—rid ourselves of the legal impositions of the past. That's all.

"But do not be deceived, the new revolution is for the abolition of debt. Old debts must be paid, but the law must set its face against the formation of new ones. Whoever sells property or loans money in the future, let him do it at his own risk. The law should not guarantee his business to be profitable any more than the State should make the corn-field or the potato-patch of the farmer sure to yield a certain number of bushels. Abolish debt, and pay cash in every deal. The government can readily furnish the currency to do this, and only refrains from it now at the bidding of those who secure slaves by the creation of debt. We do not need new laws so much as the repeal of those conferring privilege. Take away from the trade of the money-grabber and debt-maker the power of the sheriff and court, or else furnish to the farmer a *posse comitatus* with sufficient power to secure the growth of corn for 365 days in the year, and a stated price at the end of that time from the buyer, under penalty of loss of goods and confiscation of property in case of failure.

" Law is now made to give these very advantages to
the dealer in money. These constitute special privileges;
with them is created the slavery of debt. The law now
guarantees the banker's business to be profitable, if he does
not go outside of it. What folly! What injustice! Look
all around you at the results.

" Debt and the payment of interest in our modern world
make the master and make the slave. This is the great
power which threatens humanity and which must be slain.

" In the new abolition, the power of the State government will be the lever which shall lift us from the slough
of despond. Local self-government is the distinctive feature
of our republic. But for this, the war of the rebellion would
have ended freedom upon this continent. A conquered
people were never before reduced to subjection without an
enormous standing army was continued as a guard. Generation after generation but added fuel to the flame. Poland
still threatens. After centuries of government by the sword,
Ireland still longs for revenge. If, at the close of our war,
the states of the South had been abolished and the country
held as conquered territory, as was proposed, a million of
men would still be in arms to keep it in subjection. Grown
familiar with the control of the general, military despotism
would soon have swallowed all.

" But, with the power of the State in their hands, eleven
miniature republics, self-governed and self-respecting, at
once arose in the South and satisfied the natural demand of
freemen for self-control. Now a foreign war would show
them as loyal to the nation as the states of the North.

" The State governments saved our form of government
in that crisis and will do it again in another. They form
the power which would prevent the successful seizure of the
national government by an ambitious tyrant. Their very
diversity of interests form an additional security. Each is
a miniature nation in embryo, full-formed and ready to be
born.

"Kansas, under the guidance of men of nerve, such as her early history knew; men like Jim Lane and Ossawattomie Brown, can and will take the lead in a new abolition—the abolition of debt.

"The great danger of the present is that reformers may compromise the true principles of action. An increase in the amount of money in circulation would relieve, for a time, the over-burdened people; but in a few years, if debt,—the cause of all our woes,—is allowed to live and breed, the earth will be covered with a swarming brood of paupers, spawned from the hatcheries of usury.

"Debt is the cause and excuse of usury and usurers. Kill the dragon which continually sows among men the seeds of avarice, hate, crime, disease and death. Destroy at one blow the source of inequality—usury—accursed of God and all good men. Away with it, and man will be freed from the yoke of bondage. To destroy usury, kill the beast which daily, hourly and momently is bringing it forth from its hated womb. Prevent the possibility of debt, and the mother of usury is dead, and she, alone, who can bring it forth will be no more."

Grafton had now become thoroughly aroused. He walked back and forth in the little cottage, and his eyes blazed with the fire of his emotions. All this was something new to Maitland; he had no comprehension of the causes leading to Grafton's intensity of feeling, and realizing that under the circumstances he was poorly prepared for argument with such a man, he withdrew with the best grace at his command.

CHAPTER XX.

THE NEW HOME.

AVING completed his arrangements Grafton made preparations to move his children with their individual belongings to their new home. Mary wished to defer the matter till after Mr. Maitland had taken his leave, but her father would not listen to the thought of her remaining in the cottage after his departure. She knew that when once her father had made up his mind that it would be useless to argue the matter, and, accordingly, with heavy heart and many silent tears, Mary locked the door of the little home, where her mother had breathed her last. Somehow it seemed to her that here she was nearer her mother than elsewhere, and reason as she might about the matter, she could not but feel that in leaving the cottage she was removing herself farther away from the silent influences still proceeding from the dearest heart that had ever fluttered for her in human breast. In the hurry and bustle attending the change of residence Grafton had largely concealed whatever of sorrow he may have felt. Just before he was to start upon his journey, however, he called at Mr. Ellery's house for the purpose of saying farewell to his children. Mrs. Ellery was present, but very considerately withdrew. The time was short, and not much could be said; indeed, he had purposely deferred the parting until but a short time before the starting of the train upon which he was to go. Taking Charlie upon his knee, he took a seat near Mary.

. "Charlie," said he, "I have only one thing to tell you in parting. It is this: be a good boy and remember what your sister tells you."

" Now Mary," said he, " it isn't worth while for me to leave commands for you, but this I hope you will remember : Live your own life. Be true to your highest conception of right, remembering that we have each become a law unto ourselves. What to you seems just and true is binding upon your soul, whether upon others or not. I shall see you both frequently," said he, and kissing both fervently, he was gone.

There had not been time for many tears or an exhibition of deep feeling, and although both father and daughter were deeply affected by the separation, still it had occurred quietly and without excitement. Nor was it until her father had gone and the full meaning of the breaking-up of the family came over her that she realized that one of the turning points of life had now been passed—whether for good or ill, was yet to be determined.

Retiring to her room she gave herself up for the time to the most somber reflections. How full of sorrow the last few years had been ! The loss of home and her mother's untimely death again weighed heavily upon her mind. How happy the home had been, now destroyed forever ! For the moment bitter thoughts filled her heart. The loss of the home and the consequent shock, coming at a time of delicate health, had killed her mother. But for the added misery of poverty and waning fortune she would have rallied and recovered. And what were the influences which had brought all this about ? Having made a study of these, she was fully convinced that the control of the markets and finances of the country had so depressed the business of the farmer as to cause the condition of affairs which had resulted in their financial ruin. And this, thought she, is the work of men who claim the right thus to destroy homes and happiness and slowly murder by means of the market ! Freedom of contract,—there was none. That all had an equal chance in life was a delusion. If mere weight .of money was thus to rule, the combination which secured the larger sum controlled all. Far back in the history of the race brawn and the power of muscle were the arbiters of fate. All were equal—each could use the strength he had—but the giant of the iron hand took to himself whatever pleased his fancy, while petty cultivators of the ground could hide when he walked abroad.

Thus was it now, except that instead of muscle, money ruled, and cruelty and injustice were the results of the reign of both. When a combination had been formed and an agreement entered into by the controllers of the market only to pay so much, the farmer was told :

" We do not compel you to sell to us at a stated price,"—well knowing that a price had been fixed, beyond which he could not go.

" We do not compel you to ship your grain and stock upon our railroads," say the magnates, well knowing that the necessities of the producer force him to use the railway, although half the value of his property be taken for its carriage.

" If you do not like our charges, build you a railroad to carry your stuff, or transport your carcass to the city," say the sharpers who have possessed themselves of the lines of communication.

" You are not compelled to borrow our money," say the ministers of Mammon, well knowing that in modern society there is but one thing which all must have in larger or smaller quantities, and having secured a monopoly of its management, they await the homage of all.

Thus ran her thoughts, and rebellion rose within her breast. With flashing eye and quick-coming breath she resolved, with her mother's fate before her, to do whatever seemed possible to oppose giant and overpowering wrong. If rebellion against tyranny was obedience to God, she would be a rebel, whatever might betide.

———

It will not be supposed that affairs at Mr. Ellery's were unnoticed by the people of Plainville. All the actual happenings were duly reported, while many events were discussed which it was thought might possibly occur. And as all were at liberty to exercise their imagination regarding the future, the faculty was given full play by much the larger share of the villagers.

One morning Mr. Ellery found that his horse had cast a shoe, which must surely be replaced. Leading the animal over to Mr. Weldon's shop, the loss of the shoe was stated, and the blacksmith at once set to work to remedy the difficulty. But although Mr. Ellery was employed in holding the horse and Weldon in fitting the shoe, the minds of both were comparatively unemployed. It is said that a certain and unmentionable personage finds work for idle hands and minds to do, and this wise old saw probably includes in its operations the man of prayers and sermons as well as the common and undevout. However this may be, the blacksmith could not refrain from at once addressing himself to the most interesting topic of conversation in all Plainville.

" Pretty nice kind of a man that's visitin' you, ain't he? I believe he's a preacher, too ? "

" Yes; Maitland is a fine young man of generous impulses, who, so far at least, has not been spoiled by getting fastened in a groove of any kind. Most men run in a groove or rut of their own, whether of business or habit of mind, and judge everything by its relation to their particular line of thought. This they imagine to be very straight—to others it appears crooked enough—while but few are of sufficient breadth of mind to see that there is good in all and that none are perfect."

" Well, he may be an awful nice man, but he ain't jest the kind of a man I would pick out for Mary Grafton," said the blacksmith, breaking at once into the topic which interested him most.

" Well, I am not aware that anybody is ' picking him out'," said the preacher, rather coolly.

" Yes, I know; but then you see folks does n't have to be knocked down with a hint before they take it. Now, Mary was always a favorite with our Plainville people, and they don't quite fancy havin' this Boston feller come out here and carry off the sweetest flower in the whole garden. It kinder sets them agin him, you know."

"Maitland isn't from Boston, and I don't know that he has any idea of carrying off our flower. So Plainville people are altogether too fast."

"The blacksmith apparently paid no attention to the cold water which Mr. Ellery seemed disposed to throw upon the discussion, and continued : "Now, Mary always put me in mind of one of them high-strung Kentucky mares that we occasionally see ; pretty as a picture, high head, arched neck, curved and pointed ears, big, clear-looking eyes, knows everything, can do anything, and willing to do it, too, if you only treat 'em right ; but for all they are so bidable and easy managed, and sweet-tempered, jest you go to beatin' and abusin' one of that kind and see if something don't get broke, right away quick."

"That's rather a rough simile," said the preacher, "but I don't know but it is somewhere near the truth."

"Course it is near the truth ; it's right at it. Now, Mary might go through life without anybody ever knowin' the spirit there is in that girl, if she wasn't mis-used. But if she really was, she'd know it, and I'm inclined to think you couldn't strike that steel without some sparks a-flyin'."

"The great poet has said that "Hell hath no fury like a woman scorned'," said Mr. Ellery; "though I rather think that passage would be considered a good example of hyperbole ; an exaggeration of the truth!"

"Kind of high example, you think? Well, I don't know; if I was that mean that I really did deserve to be scorned by Mary Grafton, I'd rather see the devil than have her tell me what she thought of me."

The shoe was soon set, and Mr. Ellery was rather glad to seize the opportunity to break off a conversation which it occurred to him was becoming too personal in its nature.

The unexpected visit of Mr. Maitland to Kansas, the interest shown by him in Mary Grafton and the circum-

stances which had conspired, by prior arrangement, to throw
them together at Mr. Ellery's, formed a topic which was
strangely interesting to all.   Busteed had early interviewed
Mr. Ellery regarding the reported wealth of the stranger,
and had queried whether it would be possible to induce him
to invest in Plainville property, or whether he could influence the sending out of "cheap money" to his bank, which
could be re-loaned by him at heavier rates.

Mr. Ellery explained that Maitland was a student of
men and things, that he was dependent for a support upon
his father, who was a manufacturer of cotton in a Massachusetts town, and not a loaner of money.   Busteed, however, could not understand why he should be traveling over
the country, unless he was looking for a place to exercise
his calling as a preacher, or had an eye open to "the main
chance."   That a man should travel merely with the idea of
studying nature and human nature, was something beyond
his comprehension.

People, generally, in the village with whom Maitland
had come in contact regarded him as a very companionable
sort of a man, and a very good kind of a man, indeed—for a
preacher.   Preachers, however, for the most part, were regarded as lacking in those very indefinable qualities which
they summed up under the head of "manhood."   Of course,
they were well enough in their way ; but that, as a class,
they were lacking in a very important element of character,
was quite generally conceded by implication and general
understanding.   This general agreement was never obstru-
sively stated in words; still, the fact was apparent in the
daily life of the community.   It was felt that in the services
of the church and at "sociables," festivals and in the direction of Sunday-schools and the like, that the preacher could
not be spared ; that was his place; but in the real life and
business of the world, which employed six-sevenths of their
time and ninety-nine hundredths of their thoughts, he had
no place, whatever.   In fact, it was felt that his advice upon
important matters, outside of his special department, was in

the nature of an impertinence not to be endured. They were willing enough to listen to doctrines, embellished with scriptural quotations, but they must not be applied to the lives of people now on earth, unless they lived at a remote distance from the speaker and his hearers. It was felt, rather than stated, that the preachers didn't dare tell their congregations just what they thought of them and their conduct in the daily business of life. The congregation on its part feeling the force of this and the lack of moral courage which prompted it, could not fail to see that the supreme quality in man, respected in all and by all, was very conspicuous by reason of its absence in the characters of a very large number of those who were called upon to declare the whole counsel of God.

That Maitland should remain in Plainville seemed to the inhabitants of that village the most natural thing in the world. Where would he find a nicer little village than theirs, or where could he find a pleasanter place than the house of Mr. Ellery for a visit, with its kind and motherly hostess and most attractive occupant? That his visit would have been sooner concluded had he not met Mary, was beginning to dawn upon Maitland's own comprehension. Still, he was not aware that so deep an impression had been made upon himself, as to the Ellerys appeared manifest. He was interested in Miss Grafton,—he was willing to acknowledge that to himself,—and he thought that if she could only abandon, what he was disposed to regard as some very peculiar views, that she would then be quite well-informed and mentally well-furnished. As it was, the holding of these views so strenuously as she did, made quite an unfavorable impression upon him. Mary, upon her part, held much the same view of the character of the young preacher. If he could only change his notions regarding economic matters and adopt what she regarded as correct views, he would then be in position to be of great service in the world. Each had endeavored to convince the other of error, and in their frequent discus-

sions the apparent advantage had nearly always been with
Mary, because she spoke of what she was familiar with,
while Maitland, never having given special attention to
matters of that sort, was but poorly prepared for an argument.

One day, after he had stated at some length his peculiar opinions, Mary said:

"You know, Mr. Maitland, that the law of heaven as
proclaimed to Adam and Eve, when they were shut out
from Paradise, was the law of labor—'In the sweat of thy
face shalt thou eat bread.' That, I take it, applies to all
mankind. All must labor or render acceptable service,
and the laws of nature enforce the command. Some, however, escape; but no one ever escapes, or ever has escaped,
without throwing the burden of the labor thus evaded
upon the shoulders of others. Now, in your own individual
case your father has saved you the necessity of labor, so
far at least; but upon whom has the burden of your life
been placed, if not upon the operatives whom he employs?
The profits of their labor, which he has been enabled to
absorb, form the support upon which you depend. You
do not labor because an extra share has been imposed
upon them."

"What you say," said he, "no doubt is true in a certain sense, but you must remember that society, with all
its vast gains and improvements, exists upon a basis which
the literal carrying out of your opinions would destroy.
All progress, all improvement in the future, depend upon
the further spread of a civilization which you would make
impossible. If all labored, no time would be left for
thought and mental advance. Where all are equally poor,
in time all become equally ignorant; leisure to think and
plan is the very first step in the march of progress. Your
thought, allow me to say, is crude, in that it subordinates
the higher to the lower. Society has a right to exist, if it
stands for the final advancement of mankind, as I believe
it does; and this being the case, whatever is absolutely

essential to this advance must be defended against the assaults of those who would only destroy without supplying anything but mere savagery and brutism to take its place."

"You have undertaken, Mr. Maitland, as a preacher to take up your cross and follow Christ. Following Christ. I take to mean a service of the truth—to follow wherever it leads. The disciples had promised to follow Christ, and so they did up to the time of His arrest. Peter, especially, had vehemently announced that he would follow though all should forsake Him, but when he saw the Savior apprehended and in the custody of the soldiers, he, too, began to think of the rights of society, and when one of the maids came into the outer court and saw him there, she said: 'And thou also wast with Jesus of Galilee,' but he denied; social forms, 'law and order,' must be preserved even though Christ died. Peter was willing to follow until he came in contact with the law and the soldiers. You are willing to follow the truth until you come in contact with the labor question, then you deny that simple truth is to be followed, and take refuge in generalities and the rights of society, which, when inquired into, seem to be the right of the strong to impose themselves and their improvements upon those weaker brethren who appear unable to help themselves. The essence of all this is simple selfishness, the very opposite of the spirit of true Christianity and impossible of defense. Civilization will take care of itself,—it will not perish; let us do right! Surely, the self-styled upper classes have no right to exist by defrauding the poor and the weak."

"In the decision of any matter involving a question of right and wrong," said Maitland, "we are obliged to take into account the character of the people who make answer. In a question of morals, moral men would make one answer, immoral men another. This is a question of right and wrong, and in seeking an answer we can do no better than to follow the lead of the church. What it con-

doms, we may consider as against the better judgment of
mankind; what it allows, we are somewhat arrogant in
opposing."

"The church has so often been at fault," said Mary,
'it seems scarcely necessary to call attention to its ex-
.treme fallibility, but I have at hand so marked an instance
of this, that please allow me to read. As the church has
often been opposed to the principles of human brotherhood
taught by Jesus, it is not at all strange to find it now upon
the side of the oppressor.

Taking a book from the table, she read as follows:

"It is less than two centuries since seven men, of the
highest standing, a majority of whom were reverend gentlemen,—clergymen,—as good and pious men as ever lived,
as exemplary in every relation of life as it was possible for
men to be, sat in so-called court of justice, each morning
whereof was opened with fervent prayer to the divine
source of all knowledge, grace and power, to direct the
actions of his servants as the judges of that court; and in
that court were arraigned, day after day, poor, miserable,
broken-down, superstitious women and children upon the
accusation that they had commerce with the devil and
used his power as a means of spite upon their neighbors,
and as one of the means of inflicting torture because
thereof the devil had empowered these poor creatures to
shoot common house pins from a distance into the flesh of
their neighbors' children, by which they were greatly
afflicted. Being put to the bar to be tried, they were not
allowed counsel. The deluded creatures sometimes pleaded
guilty, and sometimes not guilty, but in either event they
were found guilty and executed, and the pins which were
produced in evidence, can now be seen among the records
of that court, in the court-house of the county of Essex,
Massachusetts!

"And beyond all this that court enforced,—worse than
the tortures of the Inquisition,—dreadful wrongs upon a
prisoner in order to accomplish his conviction. Giles
Corey was an old man, 80 years of age. He had a daughter some 40 years of age, simple-minded, not able to earn
her own living, and a small farm, a piece of land and a
house thereon, which he hoped to leave to his daughter at.

his then impending death. Giles was accused of being a wizard. His life had been blameless in everything except his supposed commerce with the devil. Upon *ex parte* testimony he was indicted for this too great intimacy with the evil one and set to the bar to be tried for his life.

"Giles knew that if he pleaded not guilty he was sure to be convicted, and if he pleaded guilty he would be sentenced to death, and in either case the farm would be forfeited to the king. But if he did not plead at all—such was the law—then he could not be tried at all, and his property could not be forfeited to the king and taken from his daughter. So Giles stood mute, and put the court at defiance.

"And then that court of pious clergymen resorted to a method to make him plead which had not been in practice in England for 200 years, and never here; and poor Giles was taken and laid on the ground by the side of the court-house on his back, with the flashing sun burning in his eyes, and a single cup of water from the ditch of the jail, with a crust of bread, was given him once in twenty-four hours, and weights were placed upon his body until at last life was crushed out of him, but not the father's love for his child. He died, but not until his parched tongue protruded from the old man's fevered mouth. It was thrust back by the chief justice with his cane. The cherished daughter inherited."

"Isn't that frightful? And yet, Mr. Maitland, all this was the doing of the very New England church to which you belong. You will tell me that this took place in an ignorant age and yet your church policy and even the creed itself was formed in those very ignorant times. If the church was mistaken then in matters which involve our common humanity, why may not it also have been mistaken in other things? And if this be admitted, how can it claim to be entitled to our reverence in matters of belief which contradict our reason and the compassionate dictates of our hearts when moved by the sorrows and necessities of the poor and the unfortunate? How can the judgment of men like those I have been reading of control our action, to-day?   Oh, no, Mr. Maitland, the God within is a far better instructor than those mouldy 'traditions of the elders' to which you now fly for light."

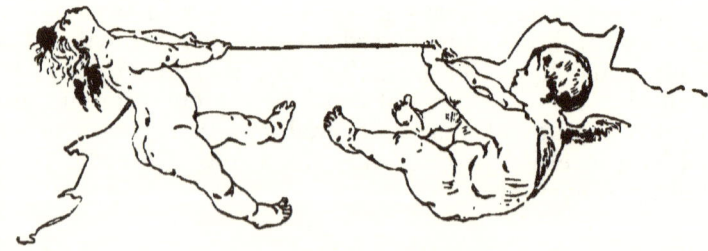

"Consider the Difference in Our Lives."

CHAPTER XXI.

GLIMPSES OF CHARACTER.

OPING for change, one may travel far, only to find that he, himself, has not been left behind. That perception which makes, for us, facts, opinions and circumstances, has not been educated or reformed by mere removal. With Maitland the fight was on.

Added to the mental struggle, which, beginning, with him, in doubt of certain tenets of a religious faith, was now leading him to review from the beginning the whole ground-work of the duty of man, was the newer complication of an awakening love. Neither birth or breeding nor the lack of them, can hide the superior soul. It looks calmly forth from the eyes of man or woman, in whatever station found, and without demanding, receives the homage of kindred spirits. Never before had he been so torn by conflicting emotions! Rights, duties, hopes and fears, took on new shapes, and new thoughts arose. He found in Mary Grafton a something which he could not define, an attraction which he could not understand, and as he queried with himself regarding it, he awoke to the fact that disguise it as he might, the influence which she exerted caused him ever to strive for that higher expression of himself for which his own better moments longed. There seemed in her presence a stimulation to which heretofore he had been a stranger. That this was true he could not deny, and yet how it came about he could not comprehend. That a country girl, with but two years' experience of life away from her modest home, and those years passed in a subordinate capacity; self-taught, the pupil only of a father whose own education was limited, should question the existence, off-hand, of the very things he had begun, only after years of scrutiny, to doubt, amazed him. And yet every manifestation of her thought was

reverent and tended toward final good, to which she looked
forward with calm and perfect confidence. He could not
fail to love her for this. Did he love her for herself?
Deeply questioned, his heart returned but one reply. But,
as he thought, difficulties arose and arranged themselves in
threatening ranks. Their opinions seemed ever to jar; the
end desired was agreed upon, but the means to be used in
attainment divided them. Several times he had been upon
the point of declaring himself in sentimental terms, but as
if warned by an unknown power, she had kept him at bay.
Did she, in this manner, conceal a tender regard? Why
was it that with him she showed none of that tenderness
and depth of feeling manifested toward others? Might it
be possible that she divined the shallowness and lack of
mental furnishing of which he sometimes accused himself?
Could he win her love?

Strange as he thought it, he was obliged to confess to
himself that he feared to make the attempt. He had never
detected in her manner anything which would encourage
him to make an avowal, and, although he told himself again
and again that a woman of spirit would quite naturally
demand to be won in bold and chivalrous fashion and would
shun the appearance of falling unresistingly into the arms
of any man; still he put off from day to day what he gradually came to think must be done. And as this feeling
strengthened, he came more and more to see that her life
was the proper complement of his own. With her, he should
improve. There was that dissimiliarity of character between them which, united, would form a perfect whole.
Each could assist the other, and if he could awake for himself that slumbering tenderness which he knew existed in
her; ah, that would be happiness, indeed! Still, strive as
he would, and did, to find opportunity for the expression of
the tender passion, she was ever, apparently, on guard, and
with clear, wide-open eyes and collected manner, made it
impossible for him to speak, except in the plainest terms
and without assistance from her.

What was to be done? He was ashamed of himself, of the length of his visit, of his lack of courage; and fairly ashamed, too, of the shame he felt, and began to wonder whether his friends, the Ellerys, might not be ashamed of him, also.

Several times he had planned to speak to Mary upon the subject nearest his heart, but each time something had occurred to prevent. At last, nerved by desperation, he gave out that on the morrow he would take his departure for California. As yet, he had never been able to declare himself, but realizing that indecision itself had already reached its climax, he resolved to tempt his fate as became, —what he had come to think of himself,—a very sheepish sort of man.

That evening, finding himself alone in the parlor with Mary, the latter made some excuse to depart and had already nearly reached the door when he found tongue to say:

"Wait a moment, Miss Grafton; I really have something to say to you!"

Mary had by this time reached the door, and stood expectantly waiting, with one hand upon the door-knob.

"You must have seen that my regard for you is something more than the ordinary respect which a gentleman may have for a lady," said he, coming towards her.

Releasing her hold upon the door, Mary immediately seated herself upon a chair, and waving her hand towards another, Maitland was forced to do the same.

"In short," said he, "I wish to make an avowal. I have long loved you—at least it seems a long time—and although you have never given me an encouraging look, I can but hope that you will now look encouragingly upon me. Will you marry me?"

For the moment her eyes sought the floor, and Maitland continued:

"You don't know how sincere I am in this matter— you can't know that—and yet my hopes are bound up in your answer. I have never met anyone whom I could so completely love and reverence as I do you. And——"

"Mr. Maitland," said Mary, "you certainly have honored me by your proposal and I thank you for the preference shown, but your own good sense will, upon second thought, show you plainly that in this you have made a mistake. You have been in exile, almost, for some time past, and being thrown much in my company of late, you have been moved to make an avowal. I must say firmly and plainly that what you ask can not be. I have certain duties to my father and little brother which I can not relinquish, and even though——"

Maitland would have interrupted her, but she continued:

"Please hear me through, because this is a subject which must not be re-opened, even though these objections could be removed, although I do not think it possible, still there are other and even more insurmountable ones which would prevent. Consider the difference in our lives: how unlike they are and have been, and must be in the future."

"Miss Grafton," said he, "perhaps I have been too rash in speaking so soon as I have, although I have charged myself with cowardice in not speaking before, still you will not utterly refuse me. I am an honorable man; no person can say aught against my character; and I love you! If I am not positively disagreeable to you, don't cast me off; give me leave to hope. I am going to California to-morrow. I may not remain there long. Only say that your refusal is not absolute and final!"

"I prefer," said she, speaking very slowly and with evident feeling, "not to discuss this matter further. What I have said is my final answer. We have been very good friends and I hope our friendship will not be interrupted."

Just at this juncture, Mrs. Ellery, not suspecting that she was interrupting, came into the room and made an inquiry regarding Mr Maitland's departure, which being answered, she, probably suspecting from the appearance of the "young folks" that matters of moment were under discussion, immediately retired.

"My father writes me," said Mary, "that he is having most encouraging success wherever he goes. All seem to approve the plans which he—and I—have so much at heart, and I do hope, Mr. Maitland, that you will see, when you have examined into it, that he is as fully doing, what you preachers are wont to call 'the Lord's work,' and that he is as thoroughly devoted to the welfare of his fellow-men as any knight or martyr of old, could be or ever was. My father is a grand man, a true man; his moral courage is sublime; and, although poor and almost unknown, I would rather share his lot and fate, whatever it may be, than wear a coronet to which I was not entitled, or live upon the wealth for which others toiled and spent days and nights of grievious sorrow."

Mary's eyes filled with tears, but her voice did not falter, as she continued: "Myself and little brother are all that is left to my father; we form the tie which binds him to life. He is not demonstrative, but a truer heart never beat. For us he would sacrifice,—has sacrificed,—ease and comfort, and I will never forsake him or follow any course which might cause him to feel that in his old age he was neglected or forsaken. He has plans which are far-reaching, and from their success we hope for much good. These plans and the hopes which they have inspired, have taken complete possession of him, and in the work which he has undertaken he is wholly enlisted with an earnest desire to benefit his fellows. What higher motive, Mr. Maitland, can actuate the human soul?"

CHAPTER XXII.

PLAINVILLE PEOPLE.

AITLAND departed rather sorrowfully and with evident regret. Somehow, the man had undergone a change and a troubled look had settled upon his face as he bade farewell to the friends he had made. Mary gave him no opportunity for the private interview which he had inwardly hoped to secure. More grave and reserved than usual, she still quite cordially took his hand in parting, while he found opportunity to say:

"May I write?"

"Certainly," said she, "I shall be pleased to hear from you, wherever you go."

"But will you answer?"

"Yes; I surely could not refuse."

That was all; the train moved off, and Mr. and Mrs. Ellery and Mary, who were at the depot to see him off, slowly retraced their steps toward their home. The house appeared lonesome and forsaken as they approached. Entering, they removed their wraps and sat down. They looked at one another for a moment in silence.

"Really, it seems almost like a funeral," said Mr. Ellery, glancing, as he spoke, at Mary.

Mary made no reply, but hastily gathering up her shawl and bonnet, went at once to her room. When she had gone, Mr. Ellery said: "Did George offer himself, do you think?"

"I think he did," said Mrs. Ellery, quite cautiously, "but I am not sure. Evidently there was something which occurred to change the current of feeling between them. They both took great pleasure in the conversations which they were constantly holding whenever opportunity offered,

almost to the last. I think, however, that I interrupted conversation of a peculiar kind yesterday. Afterward, both were quite shy and reserved."

"Well," said Mr. Ellery, "it is something with which we have no right to interfere."

"Oh no," said she, "not for the world! They must be free to act for themselves. I did think, though, that they were made for each other."

Gradually, affairs took on their wonted and rather monotonous appearance in Plainville. Mary went daily to her classes, accompanied by Charlie, who was one of her pupils; and the village gradually came to forget the fine-looking young preacher who had been for a time the center of attraction and the subject of conversation.

Mr. Grafton was heard of from week to week as he pursued his work, and tidings came that he and the other "lecturers" who had been dispatched on the same errand were meeting with great success in the work of inducing united action on the part of the farmers' organizations. The effort thus made had for its end the adoption of "the demands" by the farmers, to which they were to commit themselves. Political animosities, with them, took on so great a virulence, that it was impossible to advocate the claims of one party without securing the hatred and lasting dislike of all opposing factions, and the attempt was made to inculate a course of action within the limits of all political parties, and no favoritism was to be shown to either or any.

Bright and early one morning, Tom Jones drew up in front of Weldon's blacksmith shop; a plow was in the lumber wagon. Coming to a halt in front of the open door, he turned half way round upon the rough board seat, and putting one foot over the side of the wagon-box, rested it upon the front wheel. Weldon came to the door, and placing one smutty hand high up on its side, saluted the farmer with: "Hello, Tom! what are you settin' up there fer?"

"Can you fix my plow, to-day? Got to have it right off."

"Why, what's your sweat?" said Weldon, coming forward.

"Oh, I'm busy; got to have it."

"Busy, are ye?" said Weldon, as he pulled the plow around, that he might see what was needed. "Busy, eh; well, does it do ye any good to be busy?"

"Don't know as it does, but then I keep pegging away."

"Why, you are 'bout like the man I heard of yesterday; you see, he had the salt rheum and a Waterbury watch, and when he was n't scratching, he was winding that watch; he always kept busy; I don't know, though, as he got much ahead."

"Well," said Jones, laughing, "I'd as soon scratch and wind a Waterbury as to run around the country talkin' politics, as some of 'em do."

"I tell you what's the matter with you, Tom. You don't pay enough attention to politics to know when you are being hurt. Here, help me drag this plow in," and suiting the action to the word, the blacksmith began tugging at the plow.

The plow was soon inside the little shop, Uncle Bill began to put on coal and blow up the fire, while Jones, with monkey-wrench in hand, began to take the plow apart.

"What do you hear from Grafton?" said Jones.

"Oh, George is all right; everybody is falling in with the scheme, 'pears like. You see, they are coming the non-partizan dodge:—don't say anything about politics;—and so they have organized and gone around to all the candidates, and most of 'em has promised to support the demands; they all want farmers votes, you know."

"I don't believe I've paid enough attention to know just what the scheme is," said Jones.

"Well, there is the demands, as they call 'em; you know them?"

"Oh, yes; I've heard George talk on them things by the hour. I always kinder liked George, too, but I never had much idea how he was going to make 'em work."

" Well, I been tellin' ye, they have organized and got all the candidates to promise to help make the demands into law. The thing has gone on, 'till now opposition has about caved in Democrats and republicans, both, are going to support."

" Well," said Jones, "a Stay-law would be a good thing and I guess all right, but no law to collect debts would be pretty tough on lenders, and borrowers, too, I'm afraid."

" It ought to be! I wish it was so hard on 'em as to knock the business cold, first clatter. You never knew a man to get into the hands of the two-per-centers, but what they had his hide finally, did ye ? "

" Well, they are a bad set, that's a fact."

" Money manages everything, don't it?" said Weldon. " Can't anything stand up against the power of money, can it ? "

" Guess not."

" Well, if money is the boss, the fellows with money are masters, ain't they ? And the fellows without, have to mind their p's and q's, and sing small, generally, don't they?"

" Pretty much so."

" Well, don't you see that it's the law and the court that gives money all this power ? Money-loaners could n't take a trick without the law to back 'em, could they ? It takes your vote and my vote to make law, and in that way we put a whip into the hands of lawyers and money-loaners to lash us into poverty with. Law makes debt, and debt makes interest, and we sweat to pay it, and they grow fat a takin' it. That's what they live on : our labor turned into interest money by law. If there was no law to collect there would be no debts, or next to none. Say, Tom, we 're the damned'st fools in the business ; we hist such hogs as Bus-teed onto our backs, and then ain't satisfied without giving them the law as a whip to make us work. If it wa'n't for law we'd have no debt and have no interest to pay, and a way would be found to do business for cash. It is the cause of inequality among us, and any fellow ought to see that it's not right."

"Oh, you are a little fast there; the law applies to everybody; it will help me collect my debt, just as well as it will, Busteed."

"How many debts have you collected by law in the last year?"

"None!"

"How many in the last five years?"

"None!"

"How many since you've lived in Plainville?"

"Well, I guess just about the same number."

"Don't you see, Tom, that you fool yourself when you think that thing was made for you; course you might use it, but you'd better not. Now suppose we had no law at all, and we say among ourselves: let every fellow take what he can and hold it as well as he may; strength is to be the rule. Now we are all equal; we can use our strength. I suppose that's the way it was before men made laws. Well, now everybody is free; the law of strength applies to all alike, but you know how it would be, how it always was under such circumstances; a few strong men would own everything and the rest of us could play hide."

"Well, now, in these days, money and law play the same part that strength does among the savages. The fellow that has the most money and the most law, knocks the persimmons. I want the laws fixed so that no fellow can use his strength or his money on me, and,—honest Injun,—now Tom, he ain't got no real Bible right to do it!"

"Suppose you go back home, and you turn your sheep and hogs into the horse lot and you tell your horses, as you turn them in, too, that every fellow is free to tramp toes all he likes. When the horses got at it, the sheep and pigs wouldn't have much show, would they?"

Jones grinned, but said nothing.

"Well, the sheep and pigs have about as much use for the law you give the horses as the average debtor has for

"I tell you, Tom, I don't want no law to help me get the better of some fellow in my business, and I don't think much of the fellow who does."

the law for collecting ordinary debts. They would have too much sense to say your law of tramping was just, because you give 'em leave to tramp, too."

" I don't know but you are right," said the farmer.

" Why, I know I am! I did n't use to think much about these things, but I tell you, Tom, I don't want no law to help me get the better of some fellow in my business, and I don't think much of the fellow who does. You can bet your life he thinks he is a horse in the sheep-yard, and wants to step on somebody. Now, I've come to think it's time to stop allowing the meanest men we've got in the community to climb, rough-shod, onto any poor devil they can get their hoofs on. Laws should be made to protect the weak, not to impose on 'em. Now, if we can get the demands made into law, the big fellows will quit stepping on the little ones. Then, business will be done for cash, debts will be gradually knocked out, interest will stop, and when a poor family has a home over their heads, no interest-sucker can turn 'em into the road. Then the money-grabbers will have to buy property and go to work, or hire labor. Did you ever think, Tom, what would happen if everybody but the money-devils and their tools, the lawyers, should take it into their heads to leave the country, for good ? Supposing all the workers should git; then, Mister Money-Loaner would have to go to work, would n't he? Would n't make much difference how much money he had, would it? Could n't eat it, could he ? Could n't wear it, and so he'd have to dig in and raise crops and weave cloth, and make himself useful, generally. Now, he don't have to. Money is really no value in supporting life, when the worker is n't around. But the worker can be imposed on, with money:— but it takes the law to do it, though! Then, the money-monger goes around, stepping on folks, and he walks high ; —you hear me!—and the little fellows has to squat. And then, to think of the little fellows being pleased up with the idea that it's all right because, maybe, they can walk high, themselves, some day, and find some other little feller to step on!"

Although the blacksmith had been busy with his tongue, "between heats," his hands were fully employed, and under his vigorous strokes the necessary repairs upon the plow began to take shape. "Get that sledge, Tom, and give me a few licks," said he, as he made ready to pull a bar of iron from the fire; "don't stand there, like yer had no sense!"

"You keep your clack going so that it's a wonder I've got even a head left!" said Jones.

"Well, ain't I been a working, too? I've let you know that I can talk and work, too. Now, there's that idea of a free home: no tax and no freeze-out mortgage possible," continued Weldon.

"I thought that was a fool idea, when I first heard of it, but I tell you it's all right! Some years ago I was blacksmith on one of the smaller Indian reservations; poor kind of critters they was, but they called 'em civilized; they got nothing from the government but the land, and that couldn't be taken from 'em. They had a government to protect 'em, them Indians had. Well, they could root hog or die. Most of 'em didn't root any more than they had to, but,—Lord bless you!—they all had a plenty and some of the thrifty ones was a getting rich. One thing sure, if we had that chance, there would be no such thing as absolute poverty; everybody could make a living that wanted to. Enough to eat and enough to wear, and a roof over your head would be sure to every mother's son of us. Now, don't you forget it, there's lots of white folks would be glad of just such a chance. Them Indians didn't pay any taxes, and their lands couldn't be taken from 'em. If they had been anything like decent people they might have had almost anything they could get their eyes on; but as it was, it kept even such critters as them in comfort. Now, you see, Tom, if everybody had such a chance as that, steppin' on poor men would come to an end, and finally, after it had been in operation long enough, our 'free home' amendment would give every family an opportunity to have just that. Well, not everybody would want it, but enough would take up with it so that it would thin out the labor market and raise wages; then, when wages raised, the fellows who got higher wages could spend more and prices would rise and every-thing be put on a better footing, and—bless the Lord!— we'd get out from under the feet of money-grabbers. No harm would be done to a soul, and only the legal privilege the strong now have of imposing upon the weak, would be taken away. Nothing so very bad about that, sure!'

Jones did not reply; evidently he was revolving in his mind the propositions advanced by Weldon, who, as a par-ticular and personal friend of Grafton's, had become quite pronounced as a local advocate of the propositions included in "the demands." Although the blacksmith was hard at work upon the plow with his hands, mentally, he was strongly engaged in the efforts to "convert" Jones, watching him narrowly to see how he took what was said to him.

Tom Jones was an honest, but not very acute, sort of man; he always voted the republican ticket, had little to say, and no one was able to tell whether he really knew much or not. Weldon called himself a democrat, and thus came quite naturally into opposition to Jones. Judging from his look and actions that he was making an impres-sion, the blacksmith began again:

' "Now, you know, Tom, the big question of the future, is the labor question;—the fight between capital and labor. That's got to be settled, some way. It's a big thing, and it's liable to tear everything all up, unless some kind of a settlement is made 'fore long. Now, I've no new plan to save the world; I just want to go back to first principles, to the Declaration of Independence. We read there that gov-ernments ought to exist to secure to men their individual rights; that's the only good reason for government. Now, let our government do that thing,—that is, give men these natural rights, and there will be no trouble. Then, every fellow will have a chance, and the big horses can't step on him. Now, the adoption of 'the demands' will do that. They will say,—when put into the State constitution,—to the rich and powerful: 'Keep your hands off the poor

people; stop imposing upon 'em; give 'em a chance.'
Now, that's all any reasonable, self-respecting poor man
wants; he don't want the property of the rich, but he's
perfectly sick of the constant and continual, and never-
nding, robbery of the poor by the rich. Fact is, our great
rich people are made powerful in just one way, and only
one way—they steal from the poor and from those who are
now unable to help themselves. Course, it's done according
to law, in indirect and concealed ways. But it's done!
Fact is, that's the only way it can be done. All wealth is
created by labor, and the man who creates no wealth has
got to steal, if he gets rich. Adopt 'the demands,' and the
labor question will settle itself, because each individual will
be protected in his rights, just as old Tom Jefferson intended
when he wrote the Declaration. I'm a democrat, but I believe in that kind of protection, and I am in favor of abolition, too. I want to abolish white slavery, and I want to do
it by simply following out the lines laid down in that good,
old democratic document,—the Declaration of Independence,
—by securing to each man his rights, and taking from the
rich and powerful the power to impose upon him. That's
all,—but it's enough."

By this time the repairs on the plow had been completed; the blacksmith assisted in putting it in the wagon,
but even after this had been done, he still stood near; both
arms resting on the edge of the wagon-box, as though loth
to have Jones leave him, although the latter had climbed
into his wagon and, with lines in hand, was ready to go.

"Tom," said the blacksmith, "I think we ought to
help in this business, don't you?" But Jones would not
declare himself, only saying, as he drove away: "I'll see,
I'll see."

Casting the Ballots at the Election.

CHAPTER XXIII.

THE CONFLICT OF INTERESTS.

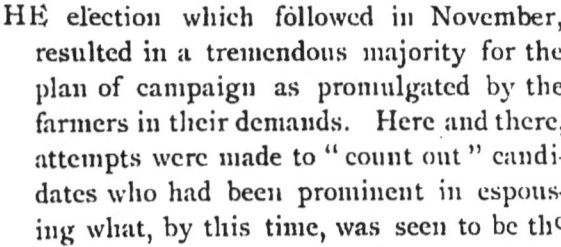

HE election which followed in November, resulted in a tremendous majority for the plan of campaign as promulgated by the farmers in their demands. Here and there, attempts were made to "count out" candidates who had been prominent in espousing what, by this time, was seen to be the cause of the whole people, but these attempts were quickly frustrated, for it began to be clear that unless the farmers were at least moderately prosperous, that it would be impossible for either merchants, lawyers or doctors, or even bankers, to live among them, since they all depended upon them, either directly or indirectly; and it was remembered that, in the past, the time in which the farmers were prosperous had always been the time of prosperity to all, including the professional classes.

But after the *furore* of the election had subsided, and men began to coolly survey the field and to think of the measures to be employed, a very natural difference of opinion regarding the proposed plans began to be manifested. And these differences, slight at first, and easily reconcilable, were magnified by the press, so that when the time of meeting of the State Legislature had arrived, a heated controversy in the newspapers being kept up in the meantime, two plainly discernible factions had ranged themselves in opposing ranks.

On the part of one it was said that while it was plain that something radical was needed, and the advisibility of some sort of a stay law was conceded, still the abolition of the collection of debts by law was furiously opposed, and an attempt was made to show that this would involve the utter prostration of business and take from the poor and industrious man the power of obtaining credit, with which he might be able to accumulate a competency. It was noticed that

the advocates of this view, although they spoke only of the
poor man and the evils which would fall upon his head by
the action of the proposed legislation, consisted almost
entirely of lawyers and men who were interested, either
directly or indirectly, in loaning money; still, they spoke
earnestly and eloquently for the poor man, and wished, so
they said, to see him secure in all his rights and privileges
which the proposed legislation would plainly curtail.

The other side stoutly maintained that debt was the
great evil, the cause of untold misery and vastly superior to
intoxicating drink as a cause of poverty and crime, and they
quoted from statistics at great length, which, so they said,
showed that in a general way crime was committed in direct
proportion to the misery, ignorance and poverty of the people. That the ability to get into debt was an imaginary
advantage, and an actual and positive disadvantage to every
honest man. "Pay as you go," said they, "is the philosopher's stone which turns all to gold!" They showed that,
by actual experience, short credits would not be interfered
with, as they were made upon the honor of the debtor at
the time, and would so continue. They also showed that,
while under laws then existing, it might be possible for a
man in comfortable circumstances to adopt for himself the
plan of cash payments, the organization of society under the
plan of universal debt, made it nearly impossible for the
man already in the meshes of circumstances to do this; and,
said they, if society, generally, is involved and depressed by
the operation of laws and customs, indirectly all must suffer,
and in the long run the general public; prosperity and
happiness will be gradually reduced to a lower and still
lower level.

During the two months which elapsed between the
election and the meeting of the legislature, if one had judged
the temper of the public mind by reading the partisan and
political newspapers published in the State, he would certainly have concluded that discord and confusion reigned.
Two things, however, operated to prevent the minds of the

farmers from being diverted to any great extent from the originally-expressed purposes of the campaign. The greatest, of course, was the thorough discussion of the questions at stake among the farmers, which had preceded the election, their organization holding solidly to their original demands and very generally refusing all overtures of compromise in the very moderate measures upon which they had at first agreed. It began once more to be seen, as has been the case throughout the history of the world, that, although tillers of the soil are usually very slow to accept changes in their manner of thought, still, when they have once thoroughly made up their minds, they are not easily diverted from the execution of their plans.

The other reason was, that the opposition, which had apparently been lost sight of at the time of the election, could not quite conceal the fact that they were now endeavoring to prevent the success of the people's cause by the policy of dividing what they had failed to conquer, when united. The character and known interests of the advocates who were industriously seeking to create divisions, appeared too plainly upon the surface for effectual concealment.

Although feeling ran high, and a subdued excitement had taken possession of the whole body of citizens, the great and distinguishing excellence of the American people, accustomed as they are to decide questions in a public capacity, became manifest to all. No disturbance of any moment took place and the greatest good nature prevailed in all public assemblies, upon the part of the participants.

Although the partisan press still kept up its weekly fusilade, it began to be noticed that the public deliverances of the farmers' organizations at their meetings and in the papers championing their cause, showed no material change in sentiment or expression. Replying to the compromisers, they showed most conclusively that any attempt to change their plans by substituting a plan for the purchase of homes by the creation of debts would inevitably result in delivering the home-purchaser into the hands of the dealers in money:

that the buyer of land under the proposed plan, in case he failed to pay in full, would be subjected to the pains and penalties of a suit at law, to obtain from the party of whom he had bought, the money he had advanced, and that it was far better for a man to be entirely free from debt, with some money in the bank, than to be the holder of land which somebody else really owned. It was acknowledged by them that in any radical change some hardships would inevitably have to be endured, but that the entire freedom from debt and consequent deliverance of a people from its galling chains, and the domination which it necessarily imposed, was a cause which fully justified any effort which might be made to escape what was clearly seen as the great evil of the time.

Thus matters stood at the time of the inauguration of the new State administration, and a general feeling of expectancy, not unmixed with alarm, on the part of so-called 'conservative' citizens, held possession of the public mind.

The inauguration of Governor Brown took place, as usual, in the capitol at Topeka, and was attended by nothing unusual beyond the deep feeling of anxiety, which appeared to take possession of the masses of people, that crowded the Hall of Representatives almost to the point of suffocation.

As the Governor-elect came forward to take the oath of office, he was seen to be a stout, well-built man of open countenance and ruddy complexion, some fifty years of age, who, though somewhat agitated by the weighty responsibilities of the hour, was yet master of himself and of the situation in which he was placed by the suffrages of the electors of Kansas. The ceremony having been quickly concluded, he stepped to the front and, producing a roll of manuscript, began the reading of his inaugural address, as follows :

" Fellow Citizens of Kansas: Impressed, as I am at this hour, with the solemn and weighty responsibilities of my present position, I should not do justice to you, nor to myself, if I failed to acknowledge, in a fitting and suitable manner, my dependence on the Supreme Arbiter of events. Appealing to Him and to that innate sense of justice which inhabits the breasts of honest men, the people whom I represent in an official capacity have declared their unalterable opposition to anything which may militate against the truest interests of the whole people of the State of Kansas. The interest of no class of citizens, even though that class should represent a majority of its people, should be fostered or advanced, if thereby the just rights of any citizen be, by such action, imperiled or put in jeopardy. The history of the past has fully proved the power of majorities to work great injustice in the dealings with the few, and the fear has been expressed that in the accession to power in this State of the present administration, that measures might be adopted which would prove both injurious and unjust to the rights and privileges of some.

" Fellow Citizens of the Senate and House of Representatives : Under these circumstances it will be right and proper for us to declare, in the most solemn manner, our determination to be guided in the legislation which may be effected by what the good Chancellor Kent has described as ' those fit and just rules of conduct which the Creator has prescribed to man as a dependent and social being, and which are to be ascertained by the deductions of right reasoning'. Let us also remember that, in the words of one of the greatest American lawyers that ' upon entering into society for the purpose of having their natural rights secured and protected or properly redressed, the few do not give up or surrender any portion of their priceless heritage in any government constituted as it should be." Let it be our duty,—and pleasure as well,—to secure to all, so far as we may be able, those inalienable rights to life, liberty and property, upon which depend our modern social life and business existence."

As the Governor began the reading of his message, the immense assemblage stood in silence and with most intense expectancy written upon their countenances. Gradually, the strained and anxious look gave way as his hearers, glancing into the faces of those about them, read the expressions of approval and satisfaction which began to be manifested there. Continuing, he took up, one after another, the questions which had so agitated the minds of the people of the State, and each in turn was so fairly and moderately stated and treated, that when he had concluded, the applause was most generous and unstinted.

The assemblage slowly dispersed, and the people composing it chatted pleasantly among themselves as they made their way out of the building; the general expression among the Topeka people being that the address was very good, indeed, for a " granger," and evinced some care in its preparation and altogether was somewhat satisfactory, being plainly intended to reassure those who had feared destruction to the monied interests from the election of a plain farmer upon a platform which had asserted some of the useful platitudes on " the rights of labor".

Among the country people present, as visitors and members of the legislature, the address was regarded as "just the thing". One of the members-elect, who had collected a little knot of fellow legislators around him in one of the corridors, declared to his interested listeners that, " Tom Brown was just as big a man as there was on the platform, for all the chief-justice and his gold-bowed spectacles. Talk about your education and polish! Mother-wit and natural good sense beats everything else, time a man gets to be forty years old."

" Then," said he, " men fall out and fight because they don't understand each other. One side means one thing by the use of a set of words, and the other fellows mean something else, and here they are at cross-purposes before they know it, when, if they only fully understood each other, there wasn't so much difference in 'em, after all."

"Well, now," said another, "what you say is all true enough; folks don't understand each other, that's a fact; and no doubt that is the cause of a great deal of trouble, but I want you to understand that there is something more than the dictionary between the two sides that's going to lock horns in this legislature, before long."

"That's all true enough, too," said the first; "but what I mean to say is that the honest men, the men who mean to do right and are disposed to do the fair thing, won't have much trouble in understanding each other, once we get to work and talk things over. The trouble will come from fellows that's hired to misrepresent and delay, and rake up difficulties, and dig pits for the rest of us."

"That's so," broke in another, "and what makes the outlook bad is that these last fellows, who mean to make trouble, are keen, bright men, who know the ropes and have a way of controlling the men they run with. Turn a lot of horses together, and there'll be one among 'em that the rest will follow anywhere. Don't seem to make much difference what kind of a horse it is; ten to one it's a worthless old plug, but he can lead 'em, and it's just so with men: they'll follow after some scoundrel, and sure's they do he'll get 'em into a bad hole."

"I tell you, Bill, said the first speaker, "there's where the good of organization comes in. Now, if there is no organization—like the old Alliance, for instance,—a lot of strange men thrown together for fifty days, as the legislature is, would be hauled around by these black sheep leaders, but when honest, well-intentioned men have an organization controlled by established principles, that sort of work gets a black eye right where it'll do the most good. The organization acts the part of the fence around the pasture where Bill's horses are running. The old plug leaders is there and the crowd run after 'em, but the fence stops 'em from going very far. You see, the fence is put up on established principles, in which the rights of men and property are settled and the bounds staked out by a force which the old plugs, men or horses, are bound to respect. Now, you turn a lot of horses loose on the prairie and the meanest horse you've got will lead the whole bunch clean off to his old stamping-ground. Then, you see, they ain't no use to you nor to themselves, and ten to one, some man's crop is a-suffering. The mischief is to pay somewheres, you can bet your life. But now you just turn them horses into a pasture with a good religious fence, with plenty of barbs on the top wire, and the next morning you know where they are. The horses ain't changed none in disposition, the old plug leader is there, but he ain't running the flesh off the bunch now; nor getting them into some man's cornfield. I tell you, horses ain't no good onless they're controlled by something they respect, and loose men ain't no better than loose horses. Principles, organization and government is good things for both men and horses, but it's mighty important which side of the fence your man or your horse gets to be."

He Fired and the Man Fell to the Ground.

CHAPTER XXIV.

DESTINY.

THE session of the legislature which followed was most exciting and troublous. Action upon the main propositions was deferred from day to day, first by one and then another motion of delay. The minor points of difference, which argument had developed during and since the canvass, were carefully kept alive and division fomented by every device know to the artful. So-called "great men," belonging to both the democratic and republican parties, strayed casually into Topeka and were "invited" to speak upon the issues of the day. Upon one point both were agreed, and on that much was said by the eminent men of either party. The sacredness of the right to have and hold property was enlarged upon and argued at great and most convincing length.' After the speeches, these eminent leaders were introduced, at different times, to the members of the legislature belonging to their respective parties; and with those who gave promise of becoming leaders, much time was spent in explaining the legal aspect of the proposed legislation. Flattered by the attention of men of national reputation, these began to waver in their adherence to the strict letter of the "demands": the "demands" were well enough,—something must be done,—but they were not in favor, now that they properly understood the matter, of anything which might savor of revolution.

Matters were still further complicated by the promises made in the matter of the election of a senator. Upon this question party lines were strictly drawn, and a heated and acrimonious discussion had so embittered the factions

that no agreement appeared possible among them upon
any question, whatever.

Thus the session wore slowly away and the fifty days,
for which the members received pay, at last expired, and
the "demands" were still unheeded. Although, at the
outset, a majority had favored them, this majority had
yielded to the powerful, and as it appeared, convincing
arguments of the visiting statesmen. However, a strong
and united minority still remained who vigorously advo-
cated the original demands,—but it was a minority.

The time for which members were paid having expired, one after another left for home, but before an
adjournment was finally had, the democrats got together
and passed a set of caustic resolutions laying all the blame
of non-action in important matters upon the wicked and
monopolistic republicans. The republicans, not to be
outdone in this matter, with the assistance of a certain ex-
Senator, possessed of a vitriolic tongue and pen, also con-
cocted "an address to the people," in which they recited
at length the doings of the wicked and whiskey-loving
democrats; charged them with the commission of every
crime in the calendar and credited them with a desire to
invent new ones that they might commit them, and upon
these degraded beings they rightfully placed, so they said,
the *onus* of the existing situation.

The minority also came out with what they termed,
"A Plain Statement," in which they showed the manner
in which the proposed legislation had been defeated.

After the adjournment, the newspapers throughout
the State which had originally opposed the demands, came
out simultaneously with a great shout of approval. Revolutionary and anarchistic doctrines had now received their
death wound, and would expire. People, said they, had at
last come to their senses and would no longer follow revolutionary and communistic leaders who aimed at the
destruction of society. The farmers, however, were ex-
asperated and moody; their scheme had failed. At first

but little was said: gradually they began, in public assemblies, to formulate and express their opinions, and it was noticed that a large share of their wrath was directed at the political leaders and organizations that had so plainly frustrated their efforts for relief, and as the feeling among them that they had been defrauded, grew and increased, here and there throughout the State, unwarranted liberties were taken with men who, as members of the legislative body, had failed to carry out ante-election promises. A number were visited at the dead hour of night by committees supplied with tar and feathers, which they, in a most illegal manner, proceeded to apply. Some were taken by masked men and stripped and beaten until they promised, if released, to undo the work which they had done, when given an opportunity. 'As this proceeded, the farmers' organizations at once awoke and took most active steps in opposition. Resolutions were passed expelling any member guilty of illegally taking part in demonstrations of a riotous character, and investigations were set on foot to discover the perpetrators of outrage, and the result of these showed most conclusively that "bummers" and hangers-on are in almost every instance the curse of either armies or organizations. And although the reign of tar and feathers quickly came to an end,—discountenanced as it was by the better elements of the State,—it is yet doubtful whether salutary effects were not produced by these overt acts of lawless citizens. But all agreed that they should come to an end.

As the season advanced, and spring, with the returning warmth of the benignant and all-creating sun, began to cause the thoughts of the farmers to return to their fields again, the wrath of the agriculturists did not abate, as had been the expectation of some.

Public meetings increased in size and favor, and many declared that until matters of importance were settled they did not care longer to cultivate land, merely that others might reap the results of their toil. So great was the

excitement throughout the State that attention was attracted to Kansas, in all parts of the country, and the great
city dailies contained standing "stare-heads," which called
attention to the situation in Kansas. As discussion proceeded, a demand was gradually evolved that Governor
Brown summon the legislature in extra session to take
action which should fairly represent the sentiment of the
people of the State. In the excited state of public feeling,
business came, very largely, to an end; and among business men, who had previously opposed the "demands" as
revolutionary, the call for an extra session found favor.
It began to be plain to them that something radical must
really be done, as, without an earnest effort was made to
pacify the excited people, they began to fear social disorder
of the worst type.

The farmers held solidy to their original demands,
and many who had heretofore been only luke-warm in
their support, spoke in the most decided manner in favor
of even more radical measures. Propositions of compromise of one kind or another were made in almost every
prominent journal—and, in short, the air was full of, what
appeared to be, a coming storm.

Mr. Grafton, as an official of the Alliance, was engaged
in delivering addresses to the farmers' assemblies at various
places in the State, in which he counseled the greatest care
in obeying the laws and preserving the peace, as well as a
united front against compromise of any character. As he
was speaking at a gathering of farmers, near Atlanta, a
disturbance arose in the audience, caused by the interrup-
tions of a drunken man, who wore the star of a detective.
Mr. Grafton bore pleasantly with the taunts of the creature,
who, from time to time, continued to apply himself to a
bottle with which he was supplied. Finally he became so
obstreperous,—supported as he was by a little knot of men
who had come upon the grounds with him,—that it was
impossible to proceed, and Mr. Grafton paused and said:

" Friends, it is impossible to proceed in this manner. That man must be removed!"

" Come and do it yourself!" said the now infuriated man, with an oath.

As no preparations had been made to enforce order, no one started to do the necessary work of removing the creature, who now, losing all control of himself, began, in the most obscene and profane manner, to scream with rage, frightening the women and children, who in large numbers were present. Seeing that something must be done at once, Grafton went toward the man, followed by some of the more resolute among the farmers. As he came near, the man flourished a revolver and bade the crowd defiance, but Grafton kept steadily on:

" You are a disturber of the peace and, as a citizen, I arrest you!" said he; but before he could reach him, the man fired, and Grafton dropped to the ground.

Immediately there was a scene of wild disorder; women screamed, children began to cry, and men to curse and swear and rush toward the point of disturbance. The villain was quickly seized and disarmed, and a cry went up of:

" Hang him! String him up! Kill the thief!" Reason appeared to have completely disappeared and its place to be taken by a wild, ungovernable fury, which converted the gathering of peaceable and easy-going farmers into a howling mob, for the moment ungovernable in its character. A lariat rope was quickly taken from a pony tethered near, and as quickly placed about the neck of the miscreant, and he was hurried to a little distance from the scene of his crime, where a suitable tree was standing.

Grafton lay upon the ground, where he had fallen. Most of the men, crazed as they were with rage, were engaged in hurrying the murderer towards the fatal tree, which already a young man had climbed and was making signals that the end of the rope might be thrown to him. As the wretch who had caused their fright was dragged

away, the women gathered about the wounded man. A
lady sat upon the ground and, taking Grafton's head in
her lap, directed the crowd to stand back. Tearing open
his shirt-front, a brother farmer exposed the fatal wound;
a small bullet hole in the left breast, with but a drop or
two of blood upon the surface told the story. He was
bleeding inwardly, and would soon be gone. He was yet
conscious, and as the death damp gathered upon his brow
he made feeble signs for water, and when his want was
supplied, he slowly and painfully said:

" Don't let——them hang——him——he was drunk!"

Meantime, although the rope was in place over a limb
of the tree which had been chosen, the crowd, revolting
from the idea of murder, had halted temporarily in its
work and sent some of their number to make sure whether
Grafton was really dead. Coming to where he lay, these,
seeing the wounded man with white face and exposed
wound, from which trickled now and then a drop of blood,
slowly sinking, without sign of life other than the sigh-
like respirations which grew more and more infrequent
from moment to moment, were seized with that intense
sympathy which the sight of blood, shed in a righteous
cause, is sure to bring to the most hardened and unthinking, and returning hurriedly, themselves seized the end of
the rope and began to pull upon it. Instantly, hands in
plenty laid hold, and the wretch was dangling in the air.

Who, that is able to look back upon a checkered life,
can fail to acknowledge that he has been " led in a way he
knew not ?" The future ever appears capable of control,
but when it is past we are forced to the conclusion that we
are, and must remain, totally unconscious of the hidden
springs from whence come the motives which impel us to
the course we pursue. This man lives a fortunate life and
that one is pursued by the slings and arrows of outrageous
fortune. And why? It is said that the one is wise in
choice and careful in council, and the other unwise and

foolish in his ways, and that thus they, themselves, have made the beds in which they lie? And who does not know that this, instead of being an answer, is but a begging of the question? For who made the one wise and the other foolish? Themselves? And can a man make himself do or be anything not provided for in the secret recesses of his mental being, when, like the infant oak within the acorn's germ, he first was fashioned as a thought of God? And shall the oak pride and praise itself that it is not a pine?

Than what they are, the oak and the pine could be nothing less and nothing more.

CHAPTER XXV.

THE ORPHANS.

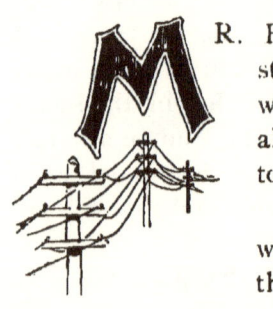

MR. ELLERY was sauntering down the street upon a pleasant spring-like day, when he met the station-agent, who was also the only telegraph operator of the town, who said :

" I have a telegram for Miss Grafton, which you ought to know of. Her father has been killed."

The kind-hearted preacher was so horrified and astonished by what he heard that for the moment he could make no sound, and stared blankly at the man. At last he found tongue to say :

" How did it happen ? Where was he ? "

" It was at a picnic near Atlanta, in Coles county; somebody shot him and they hung the fellow up without judge or jury. This I get from the wires that are sending it all over the country. The telegram gives no particulars. You better open it."

Taking the terrible missive in his hands, Mr. Ellery opened the envelope and read :

ATLANTA, KANSAS, —— ——.
To MARY GRAFTON, PLAINVILLE, KANSAS.
Your father was shot and killed near here yesterday. Will come with the body to-morrow. JAMES GREENE.

Putting the paper in his pocket, Mr. Ellery went at once to the house and without circumlocution told his wife the sorrowful news. She, poor lady, with true womanly sympathy exclaimed, as the tears filled her eyes :

" Oh! Oh! My poor Mary! What will my dear girl do? What can she? I shall fear to tell her. She was bound up in her father's welfare, and day and night her thoughts were with him."

" But you must tell her," said Mr. Ellery; " and no doubt, as it is known on the street, some one will tell her as

May God Call Me to Account.

she comes from school, if you do not. You must go to the
school-house and bring her home at once."

Hastily putting on her bonnet and shawl, Mrs. Ellery
started for the school-house. Conning over in her mind
the means she should use in managing the difficult and
most distressing errand upon which her unwilling feet were
carrying her, she was soon at the door, and although different plans had in turn presented themselves to her mind,
she had been unable to decide upon anything definitely.
Opening the door, she stepped at once inside; resolved, at
last, that, having no plan, she would restrain her own
emotions and act with the best judgment furnished her by
the inspiration of the moment. As she entered the room,
Mary, with beaming face and animated manner, was engaged
in describing to a class of little ones taking their first voy-
age of geographical discovery, the wonders of the world we
inhabit. Interested, herself, in the subject she was endeavoring to portray, the children hung upon her words with
rapt attention. Still, for the moment, undetermined, Mrs.
Ellery sank into a seat and waited her opportunity. Nod-
ding pleasantly to her, Mary continued her work. Sitting
there and noting the beautiful form and face, and the ease
with which she guided the minds of her little hearers, and
realizing the terrible shock and despair in store for her,
Mrs. Ellery could not refrain from feeling like a guilty
thing, in that she was preparing to destroy present happiness and plunge the poor girl into a sea of misery.

As ever with her, in moments of trouble, her thoughts
ascended to that "present help" upon which her mind had
come to lean. "God help her," thought she, "and may I
be enabled to render that service to a fellow creature to
which every consideration of love and duty impel me!"

Occupied with her anxious thoughts, the poor woman
for the moment forgot her determination, and as the ready
tears sprang to her eyes, half a sob escaped her. Hastily
wiping her eyes, she looked up to see if she had been observed. But the keen and observant glance of the young

teacher had already noted the trouble depicted upon her countenance and, hastily dismissing her little class, came at once to her side.

"Something troubles you, aunt," she said; "what is it? Can I assist you?"

"Yes," said she, "there is trouble enough at our house. You must dismiss your scholars, and go home with me!"

"But school will soon be out; will not that answer?"

"No, dear; don't question me, but come at once!"

Dismissing her charges, who, with wondering faces gathered about her, eager for the reason of the unusual proceeding, she gave this one a pleasant word and the next a pat upon the cheek as she prepared to close the door.

"Children," said Mrs. Ellery, "you must all run home and not trouble Miss Mary now, as I wish to talk to her. Charlie, you must go right along with us!"

Taking the arm of her friend as they set out, Mary said: "What is it, aunt; has anything happened to Mr. Ellery?"

"Yes," said the other, inwardly seeking pardon for the deception; "Mr. Ellery is in deep trouble at the house; don't ask me further until we get there!"

As they passed through the principal streets of the little village, the sympathetic and sorrowful faces of the people they met, struck poor Mary with a deep and indefinable dread. Setting out with the idea that duty was calling upon her to minister to the sorrows of others, somehow the feeling grew that she was principally concerned. What could it be? Had anything happened to her father? And instantly the thought formed itself in her mind that all was well with him. In whatever situation placed, he had done his duty and quietly and bravely met whatever of good or ill had been given him as his portion. The spirit within had sustained him. Her spirit should sustain her, and whatever burden of sorrow or care might be placed upon her shoulders, she would accept and bear it as became so true a man.

GEORGE GRAFTON.

How wonderful are the daily evidences of mind upon mind! Fix your thought intently upon another and, if not attracted by something going on about him, he turns to you as the needle to the pole, to discover the source of the unexplained attraction. And does this end with life? And if the soul still lives, why may it not continue to exert a power which does not depend upon the sight, touch or hearing of that physical body which has, alone, decayed?

Walking along the street, the unseen influences emanating from the people she met—and who will hasten to bar his thoughts against the hallowed influences which may come from those "angels which do always behold the face of My Father?"—had convinced the mind of the devoted girl that upon her head was shortly to fall a crushing blow, and as truly pointed her thoughts in the true direction.

Her resolution was taken; she would meet whatever came, with fortitude. That, for the moment, the spirit of her father was with her, she felt, rather than knew; and who shall deny?

Coming to the house, Mrs. Ellery directed their steps to the front door, contrary to the usual custom of the family. This, of itself, was a revelation to Mary; she already knew the worst.

As they entered, Mr. Ellery met them, and, opening the parlor door, they all went in and sat down. Taking out his handkerchief, Mr. Ellery began to wipe his eyes, while his wife burst into tears; but Mary sat with rigid face, the only sign of the communion within, the passionate workings of her clenched and bloodless hands.

As Mrs Ellery's feelings were now beyond control, the preacher, also deeply affected by the play of emotion about him, began in a hesitating and stammering fashion:

"Prepare yourself, my dear——for—for——the worst!"

"I am prepared," said she; and as she spoke, so hoarse and strange was the sound of her voice that she wondered if, indeed, it was her own.

"Your father, Mary," he brokenly began,—but she did not wait for him to finish—

"I know it all," she said, "he is dead! Tell me the particulars! And may God call me to account if I fail to remember the reason of the death of both my father and my mother!"

She could no longer remain in her chair, and rising, stood pale and defiant, her hands twitching nervously, one with the other. Upon the table she saw the crumpled bit of yellow paper upon which was written the telegram. Taking it in her hands, she read it calmly through.

"Where is Charlie?" said she: "he followed us through the street."

Going to the window, she saw him just at the door, playing with a dog belonging to a neighbor. Quick as a flash, she was at the door and down the steps. Seizing him by the hand, she hurried him within the house. Taking him on her lap, "big boy" though he considered himself, she kissed him again and again.

"Ah, you poor little orphan," said she, "they have killed our father! It might have been expected! We might have known it would be so! Now, you are all that is left to me."

Boy-like, Charlie began to cry, and the natural womanly tenderness, which for the moment had been in abeyance, asserted itself, as with incoherent sobbings and mingled caresses, she fondled the only remaining member of her family.

Gradually she became calm again. "And what must we do now?" said she.

"Why, my child, you need do nothing. We will see that the necessary preparations are made," said Mrs. Ellery, who by this time could trust herself to speak.

"Ah! I must! I cannot be still. I should go mad to sit and think. I will not again be so weak. Dear aunt, you have been so kind to us and I know you will bear with me now, but I must be employed at something. Please let me help! There will be so much to do."

"Why, Mary, you know I was thinking only of you,' said Mrs. Ellery, "and if it would please you better, do what you think best!"

"The short and simple annals of the poor," are, after all, not so easily told. Human hopes and fears, with intelligent people, are much the same, in whatever walk or station of life fate or fortune may place them. Hope beckons to all, and allures us on. Pleased to the last, we greet with joy the swift-coming days that bear us on to a fate hid behind the curtain of the future, and that curtain—the pall. Yet does not hope desert us, but, like an angel of light, bears us company upon the dreary road of life, and, with her sweet whisperings of a life beyond, beguiles us still. Beguiles? Ah! And hath hope a partnership with guile? Blessed vision! Art thou, too, a vain chimera of that imagination of man which forever bewilders, but to deceive?

Perish the thought! It cannot, must not, be! Hope is the evidence of sanity ; the proof that we are. For whom she hath utterly deserted and forsaken, has become a maniac, and ceased to be.

Tossing upon her bed, now lost in dreams and now staring with wide-open eyes into the dark, whose depths revealed no friendly face, Mary wore the night away. Again she was a child, and felt her mother's hand resting in peace upon her thoughtless head, and as she awoke and felt her loss, an unutterable longing for death seized upon her. Oh, that she could but die and leave a world so full of trouble as this! But the thought of Charlie recalled her. Dear little fellow, she would live for him! Again, in dreams, her father's proud and kindly gaze was upon her, his face was white as the light, care, there was none, and peace had come. She woke with a start. Alas! there was nothing real but sorrow and pain.

· Slowly, the morning dawned, and day at last appeared. A funeral day! His funeral! But she would be brave! She would so live and act as to meet their approval! If they knew? Did they know? Surely, what was so much desired must be true. No deep and holy longing of the soul could fail in its mission. It would not return void to the heart of love.

The contents of the telegram known, the idle population of the little village gathered at the station as the train drew up. An elderly, kindly-faced man in a suit of gray, was the only passenger to alight. Walking forward to the express car he assisted the messenger in depositing upon the platform the rough box containing the coffin. A few hurried words with the station-agent, who came to the corner of the platform and pointed to Mr. Ellery's house, and the stranger walked rapidly towards the point to which he had been directed. He had gone but a few steps, when he met Mr. Ellery, hastening to the train.

" You are Mr. Greene, I suppose?" said he.

" Yes," said the man, " and you are Mr. Ellery; I have come upon a sorrowful errand. I was instrumental in inducing my friend, Grafton, to undertake the work in which he lost his life, and now I am here to bury him."

A few words of consultation with friends who stood near, a little time spent in arranging the preliminaries, and the coffin was deposited in the parlor at the parsonage.

The funeral ceremonies were, as with the others, cold, formal and silent. Many were in attendance, for the tragic nature of his death attracted those to whom mere respect would have appealed in vain.

Mary and Charlie, with Mrs. Ellery, took their last look in the parlor and alone. No one was near, and no one knew the agony of that hour. Afterward, no sign was made. Heavily veiled, the daughter of the murdered man betrayed to the casual beholder no emotion, and thus the weary waitings and solemn pauses of the funeral went by, to her, unheeded and uncontrolled.

After all was over, the family at the parsonage gathered in the parlor and Mr. Greene related the particulars of the death, paying the highest tribute possible to the courage and devotion of him who had gone. Mary asked but few questions; she seemed to know it all. Charlie regarded all tearfully, but to his sister his eyes returned and from her he took the color of his thoughts; indeed, he seemed to receive his impressions as reflected from her.

Days came and went; the nine days wonder of the tragedy had ceased to attract; but from it, in part, proceeded a still stronger determination to press to a decision the questions which Grafton had propounded and for which the public had come to believe he had sacrificed his life. Monster petitions were circulated asking the Governor to convene the legislature. Immense meetings, fired with zeal, were held at different places throughout the State, and enthusiasm was at fever heat. Again, the partisan press of the State acknowledged, by their plaintive tones, the truth: that public opinion is the master of all; and to it, perforce, they bowed once more.

Finally, Governor Brown issued his proclamation calling an "extra session."

CHAPTER XXVI.

THE CONFLICT CONTINUES.

AS the legislators began to gather at Topeka, all thought was, for the time, concentrated upon the demands which had been made by the farmers' organizations. Strong ground was taken both for and against, and it became evident that dilatory tactics would no longer avail.

The opposition based its claims to support upon the assertion that the proposed legislation would be an act of bad faith and practical repudiation. On the other hand, it was argued that the political compact, which forms the foundation upon which all just states and nations, and even civilization and liberty itself, are placed, requires all legislation to be based upon the general public good.

The State was simply the agent of the whole people, and any intervention in the private affairs of her citizens could only be allowed upon the supposition that thereby the general good of all would be secured. Legislation, upon any ground other than the general good, was tyrannical and unjust. The State interfered in the dealings of citizens and proceeded to the forcible collection of debts due from one to another, not upon the ground of favoritism to the creditor, but simply because it had been supposed and held that this forcible interference had been for the general good, and if it could be shown that such interference and assistance rendered to one party, was contrary to the best interests of the general public, that, therefore, such legislation was opposed to all the requirements of a just public policy and, therefore, void, and the very ground upon which it was placed was not

MARY GRAFTON

Phinyville School Teacher.

only unrepublican in theory and untenable in law, but vicious, tyrannical, and unjust in its effects.

Previous to the meeting of the legislature, those who had engaged to support the "demands" were called together, that they might take counsel, one with the other. These came from the ranks of all parties; but as the previous session had taught them that a closer union was an absolute necessity. and that they could not succeed if they allowed the claims of other organizations, the natural and inevitable result was the formation of a new party, that bound its members to support and defend the course marked out. Having secured this closer organization, the lower house at once passed the bills, prepared at the previous session.

The Senate refused to concur, and proposed amendment after amendment, but the House remained immovable.

After much time spent in wrangling had passed, the House, by a majority resolution, adjourned, and the members repaired to their homes, with the understanding that their speaker should at once call them together, whenever the Senate was ready to pass the original bills. The Senate remained in session, and, issuing an address to the people, in which the capitalistic side of the controversy was most ably and cunningly stated, appeared to be preparing for a long and arduous struggle. No sooner had the House of Representatives adjourned than excitement among the people of the State became intense. Public meetings were everywhere held, attended by vast crowds of people. Eminent men upon both sides made the welkin ring with their denunciations, and feeling rose quickly to fever heat.

Those who held to the justice and expediency of the demands made originally by the farmers, dubbed their opponents "Monopolists" and "Tories." The so-called monopolists, however, sought to take high moral ground in all their addresses, and spoke chiefly of the sacredness of the rights of property, the inviolability of contracts, and descanted at great length upon "public honor," "plighted faith," and the rights of "investors."

The others, in making reply, denied any intention of interfering with the rights of property, and demanded that those who held bonds, notes and mortgages as property, should not be placed in a position to impose upon those interested in property of another kind. "It is," said they, "a struggle between the holders of two classes of property ; and the dealers in money, notes and mortgages refuse to be satisfied unless they and their interests are placed in a pre- ferred position, where they are enabled to impose upon the holders of productive property, while they, themselves, pro- duce nothing of value.

Thus the struggle went on and the excitement showed no signs of abatement. In many places, riotous proceed- ings were indulged in, and a general feeling of unrest and alarm began to take possession of the public mind.

Plainville showed but little change.

"Uncle Bill" continued to hammer away in his little shop and Mr. Ellery to deliver his weekly sermons. As elsewhere, the people took sides, and the questions which agitated the public mind were discussed with great heat and earnestness. As the people of the village were in close sympathy with the farmers, depending e n t i r e l y upon them for whatever business the town enjoyed, feeling was almost altogether w i t h them. Upon rare occasions, those more interested in what was going on around them went to Branchville to attend a "big speaking," when  some noted man held forth, upon one side or the other, in the great controversy, but for the most part the place was sleepy enough.

Mary was often seen in company with Mrs Ellery, upon the street or riding in the rather antiquated carriage, which the preacher called his own. She had finished her school, with only a week's intermission at the time of her father's funeral, and now, during the summer vacation, was very quietly engaged in assisting Mrs. Ellery, both in the household and in the usual visiting and managing, considered the duty of a pastor's wife. No Sunday-school picnic was,—or as it seemed,—could be conducted to a successful end without her aid. Every one deferred to her, and whatever she advised seemed to all concerned the thing to do. In appearance she had changed but little; mild, gentle and cheerful, a slightly-increased seriousness rather added to the charm of manner with which kind nature had invested her. That the trials of life have for all who will heed, a useful and benificent end, was manifest in her.

For without these, the wayward scholar in the school of life remains forever ignorant of those sublime glimpses into the depths which make the mind of man or woman the kingdom it is destined, in riper natures, to become. Children we are, and children we must remain, ever looking for the unfolding of that time when we shall be able to read the riddle of our lives.

As may be surmised, an occasional letter had reached Plainville, written by George Maitland. From California, where he had tarried during the winter, he had passed to Alaska, and his description of the great glacier and of the wonders of this new *terra incognita* were eagerly read by the little circle at the parsonage. Generally, his letters had been addressed to Mr. Ellery; parts of these, however, that gentleman, glancing hurriedly over the pages, had failed to read to his ready listeners. A few had been directed to Mary, and these and their very lively and entertaining contents were most readily shared with her friends. In one of these he had said that on his return to his home in Massachusetts he should again call upon his

friends in Kansas, but he had named no date, and his
immediate advent had not been expected.

That the people at the parsonage were surprised when,
one fine summer morning, he made his appearance and
claimed their hospitality, may very readily be imagined :
for everything, which has not become, by constant repiti-
tion, hackneyed and usual, is met by the natural mind
with wonder and amazement, more or less pronounced.

Maitland's absence from Kansas and her who had inspired in his heart that genuine admiration of substantial
qualities, which is alone the sure ground of a lasting and
life-long love, had served but to increase his appreciation
and respect for what he had come to regard as a perfect
character. It was evident to him that, so far, at least, he
had utterly failed to awaken in her that eminent regard for
himself which he had come to feel was a necessity to his
peace of mind and future success.

The thought of Mary, which in his mind's eye, had
taken shape as that of a beautiful vision, following him in
all his wanderings with a mild and seemingly heavenly
radiance, had assumed, for him, a perfect form and an
angelic significance. And yet, so wonderful is the power
of an absorbing love, that when he had felt the pressure of
her hand and looked into the liquid depths of her eyes, he
was convinced that the half had not been told—or even
thought.

"The Effect Upon His Audience was Electrical."

CHAPTER XXVII.

THE NEW CONVERT.

HE sublime poetry of the past assures us that "the Spirit moved upon the face of the waters," for the unfolding of all which has since appeared; and upon the poetical truth of this, all men are agreed. No deed, without a thought as it's father. In figurative and most expressive language we are also told that " man lives only by every word that proceedeth out of the mouth of God" The telegraphic instrument merely records the messages given to it; it does not create them. Only children think it does. In like manner, the brain of man is impressed by the thought which elsewhere takes its rise. Man is not the creator. Only fools think he is. The work of creation is still in progress.

As in the days preceding the war of the rebellion, the prevailing and controlling thought of men was directed against an evil, so in the time of which I write, the thought of the day was being moved to consider yet other evils. The ferment of Democracy was leavening the public mind, and although men still continued to hold out against its power, that it was gradually leavening the whole lump, could not be disputed. The Spirit was moving upon the face of the waters.

Maitland, too, had felt its power. His early conversations with Mary had put him upon a train of thought, at that time, new to him. Previously, he had given the subjects which she brought up, no attention. He had been reading of late, he said, and trusted that something had been learned. Like new converts, too, he was full of zeal. Something must be done!

Mr Ellery had been giving Sunday evening "talks," or lectures, in his church, upon subjects relating to the questions of the time, and he invited the young preacher to occupy his pulpit in this course of lectures on the first Sunday after his arrival. His theme was "The New Christianity," by which he explained he meant the modern application of the precepts of the religion of Christ.

The church was crowded to hear the young man, notices of the lecture having been given out in the morning, and here his college training stood him in good stead. He was what is called "a good speaker," with fine voice and commanding presence, and although his enthusiastic advocacy of what seemed to his audience to be very radical and socialistic sentiments, was listened to with the closest attention, they evidently scarcely knew just what to think or say. The abolition of competition and strife, and its replacement by association and mutual assistance, they appeared to think would be very fine in some future state of existence, but scarcely possible in this. But when, near the close of his address, summoning all his powers, he portrayed the results of such a course of action as he declared the gospel demanded, the effect upon his hearers was most marked.

" By as much," said he "as man is above money, love beyond strife, and duty higher than the promptings of selfish greed, let us, forgetting the things that are behind, press forward in the race toward that goal, now in the immediate future, which has ever held the eyes of all the poets and prophets of the past. If we but will it, the kingdom of heaven is at hand."

Coming out of the little church, Mary could not refrain from expressing the pleasure she felt in hearing what she had vainly endeavored to formulate, so well expressed.

"You know, Mr. Maitland," said she, "that our Plainville people had never heard you in public, and I am sure they will be pleased with your address."

"And were you pleased?" said he.

" Yes," said she, quite frankly, " I was more than pleased. I was surprised."

"And may I ask why you were surprised?" said he.

" No, I don't think you should inquire too closely; but one thing does surprise me somewhat, and that is that you should be able to give so fine a delineation of motives and principles to which you almost refused assent only a few months ago."

"As to that," said he, " I can only say that my attention had not been particularly called to these matters up to the time of my visit to Kansas."

Arrived at the parsonage, Mr. Ellery and his wife joined in the warmest expressions of approval and endorsement.

" I know now," said Mr. Ellery, "just what it seems to me you should do, George!"

"And what is it?" said he.

" Speaking upon the impulse of the moment, it appears clear to me that you should devote yourself to the spread of the ideas to which you have just given expression. You are young, have abundant means and are not obliged to tie yourself down to a stupid parish, or a set of stupid parishoners, and live in daily fear of saying something which they may not be able to receive. In your case and with your means and abilities I should take Wendall Phillips as my model and launch bravely forth as an agitator."

" Something of this kind has already passed in my thought," said Maitland, speaking slowly and with evident hesitation, " and I presume that I could follow Phillips,—at least, afar off."

" You would be hated and subjected to abuse, no doubt," said Mr. Ellery: "but when once fully enlisted in your work you would be happier, far, than in any other walk of life. People who know not of it, cannot understand the enthusiasm for humanity which takes complete possession of the man who gives himself to the cause of human freedom. His work *possesses* him; and even common men and ordinary natures are touched as with a coal of fire from off the altar, by their advocacy of the imperiled rights of men."

Mrs. Ellery added a few words, saying that she thought Mr. Ellery right in what he had said, as he generally was.

"And what do you say, Mary?" said Mr. Ellery

"Of course," said she, "I am not competent to advise Mr Maitland as to what he should do, but this I know: that if I were he, nothing should prevent me from making myself heard."

As Mary spoke, so firm and determined were the tones and accent of her voice and so keen the flash of her eye, as with unthinking force she expressed her thought, that Mrs. Ellery, who sat near her, said, as she placed her arm about her: "Oh, you dear little rebel! They'd just have to hear you; though I am sure they would wish to. I know I should."

Mary blushed, as she said: "Why, aunt, did I speak so strongly as that?"

"Oh, no, dear! You said nothing out of the way; but you are so earnest and determined that I should not like to undertake to thwart you. I know we all ought to be positive and determined in a good cause."

"If you will speak upon these topics," said Mr. Ellery, "I can put you in communication with parties who will be glad to make appointments for you. They will see that your expenses are paid, and may possibly be able to give you something beside; but it will be but little that they can do for you in that line. Although the work would not be remunerative, the experience would be valuable, and you could, in this way, make trial of what, no doubt, would prove an interesting experience."

Long after the ladies had retired, the two gentlemen remained in earnest consultation upon the topics suggested by the lecture.

"This is a time of great change, an era of transition," said Mr. Ellery; "the fountains of the great deep of thought are broken up; one can scarcely say what may come now."

"I look," replied Maitland, "upon the deep-seated unrest, which has taken possession of the public mind, in this way: It is the old, old struggle for larger liberty and greater freedom, now, in these later years, taking on a new phase. Once, this aspiration of men took the shape of a demand for religious freedom; that was the conception in Luther's day; next, the thought of Washington's time was political liberty. Largely, in both instances, the impulse was the same. Both steps were necessary; both were in the right direction, and both have been successfully taken. But, manifestly, all to be gained for man was not then accomplished. Now, there is another step just ahead, as important—indeed, it seems to be more so—and that is, economic liberty; the freedom of the toiler from the exactions of those who live in the sweat of his face. Of course, we must acknowledge that this is a new departure in the history of our storm-swept and sin-cursed world. Like Columbus, we sail boldly forward into an untried sea. There are no precedents. But the new theology,—that grander view of God's love and care and of the brotherhood of man,—leads us on. The first,—that is Luther's conception—meant a free mind, free thought, free belief. The second meant a free country and a free vote. Now, we want free men and free women; freedom from the control and domination of our specially and legally favored brothers and sisters. The right to life? Why, that really means a right to a living, or it means nothing at all. It means a right to the natural opportunities for obtaining one by the exercise of one's own labor, free from tribute imposed by anybody. Where did any man get "the right" to prevent his brother from enjoying the free gifts of God to all? Liberty? Why, that means freedom from the payment of tribute to those who unjustly demand it. How could a man be free who wasn't? Why longer juggle with words? The right of all to *pursue* happiness means the ability of all to obtain it. If all cannot obtain it, because denied to natural bounties, the right is denied. But we mean that in the near future all shall be put in the possession of those rights which it is a self-evident proposition, were originally given to all by the Creator. This is what we are after; that is the bed-rock fact in the whole business : the restoration of all of the rights and privileges given them by 'God. And we are going to obtain these rights by taking away the special privileges of those who now, by means of these same special privileges, are enabled to prevent, and do prevent, their brothers and sisters from enjoying the favors of a common Father. I suppose they will hire poor men to fight for them, to fight to obtain their advantage over the common herd ; holders of special privilege have always done so. Sometimes, they have fought themselves. And what a shame it is, Mr. Ellery, that in every country, the organized church has always sided with power and opposed itself to the rising demand for enlarged freedom ! But all this will make no difference in the result. The upward progress of the race cannot be stayed ; the power of God is behind it ; and just as surely as the two former steps have been taken, and successfully taken, so surely will the third be accomplished. A world of trouble and loss may stand between us and final success, but it will not prevent our ultimate victory ! "

" People will tell you, George, that you intend 'dividing up ' the wealth of the rich among the poor, if you speak so plainly."

" Yes, no doubt of it ; but it will be the ' stop thief ' cry of the thief, in his effort to divert attention from himself. The fact is, our effort is solely an endeavor to prevail on the rich to stop their never-ending robbery of the poor. Just that and nothing more. The truth is, we are willing that they shall keep the proceeds of past robbery if they will only stop stealing for the future. But this is the source of all the present social unrest : the desire of the wealthy and the strong to seize, under the name of rent, profit or interest, some portion of the product of labor. The products of labor must be had, or men will die. Now there are just three ways, and only three, of obtaining them : to work for them ; to receive them as a gift ; or to obtian them as the result of some form of fraud. 'We must all work or steal, howsoe'r we name our stealing.'"

"You put it pretty strongly," said Mr Ellery.

"Oh, yes; maybe so; but not as strongly as the facts will warrant. Why, just look at it: all the great names in the endless struggle for liberty; our own declaration of independence; all the constitutions, state and national; all the national saviours and sages of the past; all the poets and prophets of freedom, substantially agree in declaring that the end and aim of all just government among men is the preservation and maintenance of the natural, inalienable and imprescriptable rights of man. They agree that this is the sole foundation of freedom among men; that these natural, or God-given rights and privileges, cannot be rightfully abrogated or impaired in the smallest particular; that eternal vigilance is the price of liberty. And yet in spite of all this, and more which might be mentioned, the principal business of the men of wealth and 'position' among us, is in the line of hedging in, abridging or denying, in one way or another, these rights. In short, the business of the powerful, and the aim of the laws which they cause to be enacted, is to make it easy, through their control of land and exchange, to steal from the poor the sacred rights of men."

"Why, I declare, George, you are getting radical."

"Yes, I hope so; that is, that I am getting down to the roots of the social difficulty. But do I not speak the truth?"

"Yes, of course you do; but it is not usual for those who think as you do to speak so plainly."

"No, I know it isn't, and right there is where trouble begins; many of us do not dare to speak the truth. Being obliged to choose between God and Mammon, we shut our eyes to the truth, or endeavor to. But the enormous wickedness of the present Mammonistic control of things, for which we are all, in some sense, to blame, cannot be much longer hid. Look, for instance, at the ignorant and degraded children of poverty in every town! Men tell us that these poor creatures have made themselves what they are; that drunkenness and vice have made them poor. In the main, this is not true. Look at their surroundings! Why, they could n't be anything else! Good men, well-meaning men, but blinded by prejudice and preconceived opinion, have put the cart before the horse. The facts will show that nine times out of ten poverty has made them drunken and vicious; and poverty has been forced upon them by men who make the material conditions which surround the common herd. The average man don't make conditions. Conditions make him. And conditions are made for men when their natural or God-given rights are taken from them by means of the special privileges granted the few. Men tell us that no special privilege is given when wealth is allowed by law to do what poverty cannot, and I suppose some quite respectable people really believe it. Why, they might as well enact that strong men may do what weak ones shall not! Bah! what nonsense, and how easily men are deceived! Conditions surrounding the average man make him what he is; he don't create himself. God has n't given up his sovereignty; the allegory of Genesis still applies. Any man capable of thought can see that the Esquimaux, as an instance, is the natural result of the conditions surrounding him; but he is no more the product of his surroundings than are the squalid and vicious children of poverty the inevitable result of the conditions forced upon them by legal privileges in the hands of selfish men. Why God allows these men to do as they are doing, is beyond me. But it is evident in all the history of the past that He has allowed wicked and selfish men to bring great misery upon their fellows. It must needs be, I suppose, that offences come, but woe unto them by whom they come."

" It is too true, the facts are with you," said Mr. Ellery, "although they may seem to oppose some of our theology. But, George, you are dwelling too much upon the dark side of things; you forget, for the moment, that we are going to change all this. We are going to make conditions, ourselves, and make them better; and it is one of the grandest thoughts possible to man that in this way we shall be co-workers with God in lifting men. Of course it will be done by the use of ordinary and every-day methods; by the passage of laws. The household exemption will finally give every family that wishes it, a free home upon the soil. This will settle for good the labor question. An opportunity to employ one's self settles the matter of wages, and gradually a refuge of this kind will be opened up for all. Then, there need be no "unemployed". Then, the laborer can accept or reject wages offered. He will be independent. In short, he will, in this way, secure his independence. This will free him. Nothing else ever will. Most attractive and pleasant farm villages will then become possible, for under the influence of homestead exemptions it will be unprofitable to hold large tracts of land. Holding small farms with no great estates between, the farmers can be brought closely together, their available lands in long narrow fields, with common pasturage at a greater distance, as is now practiced in some parts of the world. Thirty or forty intelligent families can, in this way, form an ideal community. By co-operation they could readily avail themselves of machinery to lighten their labors; manufacturing could be engaged in and yet each family own and manage its own home. One library, lecture-room and amusement-hall, gymnasium, etc., would answer for all. It would not then be necessary for thirty or forty families to buy thirty or forty copies of the same book. Association would work wonders in many ways; the people would improve intellectually and physically, for in this way men and women would be brought nearer to nature and to healthful and natural ways. I tell you, George, that old myth of the wrestler, Anteus, has a world of meaning in it. He could not be conquered, for as often as he was thrown, coming in this way in contact with mother earth, he received fresh accessions of strength, thus finally overcoming his opponent. Hercules, detecting the source of his strength, held him up in his arms and strangled him in the air, as runs the tale.

So it is with nations and people. Divorced from the soil, they begin to die. The cities would utterly perish in two generations if not re-inforced from the country. The English people, however, seem to realize this truth, for their upper classes, (so called), keep up their country residences and their fondness for rural sports. See how it was with the Jewish people ; so long as that people obeyed the laws of Moses and held to their little farms, they could not be conquered, and more than that and better than that, they were happy ; they were fulfilling the purpose for which, as a nation, they came into existence. When they failed in this, their nation was destroyed, just as all other nations under the same circumstances have been, and will be. It is curious to note, too, how similar their history is to that of all other nations on this one point ; luxury and wealth began the trouble. Solomon's reign was magnificent. Vessels of gold and vessels of silver, men-servants, maid-servants and concubines increased in number, but the trend of affairs was more and more away from the simple and natural life of former years. Jerusalem became the desired place of residence. Taxation was, of course, heavily increased. This finally rested, as must always be the case, upon productive labor—in Judea, upon the tiller of the soil. The people became uneasy and restive. Probably they 'sold out and moved to town,' as our farmers have done and are doing. But public wealth and national glory grew amazingly. Every Jew was proud of his country and of Solomon's magnificence. And yet, while there was a great increase of national wealth, private poverty began then and there to exert its evil influence upon the national character. In a very short time this was not worth preserving. At Solomon's death the common and ordinary people,—who really pay all the taxes, finally,—complained bitterly of the taxation imposed. But Rehoboam, his son and successor, refused to listen, saying, you know : ' My father chastised you with whips, but I will chastise you with scorpions.' Well, that ended the play ; the ten tribes revolted, and the kingdom of David came to an end. And it came to an end because the peoples lost their hold upon the soil, and be· cause the healthful and natural life of the free cultivator had been made impossible. The same thing has been repeated in every one of the ruined nations of the past. Our own nation has already taken a good many steps in the same direction, and our only safety lies in retracing these steps and in getting back to the soil and to nature.

"The cities are so many plague-spots, and yet our mode of life is such that everything is made to tend toward them. The laws can easily change this current of things. Give every man a free home in the country, and the current will change itself. Of course, no one would be forced to live in the country, but if we make country life easier, pleasanter, and—all things considered—more profitable, we shall be able slowly to change the habits of society. And it is in line with natural requirements. Did you ever think, George, that the 'life, liberty and pursuit of happiness' of the Declaration of Independence, and, in fact, all the natural requirements of men upon the earth are included in Free Land and Free Exchange, or exchange at cost? Well, they are. Give a family sufficient land for self-support, free from all taxation, make it inalienable except by direct sale, and then secure to them the right of free exchange without the payment of any sort of tribute to anybody; free them completely from the claims of rent, profit and interest, and give them public facilities for exchange at cost. Then, freedom in these things and security in their results comprise all the natural rights of man; all other rights are artificial and conventional. And we must never forget that men cannot be entirely free until they come into full possession of their natural rights. And if not free, then not happy, because not in line with the great destiny God has in store for man and which is now being gradually unfolded before our eyes. Now, if these things belong to man, naturally, if they are natural rights coming from the Creator,—and we must acknowledge that they are,—then we can clearly see that there can be no right adjustment, socially, no real and lasting peace, until they are fully restored to all men, and it does seem to me that Grafton's four measures are exceedingly well adapted to bring them within the reach of all. Every one of these measures is strictly in line with the restoration to all of free land and free exchange, or exchange at cost. In each case there is a refusal of special privilege now enjoyed by the few.

First, the stay-laws give the mortgaged home-owner an opportunity to save his home and prevent, for the time, his being closed out at forced sale, in which case the creditor would probably take undue advantage of the family in his power.

Secondly, the abolition of all laws for the collection of future, ordinary and voluntary debts would, in the main, prevent the creation of such debts. They would not then exist. In this way society will be freed, to a great extent, from debt and the payment of interest. This is the great sink-hole which now swallows up the produce of the laborer. Let us close it up! It will then be 'cash or no trade',—as it ought to be. Then, we should have more money in circulation, for the right sort of a demand, such as would then be made, will bring it. Then, exchange would be largely freed from the demands of the creditor, who now tolls every deal, or he does not allow it to be made.

Thirdly, the issuance of State warrants, by the State Treasurer, bearing no interest, to each school-district, municipality and county, in amount equal to the tax levy; these warrants to be made receivable for all taxes, anywhere in the State; the State Auditor's office to be made a "clearing-house" for the settlement of balances between the various districts, municipalities and counties. This would be another long step toward free exchange and would powerfully aid in enabling people to make the ordinary exchanges of the day, free from usury.

Fourthly, making the homestead free from the claims of debt and taxation, thus creating a safe and secure retreat for every family, would, of itself, come near abolishing involuntary poverty. In this way society will be brought back to natural and healthful conditions. Now, affairs with us are artificial and unnatural, and growing more so, every day."

"Oh, we must follow nature," said Maitland; "and isn't it wonderful that when this is done, all the good things of life are showered upon the people who obey? Of course, we are only on the threshhold. Reform in the nation comes next; but its beginning in the State was the proper, and in fact, the only way. Many people seem to me to have come near taking leave of their senses in advocating practical communism in their dreams of a complete co-operative commonwealth. We must take men as they are, and the facts of human nature cannot be hid. So long as no house is big enough for two average families, the co-operative commonwealth is only a dream, an ideal. It is like the condition of sinlessness to which some of our Methodist brethren, at times, fancy they have attained. The *possibility* of a co-operative commonwealth, with godly men, is clear enough. But the *probability* of it among all classes of very imperfect men and women is quite another matter; and in the co-operative commonwealth everything would have to come in. They are going to get rid of competition, they tell us, and supply its place with 'emulation'. Surely, they ought to remember that this same emulation, in a religious way, has brought on some of the fiercest conflicts the world has ever seen. Society and social duties are pleasant in their way, but every man and every woman should be able, at times, to escape from them. Otherwise these pleasant things become, by constant and too close association, intolerably disagreeable. A meeting of kindred spirits is one of the finest things in all this world. But keep these same men together for a week, and constraint and uneasiness would arise. In a month, if they cannot escape from each other, they will be ready to fight. Even husband and wife cannot get along together, unless their interests are identical. They must be 'one flesh'. Well, the general public can hardly be one flesh, nor are the varying interests of individuals identical. It seems to me that there is a rule which settles all this. Poor Grafton's wording of it was: *'Public things to the public; private affairs to the individual.'* Whatever chiefly concerns the individual life of man must be free from the control of others. The home and the individual life of the family must not come under public inspection or control."

" Look at the clock!" said Mr. Ellery, " we must go to bed, or we shall not need to get up."

" Yes, that is so, though to tell the truth, I do not feel like sleeping at present. Now, there is that thing of having no law for the collection of debts; a good many people who never have occasion to collect a debt by law are, or seem to be, fearful that a repeal of these laws may bring on a regular social chaos, but it was just so with the samet class of people at the time of the abolition of imprisonmen for debt. Now, everybody knows that it would be a most lamentable backward step to restore imprisonment for ordinary debt; but, bless me, if it is n't after one o'clock. Well, good night!"

As stated in the last chapter, the State Senate still remained in session. On the adjournment of the lower house, efforts were made to bring influences to bear upon the senators which should induce them to vote for the passage of the bills already passed by the representatives. Disturbances in various parts of the State and the angry remonstrances of the people continued until the senators began to fear that if they longer refused assent to the action of the House, that civil discord of an aggravated kind might be the result. So, upon the presentation of an immense petition, signed by a majority of the voters in the districts represented by certain senators, they signified their intention of voting for the bills. This broke the majority, and with the passage of a resolution which was

in the nature of a protest, the missing representatives were
summoned, concurrent action was had, and the bills were
passed and quickly signed by the Governor. So far, the
victory appeared complete: still, past experiences rendered
the victors somewhat wary and suspicious. The laws thus
passed provided, substantially, for the four measures first
brought forward by Grafton.

Grafton, "the agitator," was avenged. His plans had
been mainly adopted: largely, perhaps, because his tragic
death had impressed upon the minds of an otherwise heedless people the truths he taught. Fortunate man! the
struggles and sorrows of his life and the seeming failure of
his death had permitted him to be of service in the long
and toilsome, upward march of the race.

According to the terms of the bill, all laws for the
collection of debts contracted subsequent to the fourth day
of July were abrogated and annulled. Henceforth, he who
by the power of money secured an advantage over his
fellow-men could not claim the power of the courts as an
aid to his designs. Debt, said the agitators,—that foe to
liberty and chief arm of tyranny,—will now be eliminated
and destroyed.

Great was the rejoicing among those who had from
the first seen the causes of inequality and injustice. This,
said they, is the first step in the grand march of freedom.
The people have now turned their backs upon Pharaoh.
They will go out of bondage and possess the land. But
much remains to be done; the wilderness is yet to be
passed and Pharaoh will yet pursue.

The "glorious Fourth" was now close at hand, and
immediately upon the passage of the bills which had de-
creed the new abolition, a celebration had been arranged
for Branchville upon that day, and Maitland had been
engaged as one of the speakers. Possessed of natural powers of a high order, these had been aided and assisted by
an education which enabled him to grasp at a glance the
full significance of the mighty movement yet in its incip-

iency. Entering into its spirit with all the ardor of youth and the force of a thoroughly aroused purpose, he delivered the address of the day. The man had come to himself and into possession of powers till then unrevealed and unsuspected. Heretofore, he had known no overmastering incentive; reared in luxury, his every want supplied, the man had not known himself. Now controlled by a generous purpose, he threw himself, with all his force, into the fray.

The effect upon his audience was electrical, as with ringing voice and stalwart frame he paced the platform, now picturing the beauty of that civilization which the future should yet prepare, and now in thunder tones denouncing the wrong and injustice of the past. "Yet I warn you," said he; "that the battle is but begun. New foes will rise and upon new fields our courage and our valor must yet stand the test. Let us then, renewing our vows, reconsecrate ourselves to the cause of human freedom, conscious that the battle we wage is not alone for those who stand with us to-day, but for all men and for all time."

Coming down from the speaker's stand, hundreds pressed forward to take him by the hand. But his eyes sought out the little school-teacher and the expression he read in her face outweighed the plaudits of all else beside. Evidently, her opinion of his character and abilities was subject to change.

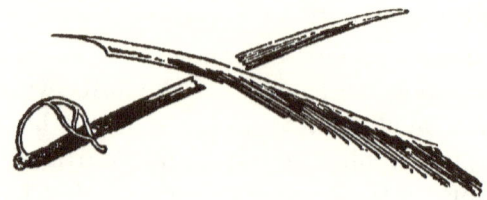

"Governor, Are You Entirely Alone."

CHAPTER XXVIII.

NIPPED IN THE BUD.

AFTER all, and as usual, it was the unexpected that happened. Governor Brown was sitting in his office one day after the passage of "the abolition bills" when John Brooks, a well-known business man of Topeka, entered and looked cautiously around, evidently for the purpose of discovering who beside the Governor might be present. Seeing no person, except the clerk or secretary, whom he had passed in the outer office, he softly closed the door of the inner or private office and said: "Governor, are we entirely alone?"

"Yes sir," said the Governor.

"Well, my business with you is private and confidential in the extreme, and I shall ask you to pledge yourself not to divulge to a living soul what I have to say," and he looked enquiringly to the Governor.

"I should scarcely like to do that," said that official; "however, I will say this: I will not disclose the name of my informant without his permission."

"Well, that's what I meant, of course. Now, because of the fact that we are members of the same lodge, I am bound to inform you of designs dangerous to you or your peace of mind. I am, as you know, a republican and so far have been opposed to the measures proposed by your party, but we've had disorder enough in this State. I'm for peace! The majority of the people have declared for what your party calls 'the abolittion laws', and I'm content to have 'em tried. Fact is, I've half a notion of late that maybe they are right. Business has been bad enough for a long time back, God knows, and any honest effort to improve it ought to have a show. Now, I went down, yesterday, to the Third

National, where I do my banking business, to make a deposit. Well, I was late, and the front door being shut, I went around to the side door, as I have often done before. I walked in as I usually do, not making a very big racket,—but gracious! I might have worn cow-hide boots and stamped all the way, they never'd heard me. Old Col. Gibson, president of the First National, you know, was talking right out in meetin' in the directors' room, which is separated from the outer room by a partition running only part way to the ceiling, so that I could hear every word he said. The front door being shut I reckon they thought they were alone. There seemed to be a kind of meeting of the bankers of the city in progress, and they had Judge Clark of the Supreme Court, who is largely interested in the First National, in there with them, by the sound. Well, by thunder I did what I never did before,—I listened; I played the Paul Pry on 'em. Now, do you know, what I heard riled my dander, and after I'd got a part of it I stayed right there for the balance, expecting every minute that the watchman or janitor would come in at the back door and find me; and then I made up my mind I'd act as though I'd just come in, and stamp along the passage-way and call for the teller. I was n't afraid of the other fellows, because they could n't get out of the directors' room into the passage-way, where I was, without going into another room, and I knew that I could have warning of their coming in that way. Well, damn my soul if them fellows did n't lay plans to knock business and everything else but their own perfesh of money-loaning, into smithereens with the cussedest cheerfulness imaginable."

"Well, what were their plans?" said the Governor, who by this time appeared greatly interested.

"Suppose I am rather long in coming to the point, but the amount of it is this: they made an arrangement with old Clark to issue an injunction, directed to the State Treasurer enjoining him against issuing the State warrants called for in what your people call the third demand. Gibson was specially outrageous in his talk. He said: 'If the State issues those warrants, as proposed, bearing no interest, receivable anywhere in the State for taxes, engraved in good style, in denominations like money, with a clearing-house provided for in the State Auditor's office, they'll pass for money; they'll circulate from hand to hand and take the place of money in their journey from the district or municipality paying them out of the State Auditor's office. Of course we can refuse to receive them on deposit and can quote them at a discount, but if they are made receivable for taxes and no more are issued than the tax-roll calls for, redemption is provided for every dollar and the discount cannot, for obvious reasons, be very heavy. They will be worth par to anybody who wants to pay taxes. Taxes being payable, at the option of the tax-payer, every three months, warrants will be in demand. No fiat money scheme in this thing; no dollar of it will be put out unless somebody has first furnished the State with a dollar's worth of labor or material; then the State agrees to take it up in taxes and destroy it. Oh, they'll go! Money is scarce and people are crazy for something to effect exchanges with, and you can bet they'll use 'em. The result will be that general business will increase in amount, exchanges will be easier

made and everybody will be convinced the warrant scheme is a good thing. Then they will issue more of 'em; begin public improvements, levy taxes and issue warrants to pay for 'em; every idle hobo will have a job and prices of property will rise, to some extent. Then,' said he, 'they will knock us out; our hold on business and business men will be destroyed. The scheme is feasible; they can make it work, and when they do,—good bye to private banking. This thing is only an entering wedge, and the amount of it

is, our business is at stake and we must nip this thing in
the bud, or not at all, for when the fools once find out that
they can get along without us we'll be like Othello in the
play, our occupation will be gone. Another thing for you
gentlemen to notice just as you turn this corner; they propose in this way to get a sort of circulating medium that
don't pay anybody any interest. Just put that in your pipe
and smoke it! You let the people get a taste of that kind
of thing and they will do us up in a rag, too quick.'

"Somebody ventured to express a doubt about the warrants being a success, but the old man pooh poohed him
down in no time. 'Why don't you know,' said he, in reply,
'that there is a vast fund of information to be obtained from
the experience of the Mormons in Utah on this point?
They issued the scrip, not half so well provided for as this
is, and did all their business among themselves with it.
Thousands of them never saw any other money from year's
end to year's end, and it made 'em prosperous, too. People
have talked about the wonderful organizing capacity of
Brigham Young and all that, but I can tell you that the
scrip which allowed very near free exchange was at the
bottom of their commercial success. They did n't borrow
any money, paid no interest, and whenever they wanted to
buy or sell there was no hindrance to the dicker, and the
profits of a trade they were able to keep. Just you look up
the facts in Utah if you want to know about scrip and what
the freedom of exchange implies. Well, they made their
scrip so common that the National Banking Association had
to take cognizance of it. Complaint was made that the
Mormons were emiting bills of credit, contrary to the United
States Constitution, and that they were liable for the ten
per cent. tax on a circulating medium, under United States
law, and the matter was taken, I think, into the United
States District Court for adjudication. Well, the Mormons
just changed the form of the scrip, making each piece
returnable to their treasury, where it was destroyed. It
was n't 'a circulating medium' then. Oh, they are smart,
them Mormons are!'

" Well, he talked on in that way, saying, substantially, that business men did n't amount to anything, that every one of 'em was in debt and under the control of the banks, and that in the ordinary run of business, as now conducted, they could be managed all right; 'but,' said he, 'if this new-fangled scheme gets a start and to running they will get out from under our control; they'll get sassy and we can't manage 'em.' He did n't say just that, exactly, but that's what he meant."

" But what did Judge Clark have to say?" asked the Governor.

" Well, he did n't say much, but he assented to what was said by Gibson and the others. They appealed to him, asking if there was n't some way in which the law could be used to beat 'that measly crowd'; though who they could mean by 'measly crowd' but the majority of the people of the State, I can't see. But the old Judge said he thought he could ' fix 'em,' and before I left he told 'em positively that he would issue an injunction in time to prevent the issuing of the warrants."

" But did you get away without being observed?"

" Yes, I did; at first I had intended only to hear a little and then steal back to the outer door, open it with a bang and then walk heavily along the passage, as though just coming in, but I had heard so much, and then, what I did hear made me so mad that I concluded to slip out as I came in and put off my deposit until another time. And this I did; the janitor was n't around; he knew, I suppose, that a meeting was in progress and so was in no hurry to go back, and his neglect in leaving the side-door open when he came out was what gave me my opportunity. I saw him in at the corner drug-store as I came away. He did n't see me; nobody saw me so far as I know, and if they did it was nothing uncommon for a depositor to be seen coming out that door. So far, the secret is safe; I know it and you know it, and you are bound by the strongest ties not to give me away."

" I wish you would come out squarely and tell it all to everybody as you have to me," said the Governor.

" Oh, I could n't do that for the world. You see, they would ruin my business, and then just look at my action in playing the Paul Pry on 'em; why, I never could hold up my head in this town again if I was to do that!"

" That's so, I suppose," said the Governor, as he thoughtfully scratched his head. "Anyhow," he added, " Mr. Brooks, I am a thousand times obliged to you for this and I'll not disclose your name to a soul without your permission. And by the way, if you get onto anything more in the same line let me know and I'll find a way to reward you; if I can't in one way, I will in another."

No sooner had Mr. Brooks taken his departure than the Governor sent a messenger to the office of the Attorney-General, the State Treasurer and the Auditor, asking their immediate presence in his office. Upon their arrival the whole story was related to them, Mr. Brooks' name only being with-held."

" It's a crisis," said the Governor; " what is best to be done ? "

The Attorney-General could n't think of anything better than to let Judge Clark issue his injunction, the State Treasurer to defy it, issuing the warrants according to law, thus throwing the whole matter into the courts for decision.

The Treasurer demurred ; he couldn't think of standing the brunt of the whole thing, and the Auditor seemed particularly glad that it was n't his office which was to be involved in a controversy. Finally, after a few expressions of opinion the four gentlemen sat and looked at each other, for the moment in silence.

" This will never do," said Governor Brown; " something must be done ; I've sworn to uphold the laws and maintain them and I am going to do it, even though a law-defier sits on the bench. One of the things I never could understand is why the people should expect an unprincipled and morally bankrupt attorney to immediately become an upright and incorruptible judge by the mere fact of an election at the polls. Going through the ballot-box does n't purify him. Usually the effect is the reverse of this. Commonly, he must make pledges to certain monopolistic influences before he can secure a nomination, even. He is the same shyster, only given more power and made more dangerous; that's all. Now, suppose we move on his works at once; suppose, that as the chief magistrate of this State I issue a warrant for his arrest, charge him with conspiracy against the people of this State in attempting to nullify the laws, and with malfeasance in office in bargaining away decisions of his court; publish the facts broadcast and summon the legislature, forthwith, to try him and take action in the emergency?"

" Would n't that be somewhat revolutionary?" said the Attorney-General.

" No, I think not; quite the reverse, indeed. It's an appeal to the people. The people are the source of all power. The laws are simply their will written down. There is nothing sacred about law, unless it embodies that will. Now, in this supposed instance, my action would be in support of the people's laws attacked by a traitor. And even suppose Judge Clark to be honest in his opinion, the case is this: one man against the people of the State; a man who sets himself deliberately to nullify the will of the people. Are the people of a whole State to confess their power to govern themselves taken away by an irresponsible shyster who, by common political methods, has been foisted by corrupt ringsters, who control party nominations, into office to do the will of corporations? We have a sample of the influence controlling Clark in that meeting at the bank. Now, are we going to let those people in that bank have more governmental power than all the people of this State? And you will remember that this is not the first time that Judge Clark has laid himself open to suspicion. Is such a man as he to be the people's autocratic ruler? Is the right of self-government gone? I will not believe it! Anyhow, the people shall decide. If necessary, we can call an election, or have it done, and let the people determine the whole matter for themselves. And something of this kind must be done if the people are to rule. Clark's will only be the first of a whole crop of injunctions unless this thing is nipped in the bud. One thing sure, we will find out, once for all, whether the voters of this State have lost the right of self-government, or not. We will put the thing to the test."

" Well, that would be one way of settling the matter," said the Auditor. " that would be the Swiss referendum in practice, straight out and right off."

" Can you think of a better?" the Governor asked. But all agreed that it would be the only way to successfully oppose the rule of Clark and his masters.

" Now, gentlemen," said Governor Brown, " not one word of all this must get out. This is a State secret and I shall hold each one of you personally responsible for its safe keeping. I have called you in consultation and in confidence, and I shall ask you to respect that confidence until I act."

Governor Brown was as good as his word, and moved with promptness. Judge Clark was arrested, a detailed account of the meeting at the bank, with the substance of what was there said, given to the public press and the legislature summoned to meet in extra session.

An immense sensation was the result. Nothing else was talked of throughout the State. The participators in the meeting at the bank were convinced that some one of their number had turned traitor and informer. Each was suspicious of the other; distrust and dislike the natural consequence, and all of them seemed willing that Judge Clark should be the victim of the occasion, for the feeling aroused by the publication of the facts was so great that it was readily seen that a victim must be forthcoming. Under these circumstances they began to talk; several acknowledging that they were at the meeting and giving

the names of all who were present. Newspaper interview-
ers soon had a full list of names and a complete account
of all that was said and done at the now famous meeting;
to the immense relief of merchant John Brooks, as our
readers will readily believe. Who had first told the Governor now seemed a matter of little importance, since all
had unburdened their minds upon the subject.

The political complexion of the legislature being
known and the necessity of a victim being apparent, Judge
Clark's title to a good degree of ignominy seemed secure.

In due time the legislature met. The fact that the
people of the State had long been suffering from "hard
times" and were exceedingly anxious to try anything
which promised relief and the further fact that they were
tired of turmoil would undoubtedly have induced the
legislature to sustain Governor Brown in the impeach-
ment of Judge Clark, but the strong and unequivocal
statements of President Gibson of the First National,
which he could not deny, that the warrants would circulate
freely, allowing exchanges to be made ; that under these
circumstances, business would increase, employment be
found for all and people be enabled to escape in a measure
from the business control of the banks, made certain the
result.

The Governor was sustained and Judge Clark im-
peached. In addition, the legislature provided for the
calling of an election at which a proposition should be
submitted for a yea and nay vote. The proposition being,
substantially: "Shall the laws passed by the legislature,
session of ——, be sustained, and is the Governor author-
ized, if need be, to employ military force in upholding the
decision of the people?"

But one answer was possible; tired of strife and now
earnestly hoping for a return of "good times," a very large
majority voted "yes." Indeed, the decision was almost
unanimous for trial of the new laws. This broke the back
of the opposition, scarcely anyone openly opposing the

issuance of the warrants, it being plain that as they were returnable to the State Auditor's office, there to be destroyed, that they could not be considered as bills of credit prohibited by the United States Constitution. The Governor being empowered to go to almost any length in support, no other judge seemed anxious to tempt the fate meted out to Judge Clark, and a general acquiescence in the new legislation seemed to be at last secured.

Slowly business began to improve, and men of means considered shrewd and "sharp" began very cautiously, here and there, to buy land offered for sale at what were considered "low figures." On account of the repeal of the laws for the collection of debt, sales were invariably made for cash or other property. Very soon, or as soon as it became apparent that men considered far-seeing in every neighborhood were buying good farms, land began slowly to rise in value. For years it had been impossible to sell land at any reasonable figure and much surprise was expressed at the turn affairs had taken. The "stay-law" having given the holders of mortgaged property able to make a satisfactory showing to the court, two years of "grace," they were not particularly anxious to sell, while Eastern and foreign holders of mortgages on Kansas property hearing extravagant accounts of "repudiation legislation" in that State became correspondingly anxious to secure their claims. "These people," said they, "have put us off for two years; now what is to hinder them from putting us off again at the end of the two years"; and they began to be afraid. The only way of securing themselves absolutely against loss seemed to be the purchase of the "equity" held by the holder of the land. The holder of the mortgage thus became the undisputed owner of the property mortgaged to him. Fear of future loss inducing many to do this, good farms rose still higher in price as the demand grew and increased. Strange as it seemed to the people who had fought the legislation proposed by the reformers, what seemed to be a regular "real-estate boom" began to show its familiar features. Unlike previous booms, however, all deals were settled on the spot. No debts were left to "draw" interest and mar the profits of transactions. Land was steadily rising in value and every one who bought was able to figure out a profit. It did not seem possible for anyone to lose in the buying and selling which now became common, nor was there opportunity for one to become largely indebted. The situation was, from its very newness and extreme unlikeness to anything before known, very peculiar. The oldest inhabitant could remember nothing like it. One thing seemed clear: it could n't last. Meantime an opportunity was offered the farmers for which they had long waited: now they could get out of debt.

At this stage of the rapidly-shifting business panorama, while improvement was the order of the day and trade extremely brisk, the only lugubrious people to be found were the followers of Henry George, who constantly filled the ears of the few they were able to "buttonhole" with doleful accounts of the ruin to come; "the land-holders were to be the new monopolists," they said; "all that had been done was for the benefit of the land-holder." But all they said had but little effect upon those who had found land for years the most unprofitable thing they could touch, and at the same time,—anomolous condition of affairs that it was,—it had seemed impossible for a poor man to hold his little homestead. The money-loaner and the tax-gatherer seemed all the time just on the point of taking it away from him. Land had n't paid anyone for its cultivation; there was no profit in that; it had been absolutely unsalable; really it seemed to be worth nothing, and yet it had been the hardest thing in the world to prevent foreclosure or sale for taxes. In short, the poor home-owner had been suffering a perfect night-mare of oppression. But this peculiar and unrighteous condition of affairs was now coming to an end. Now, if he wanted to sell his place and pay of the mortgage, he could do so, and have something left. Indeed, it began to be seen that the rise in land values was a perfect god-send to the mortgaged home-owner. In no other way could he have got out of the grasp of the money-loaner. Now, he who had a mortgaged farm could, by selling half, usually, pay his debt, leaving half clear of incumbrance, which, under the new law, could not be taken from him under any pretext, and, in addition, it was not taxable. This was a clear advantage; anybody could see that. A free home made the family possessing it free. It was better than life insurance; there were no premiums to pay and it could not be taken from the family as long as any member remained who needed it. Free homes made free men; no more fear of the sheriff or the tax-gatherer. Coming want did not scare them, nor the creditor make them afraid.

From appearances, a regular land boom had been engineered, evidently by design; or, so it seemed. Among the people who had opposed "the demands" the greatest wonder was manifested. Had "that measly crowd" sense enough to work such a scheme? And how curious—to them—the working out of the plan! Previous land speculations had left everybody in debt. This one got people out of debt and made it practically impossible for them to get in. Another thing was a great surprise to them: all enquiry was for farms and rural homes which, under the new law, would be free from taxation. "Town property" didn't figure in real estate deals, as formerly. Public attention was attracted away from the cities and to the country. Meantime, business of every legitimate sort was pressed to the sky line; in fact, the large amounts of money sent into the State for the purchase of equities made exchanges and the payment of debts easy. Under these circumstances no one could be found to say anything against the abolition laws, and the strongest opposers freely acknowledged that they had been mistaken. But shrewd observers began to say: "If the people who have run this deal, so far, were bright enough to do what they have done, we may be sure they have something else 'on the string'. Better look a little out!"

CHAPTER XXIX.

A NEW DEAL.

 UR story approaches its end. What remains to be told must be hastily sketched.

"The boom" quickly came to an end. Like all other and previous booms, it left a large number of people, who had prided themselves upon their shrewdness, heavily encumbered. Not with debts, as had formerly been the case, but with land. The eagerness of the mortgage holders to secure their claims had made a demand for farms, and demand had largely increased price. Thus the speculative fever had taken its rise. Seeing that the price of land and farms continued slowly and steadily to rise, all who could obtain money began very cautiously to buy land. What was bought this week was rated at a higher figure next. In every neighborhood certain parties were said to have "made" large sums in buying and selling land. This operated, as it has ever done, to temporarily craze whole communities. Any resident of one of the affected communities could easily prove to himself that the then present conditions were not temporary, but permanent. "Things were now just where they should have been all along; and, as a matter of fact, were simply assuming their normal relations." Argument was lost on him. "Look at the steady rise in prices!"

But when the mortgaged home-owners had been able, by the rise in prices, to get out of debt, and in most instances still retain a somewhat smaller and less expensive home, genuine and legitimate demand, for occupation and use, backed by money, came to an end. The fever of speculation, however, did not at once abate, and large investments of money continued to be made for a time. Suddenly a halt was called and speculation stopped. Facts began now to be

fully realized and investors slowly regained their senses.
It was all very clear, now. They had started the boom.
They had furnished the money, *without interest*, to run it
and make all the necessary exchanges, by means of which
most of the farmers were now free. They had given up
interest-bearing obligations and, in the aggregate, had in
addition furnished the owners of land with large amounts of
money. Fear had induced them to begin buying, and greed,
or the hope of gain, had urged them on in what all could
now see was a wild speculation. Now, they began to think.
Income from the payment of interest money had largely
ceased. A large share of the people still had homes and
yet could not be taxed; had, in fact, secured their independence. "Investors" and land speculators, however, held
large numbers of farms and great quantities of land, which,
on the subsidence of the speculative fever, remained unsalable, and quoted prices began to recede. All this was taxable. , This was a very important fact, the importance of
which began, now, to be fully appreciated. The prospect,
too, in the eyes of the large land-holders, seemed extraordi-
narily good for a great increase in taxation. Under these
circumstances, a new terror took possession of them. They
were worse off than ever. Plainville had already built a
new bridge across the creek and paid for it in warrants
issued to her own citizens. Nobody seemed to feel that it
had really cost anything, and now they were talking of
building a flouring mill in the same way; that is, by taxation. Other towns had done the same and the seemingly
unlucky investors in land already felt in their minds the
pangs of approaching loss.

The speculators thus self-entrapped made a great out-
cry. True, however, to their never-failing duplicity, it was
not of their own woe that they spoke. As usual, "the poor
man" was the subject of all their conversation. "Credit
being destroyed by the most disgraceful legislation which
ever cumbered the statute-books of a civilized state, the poor
man was now deprived of the opportunity of obtaining a

home"; this was the burden of their cry. What it really meant was this; their occupation of "drawing" interest and clipping coupons had received a set-back, the first it had ever known. Now, their power to sell land, or anything else, "on payments" at an exorbitant price, "draw" interest for a series of years, often in amounts greater than the value of the property sold, and then on the appearance of the usual panic, caused by the concerted withdrawal of loans and credits, foreclose and seize the land, or other property, to be "sold" to the next comer who could be induced to bet against their control of the money market. That game had come to an end. Hence the disturbance.

Poor people, for themselves, were not specially dismayed, for even those who had lost their farms were now able to rent one for less than they had formerly paid in interest, taxes and insurance. Rents fell with the price of land. Business was good. Exchanges were freely made and "trading" brisk. Any man could get work at good wages. Public improvements were everywhere projected, warrants circulated freely from hand to hand, and as the interest drain upon production had largely ceased, more money circulated among the people than had been the case for years. Even the poor man, who wished to do so, could now save a little money.

Although a furious effort was made in the newspapers to influence public sentiment against the new legislation, it miserably failed. It was too plainly in the interest of speculators and investors. Evidently they were the only people dissatisfied. They had brought on the boom. If caught in their own trap no one outside their ranks felt specially responsible for the situation. And thus the matter stood.

But the investors were energetic people and well supplied with brains. Something must be done! If thrown upon their own resources they could at least make shift to rid themselves of the worst features of their present condition. Even though the opportunity for profit had gone glimmering, they could at least save themselves against loss. So, after much talk and many conferences, which included leading men throughout the State, what was called "A New Deal" was published, as agreed upon. Substantially, the scheme was as follows: The speculators were to divide their offerings of land into small tracts suitable for homes, of about $1500 valuation. Of farming land this would cover, generally speaking, from 40 to 80 acres. These small tracts were to be "rented" to suitable families making application; the "rent" paid to be one-tenth of the valuation, annually for ten years. The owner of the land to execute an approved bond to deed to the renter the tract thus "rented" at any time upon the payment of the ten annual installments; the rent paid to be and remain a lien upon the land. If a renter failed to pay his rent, the owner of the land to be able to eject him during the month of March following his failure to pay; arbitration, and not a suit at law, to determine the resulting damage to either party. As no interest could be collected upon payments of "rent," at the earnest solicitation of the large land-holders and for the purpose of further protecting "the renters," the Governor and most of the members of the legislature promised to favor the passage of a law at the next session exempting from taxation small homesteads "rented" under the the terms of "The New Deal."

The effect of this was wonderful. It being noised abroad that every family possessed of a few hundred dollars could, in Kansas under the new laws, in a few years be able to acquire a sufficient portion of the earth's surface for self-support, which could neither be taxed or taken away under any circumstances, attracted to the State world-wide attention. Even in foreign lands men and women were intensely interested in this new step toward the enlarged and greater freedom for oppressed humanity thus secured. A very large immigration to the State was the immediate result. All the immigrants brought more or less money, and, what was of vastly greater importance, a new hope filled them with the spirit of endeavor. The conditions prevailing were such that all were able at once to begin the production of values. Added to the previous very general prosperity, all this made Kansas and its people happy, indeed. Once more, the very name was an inspiration. Once more, Kansas led in freedom's march! Free Land and Free Exchange were partially secured!

"The investors" were able to "rent" all their land without trouble and so great was the desire to possess a free home, and so hungry is humanity for land freed from the demands of those who desire to eat bread in the sweat of other men's faces that large numbers of dejected and almost hopeless people heretofore considered "shiftless," lazy and improvident in the extreme, submitted cheerfully to many privations when once more able to hope in the future opportunity of escaping from the control of other men. Even the happy-go-lucky negro of slavery days would fight like a devil for his freedom when once he had a clear opportunity of obtaining it.

Of course it was recognized that benefits so far received were, and could be, only partial and local in their effects;—the conditions prevailing in the nation at large preventing full success. And yet, those who were in possession of free homes and had in some measure succeeded in freeing themselves from the burdens formerly imposed upon production and exchange had, in these things, come near securing that free access to nature's bounties which will finally enable the poor and the weak to escape from the exactions of the rich and the strong.

If the cities have favored positions and peculiar privileges let the people most benefitted pay for what they, only, enjoy; if corporations and "property" demand "protection" and an army, let them tax themselves for what they desire! Let them stop stealing from the poor, and the poor will never threaten or harm them—have never done so, as a class, in all the history of the world! Fear is the sure sign and evidence of wrong; men who fear the mob bear evidence of having wronged it, as men who fear God usually have good reason to do so. If wealth and power and position demand "stronger government" let them pay for the bauble. Decent men,—not to speak of Christians,—should be ashamed of present methods, which in most crafty and indirect manner tax production and exchange in such a way as to force poverty unknowingly to pay for the luxuries of the rich.

But the people of Kansas, for the most part, were now able to live. They could no longer be starved into submission. Meantime, and until national measures of relief should come into play, they could, now that they were partially free from rent, interest and taxes, take Senator Plumb's advice, "live within themselves" and wait for the opportunities of the future.

Some of the reforms effected were these: Taxes were very much reduced and county government, in particular, condensed to the merest skeleton of what it had been. Township and municipal government took its place. The New England town meeting—the Swiss Initiative and Referendum practically—furnishing the model. People governed themselves, as their grandfathers had done, almost without cost. The abolition of all laws for the collection of debt had largely done away with courts, lawyers and court expenses. In all ordinary cases of misunderstanding and difficulty between citizens arbitration was made compulsory. The rich and the contentious were unable, as formerly, to terrorize the timid and the peacefully inclined with the disaster of a suit at law.

A general uniform system of State education was established, known locally as "the barefoot schoolboy law." The State undertook the education of every child; each pupil drawing from the proceeds of State taxation the sum of ten dollars per annum. This paid the total running expenses of most schools. Districts, towns and counties desiring to do so could, of course, tax themselves additionally.

Hopefulness ruled the hour. What the toiler earned, he was able to keep and all looked forward with the greatest confidence to that "good time" sure to come in the not distant future.

During all this time Maitland had been incessantly engaged. He was called for from every point of the compass, and, like the trusty soldier, was ever found in the thickest of the fight. Several times the forces opposed had seemingly been on the point of gaining a victory and thus delaying the final and inevitable result, but each time his splendid powers and matchless oratory had turned the tide. Hopeful and buoyant, his speeches rang with good cheer and that hope and confidence in final victory which encouraged and inspired success.

At the time of which I write he was in Iowa, engaged in the work which had employed all his powers since his first effort at Branchville.

The following letter written by him at that time will explain itself:

DES MOINES, IOWA, ———— ——————.
REV. MR. ELLERY.

My Dear Friend:—As you are aware, we have gained a great victory and have now secured for Iowa the legislation which has resulted in so much good to Kansas. But we have only just begun, and much remains to be done. Our enemies taunt us with destroying credit and say that we have made it impossible for private parties to obtain large amounts of money for great and necessary works of public utility. This is doubtless true, and from my standpoint is not the least of our victories. Let us make it impossible! For great works, the nation, the State, the county or the municipality must in future take the place of private and irresponsible corporations and companies. At present, many of these are our masters. In a republic the people, in theory, rule. Let us not rest until this theory has been reduced to practice, for in no other way can we escape that taxation without representation against which our revolutionary fathers rebelled. The money power, the railroads

and the trusts, tax us freely; we are without representation
on their boards.

Let us rebel!

But I sat down to write for another purpose. I am·
coming down to see you again. From what you write, I
hope to receive a different answer from Mary Grafton from
that given me, now some years ago. I felt terribly repulsed
at the time, but it was the answer I should have been given.
I ought to have known better. As sure as you live, though,
I think her influence has made a man of me. But I will
not bother you with the thoughts of a man in love. You
may expect me on Saturday the 10th.

As ever, yours truly,
GEORGE MAITLAND.

CHAPTER XXX.

CONCLUSION.

T is now nearly ten years since our readers were introduced to the people of Plainville. Many changes have taken place and all our old friends show plainly the passage of time. Mr. Ellery had been, for some years, occupying the debatable ground between middle life and old age. Now, the matter had been decided for him, and it was clear that he was no longer young. But age, with him, while frosty, was yet kindly. To meet him was a pleasure, to know him a benediction, and to be near him an assurance of high thoughts and noble impulses. In the troublous times through which they had passed he had never failed to speak clearly and plainly upon the topics of the day. All knew him to entertain the most radical opinions, and yet his utterances had been tempered with so great and plain a love for all, in every station of life, that none dared take offense.

Mrs. Ellery,—dear, kind, motherly soul,—had changed but little. Life, to her, was a pleasure. Long years before she had learned the truth that self-seeking surely ends in loss of that happiness for which all, without exception seek.

That our love can create happiness in others and that its reflection upon ourselves is absolutely the only source we have of true and lasting pleasure, she had mastered. What wonder, then, that she was happy and beloved? With no thought of self, she had devoted herself to the distressed and forsaken. None appealed to her motherly heart in vain; the sorrows of all were her sorrows, and in their joys she rejoiced. Though pinched by "genteel poverty" herself, she had opened wide her door and her heart to Mary Grafton and the motherless boy, at the time of their greatest need.

The Meeting of Mary and Mr. Maitland.

But she had been repaid by the love of children, more fond, mayhap, than that of her own might have been.

Mary—our Mary—now a beautiful young woman of twenty-five, still taught in the village school. She had always been the pride of Plainville, but since her father's tragic death had been adopted as the daughter or sister of every loyal resident. With a pleasant nod for all, she yet maintained that calm equipoise of manner which betrayed what she could not hide,—the superior soul. How much of Mr. Ellery's radical stand for truth was due to her influence, could not be determined; psychology and philosophy as yet are but words used for the concealment of thoughts which take hold upon the verities of life. Much remains for which words afford no expression.

And she, herself, whence did she derive that superiority which, without a word from her, impressed itself upon all? The daughter of her father, were the hopes and aspirations, which in him had been but as the shadow of power, recreated in her to blossom and bloom with a fragrance and beauty which compelled that of which he only dreamed?

Or was her life her own, and is each vital spark but a flame, whose source is the Eternal Light, which must needs take character from the mortal body upon which it temporarily depends?

Charlie was now a bright boy of twelve. His sister had exercised over him, as she had promised, a mother's care, and with such a mother and such a household as that in which he found his home he could not be otherwise than obedient and affectionate.

Plainville was "looking up" they said, New buildings were appearing on every hand and an era of thrift and substantial improvement seemed setting in. No large and pretentious brick and stone palaces, constructed with borrowed capital and covered with mortgages, to pamper the pride and eat and corrode the substance of the builders, were attempted, but better yet, the modest dwellings of the residents began to show, by here a coat of paint and there an added room or a new "piazza," the solid and substantial progress of a people, who, having learned the hatefulness of borrowed finery, were resolved henceforth not to spend money before they had it.

Upon the receipt of Maitland's letter, Mr. Ellery resolved, like the true and loyal friend he was, to learn from Mary the probable result of the suit, which he had written he should again resume. Of course, Mrs Ellery was to be the medium through whom the desired information might be obtained. Reading the letter to her, he said:

"Don't you think you ought to acquaint Mary with the substance of this letter and learn from her George's probable answer? This would save them both some embarrassment, and possibly, pain."

"Perhaps so," said she, "and yet I dislike to appear to intrude. Affectionate and loving as she is, no one would ever know the secrets of her heart unless she saw fit to reveal them."

"True enough, but I know George, now, intimately. I have been his confidant in this matter, you know. He means just what he says, and it occurs to me that as his friend I should make an effort to save him a possible refusal. Aside from the claims of friendship, the gifts we have received from him, surely call for at least the effort to serve him.' And as we are not called upon to exert any influence we may possess, but simply to find out the state of her mind, it does seem that you ought to make the attempt."

"It does seem strange that we are obliged to ask her, and that we have no idea what her answer may be," said Mrs. Ellery; "and yet, when we think of her, as she is, we know that she would sooner die than reveal by a look, a feeling which she might wish to conceal."

At the next favorable opportunity, Mrs. Ellery said:

"Mary, Mr. Maitland will be here on Saturday!"

"Will he? Well, now we shall hear the story of the Iowa campaign. Was n't that a grand speech at Fort

Dodge? Even the *Register* could not refrain from words of praise."

"Yes, it was grand just to hear it read, but to have heard him deliver it must have been impressive, indeed. But, Mary, he is coming to again ask you to marry him, and both Mr. Ellery and myself are anxious to know whether you have another refusal in store for him, or not."

Mary blushed, but her eyes were steady, as she said: "Has he requested you to ask for him?"

"No, indeed, he has no idea of such a thing, but our wish is to save you both possible annoyance and pain. That is all. I am sure nothing would have induced me to speak as I have if I did not know that you had once refused him."

Mrs. Ellery said no more. She knew Mary too well to add anything to what she had said. Mary was silent; her eyes sought the floor and only the clasping of her hands, one with the other, revealed the emotion within. At last she said, speaking very slowly:

"Mr. Maitland is a man whom I respect and admire. Let him speak for himself."

That was all, and although Mrs. Ellery remained in an expectant attitude, the subject was not again alluded to.

Speaking to Mr. Ellery of the matter afterward, she said: "Mary is a wonderful woman; she treated the matter as a queen might have done; gracious and cordial though she was, she yet reserved her thought. Of this, though, I feel sure: George need not fear."

Saturday came at last, as looked-for-days have ever done, and with it the expected arrival. Mr. Ellery was at the depot and warmly greeted his friend. On the way to the parsonage many hands were to be grasped and hearty greetings exchanged, for Maitland had now become not only a noted man but a general favorite. "Uncle Bill" grasped his hand with a terrible squeeze, saying:

"God bless you, Mr. Maitland, for what you have done and for what I believe you will yet do!"

And as Maitland, for the moment engaged in conversation half a dozen others, who gathered to speak a word of welcome, he said, *sotto voce*, to Mr. Ellery: "I take back all I once said to you agin him," indicating Maitland with an inclination of the head; "he is a royal man, if he is a preacher, and now I sha'n't say a word agin his carrying off our favorite. Poor Grafton, I hope his daughter will be happy! She is a splendid woman and the man that gets her will have a treasure, sure."

Arrived at the parsonage, Mrs. Ellery kissed the traveler as she would have greeted a son and appeared overjoyed to see him, but as Mary gave him her hand her usual self-possession failed her, she blushed deeply and the telltale color overspread her face. Presently she recovered, and the conversation became general regarding the Iowa campaign and the wonderful success which had followed the efforts of the "agitator," as now he was willing to be called.

Mr. Ellery was so much interested in the details, as related by his friend, that he did not notice that Mrs. Ellery had left the parlor where they sat. Casting his eye toward the open door he saw his wife, who, standing where she was only to be seen by him, stood, beckoning him to follow her. Excusing himself as best he could, in a few moments he, too, departed.

How it came about he never could tell, but no sooner had the Ellerys left the room than Maitland, seating himself by Mary's side, took her hand. She did not withdraw it. Emboldened, he placed his arm around her and drew her head upon his shoulder. The ready tears,—her mother's legacy,—came into her eyes, but he kissed them away as he clasped her to his heart. Whispered confidences and sweet embraces followed in rapid succession. How long they were thus employed neither knew, when Mrs. Ellery, with much rattling of doors, returned to summon them to supper. Rising to his feet, Mr. Maitland said:

"Aunt Ellery, allow me to present the future Mrs. Maitland!"

Mrs. Ellery could scarcely keep back the tears as she pressed her foster-child to her heart. "Ah, children," said she "you don't know how happy I am for you! God bless you both!"

But little remains to be told. At the time of the marriage, which occurred shortly after Maitland's return, the elder Maitland, now advanced in years and thoroughly proud of his gifted son, came to Plainville, entreating his old friend Ellery to return to Massachusetts with him, offering to place him in comfort for the rest of his days. But the old preacher would not listen to it. "I have put on the harness," said he, "and I shall die at my post." Not to be balked, however, the other, saying that he wished to have the privilege of subscribing to the "cause," settled $500 a year upon his old friend, which was regularly thereafter paid.

John Busteed had been convicted of a crime and sentenced to the penitentiary, but his father secured a pardon for him and established him in business in Idaho, where report says he is "doing better."

Charlie, although the little fellow scarcely knew what to make of the turn affairs had taken, was completely assured by his sister, who said: "You haven't lost anybody, have you, dear? You've only gained a big brother," (glancing shyly at Maitland), "and he is just as good as he can be, too!"

www.ingramcontent.com/pod-product-compliance
Lightning Source LLC
Chambersburg PA
CBHW060516030726
47498CB00004B/964